The Able Seaman's Mate

William Cheevers

WingSpan Press

Printed in the United States of America
Published by WingSpan Press, Livermore, CA
www.wingspanpress.com
The WingSpan name, logo and colophon are the
trademarks of WingSpan Publishing.

First Edition 2010
ISBN 978-1-59594-409-2
Library of Congress Control Number: 2010931108

...look at a stone cutter hammering away at his rock, perhaps a hundred times without as much as a crack showing in it. Yet at the hundred-and-first blow, it will split in two, and I know it was not the last blow that did it, but all that had gone before.

— Jacob A. Riis

CONTENTS

One

The Road to Ballinasloe

His secret place was an old castle, the earthly remains of the O'Conors of Connaught. He scaled the vines clinging to the stones and from the highest reach of the castle ruin surveyed his realm and imagined the world beyond the river, five miles away and almost visible. When Jimmy Delaney's schooling was over, Mary Delaney asked the priest to speak to him and the priest said, "You have your health, lad...what more would you be wanting?" Jimmy Delaney said it was nothing he was wanting. He dug peat in the bog when the foreman fell behind and took no notice of openings for steady work. At fourteen or nearly so, his secret world had spread along the River Suck to Lough O'Flynn and back through the hard turn of the river at Castlerea to Dunamon, well south of the bridge at Ballymoe. Often he stood in the road at Dunamon and to the south his mind's eye formed the village of Ballinasloe where his grandfather married Sarah O'Neill before the great hunger. Further on was the River Shannon running through Lough Derg and out again to the head of the bay slapping against the docks trod by Big Tommy Delaney.

"The priest, he is pestering me," said Jimmy Delaney.

"Fellows running loose," said the schoolmaster. "And what is it you say to him?"

"I say nothing."

"You say nothing?"

"What is it I want? I tell him it is nothing I want."

"It is wise, Jimmy," said the schoolmaster. "It is wise to know the value of silence in the matter of priests."

"And, as you say, most other things as well," said Jimmy Delaney.

"And most other things as well," said the schoolmaster.

"What do you know of the great hunger?" said Jimmy Delaney.

"You cannot choose your moment in history, Jimmy," said the schoolmaster. "And if you could, you would not be choosing the dark time of the great hunger. Fifty years ago it was, and many perished. I have seen drawings... itinerant artists, one supposes. It's the eyes, Jimmy. You cannot forget the eyes. Always the same...the eyes..."

"My pa is forty-four and he does not speak of it," said Jimmy Delaney.

"Fifty years ago...he likely knows little of it," said the schoolmaster. "It is not a thing to be remembered. The faith...the great hunger tested the faith and the sooner forgotten, the better."

"The faith cannot be tested?" said Jimmy Delaney.

The schoolmaster smiled. "It cannot," he said.

"I have seen the old ones," said Jimmy Delaney.

"A few," said the schoolmaster. "A few are left who did not die or flee."

"I think they live in the days gone by...with the memories," said Jimmy Delaney.

"They do, Jimmy, they do," said the schoolmaster. "And when they are gone, the famine will be no more."

Jimmy Delaney watched the elders on the road, pushing carts loaded with peat. He walked with them, lagging behind, and one day an elder motioned for Jimmy Delaney to come forward and walk beside his cart.

"Ye're Little Jimmy Delaney...grandson of Big Tommy Delaney," said the elder.

"Aye, son of Jimmy Delaney, son of Tommy," said Jimmy Delaney.

"Big Tommy Delaney," said the elder. "Never was another like him. Come here even afore Sarah bore him a son an' he got to be Big Tommy. Afoot, they were...Tommy an' Sarah, just out of the workhouse in Castlerea."

"During the great hunger?" said Jimmy Delaney.

"Aye, lad...they couldn't keep Big Tommy in the workhouse," said the elder. "Walkin' tall with their heads up...stout people, they were, Tommy and Sarah. The old priest...sayin' how the sins brought on the hunger, he was, an' Big Tommy sayin' that's blarney...how the priest, he's just sayin' that to keep a hold of the people. An' they died refusing the rites...Big Tommy an' then Sarah... died, they did, spurnin' the rites. How do ye get a fellow like that out of yer mind? An' Sarah...did ye ever hear of a woman what refused the rites? An' yer ma, lad...it was yer ma what saw Big Tommy off...an' then Sarah, even when they was refusin' the rites. It's a woman among women, she is."

Mary Delaney turned from the stove, not expecting to see anyone standing in the doorway.

"Jimmy, you startled me," she said.

"Sorry, Ma," said Jimmy Delaney. "Are you needing more peat?"

"I've enough," said Mary Delaney. "Is there something?"

"I'm wondering, Ma...did Big Tommy refuse the last rites?"

"Your grandfather refusing the rites?" said Mary Delaney. "And who is it saying that?"

"One of the old ones...out on the road," said Jimmy Delaney.

Mary Delaney sighed. "Aye, Big Tommy refused the rites...and Sarah," she said. "But it did not go against them. You mustn't dwell on those old men."

"Aye, Ma."

"It did not go against them," said Mary Delaney. "Those old men, Jimmy...Big Tommy, he was a powerful presence, but the telling gets bigger as the telling gets longer." She paused. "Legends are a burden to their sons, Jimmy," she said. "And there's no stopping them growing in the minds of those needing a legend."

"Aye, Ma, I understand you," said Jimmy Delaney.

"It did not go against them," said Mary Delaney.

3

"What happened to Little Tommy?" said Jimmy Delaney.

"Sarah's first-born?" said Mary Delaney. "He died before your father was born...a sickness going through the land."

Big Jimmy Delaney and Mary Delaney arranged themselves at the kitchen table with a solemnity appropriate to a special occasion. A letter had come from Timothy O'Brien, Mary Delaney's older brother. Jimmy Delaney read the letter aloud. Timmy and then Tim, as everyone had known him, had settled into a steady job after years at sea.

Jimmy Delaney paused and removed a second sheet from the envelope. Folded into the sheet were silver certificates and coins totaling 80 dollars, an explanation of American currency and a third sheet of paper. Written carefully and embossed with a notary's seal, the document attested that the bearer, James Patrick Delaney, born 1858 in County Roscommon, Ireland, was the brother-in-law of Timothy Eugene O'Brien, boilermaker, residing at 73 Ludlow Street in the city of New York, America.

Jimmy Delaney laid the money and the document aside and read: "Take this money and letter of introduction and get Mary and the boys out of the peat bogs, Jimmy. I'm to be married soon and we should get the family together and a fellow can get ahead here. I'll be waiting to hear that you have booked passage for the spring. It won't do to make a winter crossing, Jimmy...it is not for landlubbers. In the spring I'll be meeting you at the dock." Jimmy Delaney hesitated, then read: "Get out of the bogs, Jimmy, or I'll take a shillelagh to your backside, lad."

Big Jimmy Delaney laughed heartily. "That Timmy... never a jibber and full of the malarkey," he said.

"I wonder if it is my destiny to follow in the steps of my grandfather," said Jimmy Delaney.

"You may be reminded that you are not your grandfather," said the schoolmaster.

"And if I find otherwise?"

"Then it will not be your destiny."

"I do not understand. I think it is not much you think of destiny."

"It is something you say to add glow to a lifeless thing," said the schoolmaster.

On a misty day Jimmy Delaney crossed the bridge at Ballymoe and followed the river to Dunamon and stood at a place in the road where Big Tommy Delaney had summoned him from the castle ruin. Toward Ballinasloe and the River Shannon and beyond through Lough Derg and Limerick lay the docks at the head of the bay.

"We are kindred spirits just the same," said Jimmy Delaney.

On the road to Castlerea there was a man who had come back from America. The man said that America changed fellows. He said it was a place where even lads turned on other lads. Jimmy Delaney bade the man a pleasant day and watched until he was out of sight.

"You weren't born for it," he said.

Two

The Foreman's Nephew

Jimmy Delaney tucked the loaf of bread for the evening meal under his oilskin slicker and nodded to the proprietor of the general store. He pushed his way through a group of men standing in the doorway. One of the men drew on his pipe and said that the rain and wind seemed heavier and the others nodded agreement. Jimmy Delaney left his slicker and muddy boots in the pantry and came through the back door into the kitchen. The aroma of simmering stew filled the room.

"It's a tear in the peat canvas," he said. "It's under the shed. The peat is dry, but I'll be after sewing it up."

"The river...they say the bogs may flood," said Mary Delaney.

"Lough Derg will drain the river...always it has," said Jimmy Delaney.

"Um," said Mary Delaney.

"Ma, we are not making any plans," said Jimmy Delaney. "It is weeks since Tim's letter. Is it staying here? Is it really to be staying here?"

"It is your father deciding these things," said Mary Delaney.

"Is he not thinking about it even?"

"When he speaks of Tim's letter, he speaks of what is good for the family," said Mary Delaney. "You must prepare yourself, Jimmy. This is not a thing your father would do and he will come to believe that what he would do is best for the family."

"You cannot change his mind?"

"It is your father deciding these things," said Mary Delaney.

"Tim's letter, Ma...it sets things straight," said Jimmy Delaney. "There is nothing here for me."

"You have your family and your health," said Mary Delaney.

"There is more, Ma. There is more than just breathing and digging peat. Just because Pa is afraid..."

"You'll keep a civil tongue in your head, Jimmy," said Mary Delaney.

"Ma, this is not a chance I can be passing on," said Jimmy Delaney.

"We'll see," said Mary Delaney. "We'll see."

Big Jimmy Delaney sat on the edge of the bed, his palms on his knees. Mary Delaney sat next to him. Jimmy Delaney and his brothers, Michael and John, stood in the doorway.

"This going to America...it is not a good thing, a right thing," said Big Jimmy Delaney. "It's a good life we have... and we have our health. We must return Tim's money."

Jimmy Delaney took in his mother's stern expression. He turned and left the room. Later in the night, after Big Jimmy Delaney was asleep, Mary Delaney went into the kitchen. She paused in the doorway, watching her son. He sat at the table, looking out the window at the rain.

"I'll be going, Ma," said Jimmy Delaney. "It's the bogs for me and I'll not be wasting away."

"I know, Jimmy," said Mary Delaney. "I'll not be trying to stop you. You'll not be going with the rains, I'm supposing."

"In the spring," said Jimmy Delaney. "Schoolmaster O'Donnell...he is advancing my passage and something to get started and when I am having a fine job in America, I'll be sending the means to buy new books for the school."

"Even before your father..."

"Pa did not think about it, Ma," said Jimmy Delaney. "And when I knew he would not..."

"Schoolmaster O'Donnell has this money to spare?" said Mary Delaney.

"Aye, he does...he does not say how this comes about. He has family in County Cork, people of means, I'm supposing. It is not wise, I think, to use the other

7

money...the money from Tim. And too, the postman from Dublin will make his rounds before it is time."

"Are you sure this is a door you want to go through?" said Mary Delaney.

"Aye, Ma...it is the only door I have," said Jimmy Delaney.

"Your father will not understand," said Mary Delaney.

"I'll not be telling him," said Jimmy Delaney. "There is no good that comes from it. I'll not be moved...and he'll not be either."

"You must talk to him," said Mary Delaney. "Even if you cannot agree..."

"Aye, Ma, when it is time," said Jimmy Delaney. "You must allow that I will know when it is time. I cannot be fighting with Pa. Sure I do not want to."

"Aye, I know it," said Mary Delaney. "Going to America...it must be, I'm thinking. The Lord will protect you."

One week before he would sail from Galway City, Jimmy Delaney found his mother waiting for him in the kitchen, facing the door. He walked past her and draped his denim jacket over the back of a chair.

"I have not forgotten my promise," he said. "I will talk to Pa."

"It's a sign, Jimmy...a good omen," said Mary Delaney.

"Aye, Ma...what is?"

"We are all going to America," said Mary Delaney.

Jimmy Delaney studied his mother's face, straightened the jacket on the back of the chair.

"Why would Pa change his mind?" he said.

"Things will be better in America, what with Tim already being there."

"What is it you are not telling me, Ma?" said Jimmy Delaney.

"Your father must not know," she said.

"Aye," said Jimmy Delaney.

"The foreman's nephew...he needed the steady work," said Mary Delaney.

"What? Are you saying..."

"There is nothing to be done, Jimmy," said Mary Delaney. "We will be together...it is the fate of our family to be together. The passage money not going back to Tim, the postman passing through early...it is a sign. I have thought it through. Michael and John will stay in the orphanage in Castlerea and finish their schooling and join us in America. We will all be together...that is the important thing."

Jimmy Delaney looked away, took in a deep breath and let it out slowly.

"Aye, Ma," he said. "That is the important thing."

Lough Derg carried away the swell of the river into the bay and the winter rains subsided. A farmer waited on the seat of his ox cart in front of a stone cottage on a treeless plain where the village merged into the bogs. A thin mist, silent and ghostly, hung in the air. The farmer clapped his gloved hands together against the chill and looked around toward the lane to the village. He was anxious to leave for his brother's farm on the River Clare.

Jimmy Delaney and his father stood next to the cart. They had the woolen clothing they wore, three suitcases tied with heavy cord and a rucksack containing bread and cheese, three tin cups, Tim O'Brien's letters and the American money. They waited for Mary O'Brien Delaney, who had left her two younger sons, aged twelve and nine, in the care of the priest. The father and son saw her as a dot on the horizon and stood waiting as she took form on the lane. She approached the ox cart and Jimmy Delaney studied her face and he knew that much was expected of him.

The farmer coaxed the ox. The cottage faded from view. They sat silently, hunched over, and the wheels of the cart clattered on the wooden bridge at Ballymoe.

Three

The Stranger and the Coachman

The narrow cobblestone streets of Galway City were filled with people and horses and carts and makeshift stalls where vendors hawked their wares and all seemed to flow as a single entity. Jimmy Delaney could not see the end of the stone buildings fading to a point in the distance. The photographs in books at the schoolhouse did not capture the colors and smells and sounds. Jimmy Delaney consumed the pulsating seaport where everything clattered on the cobblestones and no one said, "Slow down with ye, lad," and he was warmed against the wet chill by a dreamy eagerness.

"Look out," shouted a man in the street, lunging forward with his arms outstretched and pushing the Delaneys against a store front.

A whip cracked over their heads and someone shouted, "Outa the way, ye waifs," and a horse drawing a carriage at full trot charged past them.

"Ye're after gettin' kilt, are ye?" said the stranger, flipping his thumb toward the carriage. "Them's a laudy daw...a dickey dazzler at that...an' 'is lady muck."

People began moving back into the street. The horse drew up a short distance away and the stranger turned abruptly and disappeared into the crowd. When Mary Delaney had recovered her balance, Jimmy Delaney released her arm and turned toward the coachman, who had stepped down from his perch and opened the carriage door. A man and then a woman holding the man's hand stepped out of the carriage. Jimmy Delaney knew them from photographs. Their clothing was black, followed the contours of their bodies and seemed not very durable. The man released the woman's hand and turned toward the coachman. The woman opened a delicate parasol adorned with lace and looked away. The man said something to the coachman, wagging his finger in the coachman's face. He then turned back toward the woman, who folded the parasol and laid her hand on the man's extended arm. They went into a store, the man removing his top hat as they passed through the doorway.

The coachman closed the carriage door, looped the whip into a coil and stood with his heels together, holding the whip behind his back. He began scanning the crowd and his gaze fell on the boy staring back at him. The coachman looked away, back again and then left his post. He walked along the sidewalk deliberately, stopped and leaned in toward Jimmy Delaney's face.

"Culchie, are ye," he said. "Ye lower yer eyes in the presence of yer betters, boy."

"And what betters would that be?" said Jimmy Delaney.

"Jimmy," said Mary Delaney, as the coachman raised the whip.

Big Jimmy Delaney moved quickly and took Jimmy Delaney's arm, pulling him away.

"He's only a lad," said Big Jimmy Delaney.

"He's a muzzy after gettin' 'is arse bopped," said the coachman.

"Beggin' yer pardon, we'll be goin' now," said Big Jimmy Delaney, tugging Jimmy Delaney's arm.

"Gammy bogtrotters," said the coachman, walking away.

"That fellow's off his nut, Pa," said Jimmy Delaney.

"Shush," said Big Jimmy Delaney. "We need no trouble."

The coachman returned to his spot next to the carriage and looked again toward Jimmy Delaney. Their eyes locked as before. Jimmy Delaney heard his father's voice and felt the tug on his arm. When the coachman looked away, he yielded, allowing himself to be dragged along the street.

Schoolmaster O'Donnell had once said that the more

insignificant a man, the more objectionable he is when given a modicum of authority. Jimmy Delaney smiled.

"We're out of sight now, Pa," he said, pulling his arm free.

"There are always people of that sort, Jimmy," said Mary Delaney.

"Aye, Ma...and people of my sort," said Jimmy Delaney.

"Jimmy..."

"Aye, Ma," said Jimmy Delaney.

Big Jimmy Delaney settled on a rooming house in Dominick Street. Jimmy Delaney glanced around the parlor and noticed that the gas jets on the walls had been fitted with bulbs which emitted a soft orange glow.

"Electric lights," he said. "It's many of these we'll be seeing in America."

"Light without the lamps," said Mary Delaney. "How could it be?"

"The light, it comes from a wire," said Jimmy Delaney. "Some in Castlerea have them. Electricity, it is. Schoolmaster O'Donnell said electricity is made at a station far away by burning the coal and comes to the house through a wire and lights the globes."

"The light is so warm," said Mary Delaney.

"Our lodging is on the second floor," said Big Jimmy Delaney.

From the room in the back of the house, Jimmy Delaney could see the merchant ships in the harbor of Ballyknow Quay and the teeming commerce on the pier. Dun Aengus Dock, hidden in a forest of masts and rigging, lay on the far side of a spit of land in the harbor bounded by Dock Street and Long Walk. Mary Delaney called his name and Jimmy Delaney turned away from the window.

Mary Delaney dispensed bread and cheese and the family ate in silence, drinking water from tin cups. Jimmy Delaney watched his mother and father, one and then the other. Soon his father's watch would show the time for retiring and they would darken the room and awaken with the dawn and the unknown. Jimmy Delaney supposed that neither of his parents wanted to believe that Dun Aengus Dock would be the last piece of Ireland they would touch.

Jimmy Delaney switched off the bulb in the ceiling and lay awake in the darkness with his head propped against the wall. No one in the village hurried and everyone in Galway hurries. Hurrying is the tide of the street and has with it a language thrown upwards and downwards and the language tells as much as the hurrying. The man on the road to Castlerea said that lads can turn on other lads. The stranger on the street, he is no turner, but the coachman, aye, he's a turner, and being a turner, he spits on a muzzie when the laudy daw spits on him. Sure the stranger who ran away is afraid of the coachman and the coachman...aye, he is afraid of the laudy daw. Maybe afraid is a door both turners and not have been through.

Four

The Setting Sun

From Dominick Street they joined the flow across O'Brien Bridge and made their way through the alleys to Long Walk and Dun Aengus Dock. Jimmy Delaney stood against the heavy mist waiting for the steamer *Edinburgh*, sailing from Glasgow and calling at Galway and New York.

"The weather is poor...do you not see that?" said Mary Delaney. "Come under the shed."

Jimmy Delaney waived her away. His mind's eye looked back from the ox cart toward the village. He saw the highest tower of the castle, the north tower, where birds of prey on wing lifted him into a world beyond the river. He saw the schoolmaster, who said there is value in silence and fate is coincidence that does not seem so and destiny is only something you say. The village blurred and faded, leaving Schoolmaster O'Donnell and the north tower of the castle ruin, and Jimmy Delaney turned away and heard the sound of Big Tommy Delaney's boots against the pier along the Shannon.

In the early afternoon, a ship sounding a foghorn emerged out of the mist. Jimmy Delaney narrowed his gaze toward the mouth of the harbor. He could make out masts and yards fore and aft and a single stack discharging black smoke and the ship was longer and wider than any other ship in the harbor. Passengers gathered their possessions, moved out of the sheds, drew into family islands. Big Jimmy Delaney and Mary Delaney made their way to the edge of the dock where Jimmy Delaney had been waiting. As everyone watched, the ship turned away and tied up at the mooring posts along Nimmo's Pier on the other side of the River Corrib.

The smoke from the stack faded and there was no sign of activity.

"Is it the Edinburgh?" a man asked.

"Aye, it is," said another man. "I see the name is on the side."

"Aye, it's there...I see it as well," said another man.

"They load up the first and second cabin blokes from the pier on the other side," said a man with an English accent.

"Away with ye," said the first man.

"Aye, it is so," said the Englishman.

"There," said another man, pointing toward the ship.

Everyone on the dock fell silent. Crewmen had begun moving around on the deck of the *Edinburgh*. Two men in a long boat suspended by ropes from a boom descended toward the river and another crewman extended a gangway outward over the water. The men in the long boat untied the boom ropes, lashed the gangway into place along the ship's hull and rowed the long boat across the river. One of the men tied the boat to a mooring post and the other man climbed the ladder to the dock. He was a burly Scotsman wearing a wool sweater and a stocking cap drawn over his ears. He took a clay pipe from his mouth and rapped it against the mooring post. Ashes fell into the river.

"Steerage launch for Edinburgh, sailing for New York," said the Scotsman, pushing the pipe into his pocket and regarding the crowd with a scowl.

"Aye," said Jimmy Delaney.

The Scotsman eyed Jimmy Delaney. The scowl was replaced by a thin smile.

"In a hurry, are we?" he said.

"Aye," said Jimmy Delaney.

The Scotsman began tossing suitcases and boxes into the long boat and directing people down the ladder.

"Watch now, to the front...mind your step," said the other crewman, as he steadied the boat against the dock.

When the boat was full, thirty people and their belongings by Jimmy Delaney's count, the Scotsman descended the ladder and he and the other crewman rowed to the other side of the river. The Scotsman lashed the long boat to the gangway.

"Everyone up the gangway...and mind the step," he said.

Jimmy Delaney paused on the swaying gangway and then stepped off and positioned himself in the long boat behind his mother. With no heed of the crewmen, who were shouting instructions, Jimmy Delaney told Mary Delaney to hold the rope railings with both hands. He guided her up the gangway to the deck and then made his way down to help Big Jimmy Delaney with the suitcases. From the deck, Jimmy Delaney watched all the ways the families behind were climbing the gangway. He saw that everyone tried to hurry in response to the crewmen. He watched the crewman who was not a Scotsman. The man was steadfast, waving his arms and talking louder than was needed, but he did not use the language of the coachman. Sure there is something about that coachman more than hurrying. Jimmy Delaney felt the tug of his mother's hand on his arm and turned away from the gangway.

The master of the steamship *Edinburgh* wore a dark blue great coat with a double row of brass buttons and four gold stripes on the sleeves and a seaman's cap. He had a full gray beard and stood erect. He held an open ledger balanced in his left hand and a writing quill in his right hand and stared straight ahead. Next to him was an inkwell resting on a tall stool and next to the stool stood another man wearing a great coat and seaman's cap. He confronted Big Jimmy Delaney with a steady gaze.

"Just you three," he said.

"Aye...me myself and me wife and son," said Big Jimmy Delaney.

"What is the state of your health?" said the man.

"Health?" said Big Jimmy Delaney.

"We are all able," said Jimmy Delaney.

The man scanned the Delaney family and then moved forward and lifted Big Jimmy Delaney's eyelid with his thumb.

"What?" said Big Jimmy Delaney.

"I am the medical officer...stand still," said the man.

The medical officer examined Big Jimmy Delaney and Mary Delaney. Jimmy Delaney's jaw tensed as the man's hand approached his face. Feeling the pressure of his mother's hand gripping his shoulder, he stood rigidly as a thumb quickly lifted each of his eyelids and fingers probed his neck near the angle of his jaw on both sides.

"No trachoma and passable," said the medical officer.

Dipping the quill into the inkwell, the master said, "Name, age, number in your party, their names and ages."

As Big Jimmy Delaney answered, the master made entries in the ledger and wrote their names on three cards. He handed the cards to Big Jimmy Delaney.

"These are your medical inspection cards," he said. "You will need them for the American authorities."

"Aye," said Big Jimmy Delaney.

"Down the stairs to the right and mind your step," said the master. "At the bottom of the stairs is a corridor directly in front of you. Take any open cabin along the corridor and stay there. I shall come around in due course to collect the passage, give you further instructions and take down additional information."

"How long for getting across?" said Jimmy Delaney.

"Eleven knots, eleven days," said the master, gesturing for the Delaneys to move along.

The cabin had two lower bunks and two upper bunks abutting the common walls of the adjacent cabins. A narrow space between the bunks ended in a small table against the ship's hull. There was a wash bowl, a pitcher and six metal cups on the table and just above the only porthole was a sign directing the occupants to the pump and washrooms at the end of the corridor. A change of bed linen and several towels lay on top of a chest with three drawers; the drawers could be opened when the door to the corridor was closed. Next to the linen and towels was an oil lantern attached to the chest with bolts.

"Aye, this will do," said Big Jimmy Delaney from the doorway.

"Where shall we change?" said Mary Delaney.

"I'll be finding the loo," said Jimmy Delaney.

"You'll not be scampering about," said Mary Delaney, handing Jimmy Delaney the pitcher from the wash stand. "That Scotsman will be coming."

"Aye, Ma," said Jimmy Delaney, understanding that the master would have questions and possibly papers and that he would represent the family if there was any writing to be done.

Jimmy Delaney found the pump in a closet near the end of the corridor, filled the pitcher and returned to the cabin. Mary Delaney passed out bread and cheese from the rucksack and poured water into the cups. They ate sitting on the bottom bunks with their knees almost touching.

"I'll be looking around a bit, Ma," said Jimmy Delaney.

"You'll not be scampering about, Jimmy," said Mary Delaney. "That Scotsman..."

"I'll be staying close, Ma," said Jimmy Delaney.

Jimmy Delaney explored the steerage deck. There was not much to see. A narrow corridor began at the bottom of the stairs to the main deck and ended in an iron door. The door was open, revealing another stairway descending into darkness with an oily smell. The corridor provided access to the cabins, the pump closet, two washrooms and another large room with tables set end to end. Jimmy Delaney climbed the stairs to main deck, but did not venture far from the door. After an hour he returned to the cabin. After another hour he rose quickly in response to a knock on the door.

The master and a crewman were in the corridor. The master held the ledger and the quill; the other man carried the inkwell and a metal box under his arm.

"This is your cabin?" said the master.

"Aye," said Jimmy Delaney.

"Name," said the master.

"Delaney," said Jimmy Delaney.

"Pounds or dollars," said the master, turning pages in the ledger.

"No other Delaneys?" said Jimmy Delaney.

"No others," said the master. "Is it pounds or dollars?"

"Dollars," said Jimmy Delaney. He turned to Big Jimmy Delaney. "The passage, Pa," he said.

"Eighteen dollars for the three of you," said the master.

Big Jimmy Delaney took the money from a suitcase and handed it to Jimmy Delaney, who counted out several bills into the master's hand and returned the other bills to his father. The master gave the bills to the crewman, who placed them in the metal box. The master made an entry in the ledger and then wrote on a slip of paper and handed it to Jimmy Delaney. His movements had the precision of practiced repetition.

"Keep this receipt along with your medical inspection cards in your luggage or some other place where they will not be lost," said the master. "I have entered your name and cabin number in this ledger with a notation that your passage has been paid. However, should anyone wearing a uniform similar to mine inquire of the receipt, please show it."

"Aye," said Jimmy Delaney, handing the receipt to his father.

"Your bunks are made up with fresh bed linen," said the master. "There is a change of bed linen here on the chest to be used as you please. The towels will be replaced by a steward just after the evening meal each day."

The master handed the quill to the crewman and

turned a switch on the wall next to the door. A bulb encased in a wire cage on the ceiling glowed.

"This switch turns your light on and off," he said. "It is likely you shan't need the lamp, but if you do, it has been filled with oil and there are matches in the top drawer of the chest. Notice that the drawers have latches to secure them at sea...just hold in the latch to open the drawer."

He turned off the light and took the quill from the crewman, who had cleaned the nib with a cloth.

"There are two meals per day included in the passage... breakfast and supper," said the master, examining the nib. "Listen for the bell in the morning and evening. The dining room is aft...that is, to your left...at the end of the corridor. The dining room is also a recreation area for social gatherings when meals are not being served."

"Where may we go to mass?" said Mary Delaney.

"The ship does not sponsor religious services," said the master. "There is a priest aboard on this crossing. He will post a notice for mass in the dining room when it is not otherwise occupied."

Mary Delaney nodded.

"Now, beyond the dining room, you will see a bulkhead closed off by an iron door," said the master. "You are not allowed through this door, even in the unlikely event you find it open. The fore deck..."

"The door is open now," said Jimmy Delaney.

"Jimmy," said Mary Delaney."

"After we are under way, it won't be," said the master. "However, as I said..."

"Aye," said Jimmy Delaney.

"Where was I?" said the master, looking at the crewman.

"The fore deck, sir," said the crewman.

"Aye, the fore deck at the top of the stairs is for steerage passengers," said the master. "You may take fresh air on deck as you please. The limits are defined by a railing...you will please respect this railing. Do you have any other questions?"

"May we change in the washrooms?" said Mary Delaney.

"Aye, madam, facilities for ladies and gentlemen are aft across the corridor from the dining room," said the master. "You may leave the used towels there or bring them back here. In any case, the steward will leave the clean ones here in the cabin...on the chest. One thing more...if the facilities are occupied, there are two chamber pots under your lower bunks. You may empty them in the washrooms. Now, if there is nothing more, we shall get to the matter of the American authorities."

"Aye," said Jimmy Delaney after looking toward his father, who nodded.

"Are you visiting America or do you intend remaining there?" said the master. He balanced the ledger in his left hand and dipped the quill in the inkwell.

"We are staying in America," said Jimmy Delaney.

"Then I must put some questions," said the master.

"Aye," said Jimmy Delaney.

"I assume your mother and father are married," said the master, his quill poised over the ledger.

Mary Delaney looked away.

"Aye, married...in the church," said Jimmy Delaney.

"No offense intended," said the master. "Occupation... how do you earn a living?"

"Peat," said Jimmy Delaney. "We cut peat."

"Laborer," said the master. "Can you read and write?"

"Aye," said Jimmy Delaney.

"All of you?" said the master.

"Aye," said Jimmy Delaney.

"Where do you come from?"

"Ireland," said Jimmy Delaney.

"I mean, where in Ireland," said the master. "Where did you come from to get here?"

"County Roscommon," said Jimmy Delaney.

"Nearest relative," said the master. "In Ireland, that is."

"My father is William O'Brien," said Mary Delaney. "He is a tenant farmer near Cloonyquin, County Roscommon. My mother's name is Catherine."

"Do you have relatives in America?" said the master. "If so, who is your nearest relative in America?"

"Timothy O'Brien, boilermaker...brother of my mother," said Jimmy Delaney.

"Do you have his address?"

"New York," said Big Jimmy Delaney, holding Tim O'Brien's letter for the master to see.

"The address?" said the master.

"Ludlow Street...Seventy-three Ludlow Street," said Jimmy Delaney.

"You're destination is New York?"

"Aye," said Big Jimmy Delaney.

"How much money do you have left there?"

"Fifty-eight dollars," said Jimmy Delaney.

"Aye," said Big Jimmy Delaney. "We have used a part of the dollars for lodging and the like and we gave the money we had before to Father Callaghan. He is caring for the two younger lads."

"Quite," said the master. "Did Timothy O'Brien pay your passage?"

"Aye, me brother-in-law sent passage money from America," said Big Jimmy Delaney.

"Have any of you been to America before?"

"We've not been there before," said Jimmy Delaney.

"You're joining a relative...Timothy O'Brien," said the master.

"Aye, Tim O'Brien, me brother-in-law," said Big Jimmy Delaney.

"Have any of you been in prison or an almshouse or a bedlam house or supported by a charity?"

"What house?" said Big Jimmy Delaney.

"None of that," said Jimmy Delaney.

"Are any of you a polygamist or an anarchist?"

"The antichrist," said Mary Delaney, crossing herself.

"Anarchist, anarchist," said the master. "Have you attempted to overthrow the authority?"

"We're not after overthrowing anyone," said Jimmy Delaney.

"If you wish not to be turned away in New York, lad, you must answer these questions," said the master. "It is the American authorities who pose the questions. The answers are of no consequence to me. It is not personal."

Jimmy Delaney nodded.

"Do you have an offer, promise or agreement of work?" said the master.

"Me brother-in-law will get me on at the boilermakers," said Big Jimmy Delaney.

"But you don't have that in writing."

"What writing?" said Big Jimmy Delaney. "Me brother..."

"Very well," said the master. "What is the condition of your health? Anyone deformed or crippled? Any scars to speak of, moles that seem angry? Is there anything? If you are trying to conceal a medical condition, you will be turned back in New York...and I shall be obliged to collect another eighteen dollars to bring you back here."

"We are all able," said Jimmy Delaney.

"Very well," said the master. "All of you were born in County Roscommon?"

"Aye, County Roscommon," said Big Jimmy Delaney.

"That is all," said the master. "By all accounts, I shan't see you again until the day before we arrive in New York harbor or possibly after we have anchored in the harbor. At that time, you will receive instructions regarding your interview with the American authorities."

The master handed the quill to the crewman. He blew on the entries briefly and closed the ledger. Nodding curtly, he backed out of the cabin. The crewman followed and closed the door behind them.

"Jimmy, it's not trouble we need," said Mary Delaney. "You'll be keeping a civil tongue in your head."

"It's glocky, Ma...if I was after overthrowing the authority..."

"Jimmy," said Mary Delaney.

"Oh, I'll be taking your ship...and him asking after a bedlam house..."

"Jimmy," said Mary Delaney.

"Ma..."

"A bedlam house?" said Big Jimmy Delaney.

"A place for lunatics, Pa," said Jimmy Delaney.

"Jimmy..."

"Aye, Ma," said Jimmy Delaney.

The sky had cleared in the late afternoon, odd for March, and the master ordered full steam in the calm waters of Galway Bay. Near the bowsprit Jimmy Delaney had the breeze in his face and unfettered scrutiny of the ocean world he had promised to embrace and remember. Leaning over the side, he watched the prow knife through the calm water until the sun was on the horizon. The Connemara was a ghostly silhouette in the moonlight and west of Inishmore the coastline faded into the recesses of Kilkieran Bay and Bertraghboy Bay and then returned and to the west of Ballyconneely Bay returned only briefly before the lighthouse at Slyne Head and to the west of Slyne Head there was only water. Jimmy Delaney kept the lighthouse in sight until it fell away and now the sea was dark and seemed to breathe with an authority he had not sensed in Galway Bay. Thick smoke poured from the stack and the deck shuddered under the force of full steam. Jimmy Delaney fixed his gaze to the west and pondered what the next light would bring and when the last sliver of the moon disappeared below the horizon, he was struck by the frailty of a tiny ship holding back a menacing abyss. His eyes blinked and the spell was gone. He made his way back to the cabin.

Big Jimmy Delaney and Mary Delaney were in their bunks. The electric light had been turned off and the oil lantern produced a dim flame which cast ghostly shadows about the cabin. Jimmy Delaney smiled, blew out the flame and climbed into his bunk.

"Did you not hear the bell?" said Mary Delaney. "You missed the evening meal...mutton, boiled potatoes and bread. Are you not hungry?"

"Just taking the night air, Ma," said Jimmy Delaney. "I'll take extra at breakfast."

"The light was so bright," said Mary Delaney.

"I know, Ma," said Jimmy Delaney.

Five

Murphy

On the fourth morning Jimmy Delaney was awakened by regular blasts of the foghorn. A thick gray fog awaited him at the top of the stairs. Making his way along the railing and squinting over the side, he was suddenly aware of someone else.

"A pea souper it is," said a husky voice far above his head.

Jimmy Delaney looked toward the voice and realized that his line of sight was cut off by the man's chest. Moving back a step, he mumbled an apology.

"And it's a wet railing and a sliding deck as well," said the man. "A rolling sea would put a seal on it."

The man spoke the brogue of a Londonderry seaman, a dialect foreign to Jimmy Delaney. He seemed near seven feet tall and had red hair not contained by his wool cap, a square jaw with a full beard and a chest the shape and size of a stout keg. His heavy pants were tucked into rubber boots and his sweater smelled of damp wool. Jimmy Delaney was put at ease by the man's broad smile and the feigned roguishness of his vivid blue eyes.

"Did not see you there, though I do not see how I missed you," said Jimmy Delaney.

"A bit early for a sprog," said the man. "The name's Murphy...Ulsterman, hailing from Derry. Drowned once in the Lough Foyle and came back to life. And who might ye be?"

"Delaney...Jimmy Delaney, sailing for America."

"Then America it is," said Murphy. "I'm off to me duties. Come along if ye're a mind."

"The fog," said Jimmy Delaney.

"A mere annoyance, lad...'tis a mere annoyance soon gone the way of a scuttered wave hand at the local," said Murphy. He pointed toward a light gray spot in the thinning fog. "Look there," he said. "The sun will be poking through before ye can say Murphy."

"Murphy," said Jimmy Delaney.

"Aye, and ye see...that spot is brighter," said Murphy.

Jimmy Delaney laughed, pulled his wool hat over his ears and drew his arms in close to his body.

"Ye're cold, lad," said Murphy, frowning. "That flimsy coat...ye've not enough clothing for the North Atlantic."

Jimmy Delaney shrugged. "I had a slicker...we had not room for it," he said, tugging the tail of his denim coat. "This will do until I'm getting another slicker in America."

"Blarney, ye wait here," said Murphy, and before Jimmy Delaney could answer, Murphy had disappeared down the stairs. He returned carrying a dark blue coat of tight worsted weave with a frayed collar and cuffs and gray spots of encrusted salt. "Yer lucky day," said Murphy, offering the coat.

"I cannot," said Jimmy Delaney.

"I've a new one," said Murphy. "Ye'll not be treading this deck with Murphy without a proper coat." He swung the coat out into an arc around Jimmy Delaney's shoulders. "Put yer arms in the sleeves, lad," he said.

Murphy's coat hung below Jimmy Delaney's knees and the sleeves hung below the tips of his fingers.

"It is much too large," said Jimmy Delaney. "The coat I have..."

"Blarney, we'll roll up the sleeves," said Murphy. He put two tucks in the sleeves, which now ended in bulky cuffs at the top of Jimmy Delaney's wrists. "There...'tis a proper coat for the North Atlantic," he said.

"Murphy..."

"Ye do not fancy a warm coat?" said Murphy.

"Aye...'tis a proper coat," said Jimmy Delaney.

Jimmy Delaney learned that the *Edinburgh* had no first class cabins apart from the master's quarters and the owner's cabin. Murphy said the owner's cabin had not been occupied since he had signed on, as no one from Allan and Company of Glasgow had ever been aboard. On this crossing, though, there were two American men in the owner's cabin. They wore soft wool suits and hats and carried canes. Murphy said they often stood on a patch of deck amidships near the stairway to the bridge.

"Aye, seen 'em there," said Jimmy Delaney. "Their clothes are fine and hang trim, as my ma would say. Laudy daws, they are, but durable."

"Aye, laudy daws," said Murphy.

"There's other laudy daws...dressed different...not like these," said Jimmy Delaney. "They wear fine dark clothes...frock coats, my ma says. I saw one in Galway City...with a lady. Delicate, she was."

"Aye, I know them kind," said Murphy. "They's dickey dazzlers...born that way. These here laudy daws in the first cabin...they was regular fellows 'til they got money."

Murphy talked as he worked. Jimmy Delaney watched and listened and after two days he had learned many of the duties of a deck hand on a steamer at sea. He watched Murphy tie bowlines, figure of eight stoppers, clove hitches and sheepshanks and learned to make fast to a cleat and late in the day he leaned over the railing and watched the prow slice through the water.

On the seventh day Murphy said the ship was carrying thirty-four second class passengers in two clusters of cabins amidships and aft on the main deck. His tone was darker, not carefree as it had been. There were seven kinsmen in second class, he said, and one hundred and twenty-two souls below decks in steerage and ninety-two of those were kinsmen. Murphy held Jimmy Delaney sternly in his gaze and said that kinsmen were always in steerage and would be until all the foreigners were tossed out of Ireland. The Scots had surrendered, he said, but kinsmen would never surrender.

Jimmy Delaney regarded this intense man, in turn compassionate and defiant.

"I know how to get to the engine room from the steerage deck," he said.

"Ye're after getting to the engine room, are ye?" said Murphy.

"Aye, I might be after doin' that," said Jimmy Delaney.

"Well, ye don't go through the steerage door, lad... the officers, they take a dim view," said Murphy. "Here, behind that funnel is the forward hatch what goes down to the fireman's walk."

Jimmy Delaney could see the hatch in the side of an iron box the size of a large closet protruding from the deck near the cargo boom.

"Fireman's walk?" he said.

"Aye, the fireman's walk...'tis a walkway along the keel, bow to stern...coal bunkers, boilers, engine room... aye, and fresh water tanks and waste tanks and the cargo hold."

"It is not forbidden?"

"It's not a bold lad ye are?" said Murphy.

"Aye," said Jimmy Delaney.

Murphy opened the hatch and warm moist air rushed out. Inside the iron box, Murphy turned a switch and bulbs encased in wire cages attached to the bulkhead glowed orange. A stairway with iron railings was visible in the dim light. Murphy closed the hatch.

"In our cabin the globe is in the ceiling...in the wire cage like these," said Jimmy Delaney. "My ma is not so sure about electric lights."

"Aye, the ship got the lights in the last refit," said Murphy. "Know what makes 'em shine?"

"Aye, learned that," said Jimmy Delaney.

"More'n me, lad," said Murphy. "They tell me it's a generator...runs off the engine."

"Aye," said Jimmy Delaney. "The electricity comes through a wire and lights the globes."

"Fancy that," said Murphy. "Well, Murphy, he just switches 'em on and he switches 'em off. Improvement on them feeble lanterns...I'll say that."

"Warm with the door...hatch, closed," said Jimmy Delaney.

Murphy smiled. "Aye, hatch it is," he said. "The forward hatch stays closed, what with passengers up there. The engine room is vented astern."

The orange light from a row of bulbs aligned along the low ceiling penetrated the humid haze only a few inches, leaving the fireman's walk dark to the unaccustomed eye. Jimmy Delaney sensed the iron grating and then distinguished the narrow walkway fading into the dimness toward a faint red glow and the steady din of machinery. The walkway had no railings and water flowed through troughs on both sides.

"Water," said Jimmy Delaney.

"Aye, bilge," said Murphy. "Now, stay close to me and don't go off the walk."

The steady pounding of pistons filled the engine room and sweat glistened on the shirtless forms of men shoveling coal into the boilers. Cameron, master of the engine room, stood on a platform overlooking the floor. Every man fell under his gaze.

"O'Leary," shouted Cameron through a megaphone. "Ye're leavin' that fire box door open too long. The pressure is low. Put yer back to it, man. Cap'n wants eleven knots and by the devil he's going to have eleven knots."

"Gammy Scot," said Murphy. "Scots and peelers... wouldn't give a farthing for either of 'em."

"Peelers?" said Jimmy Delaney.

"Coppers," said Murphy. "Officers of the law what keeps the boot on the neck of kinsmen."

"You, Murphy...you off your nut?" said a loud voice. Murphy and Jimmy Delaney turned. Cameron was shouting from the catwalk through the megaphone. "Who's that muzzy?" he said.

"He's not a muzzy," said Murphy. "He's just a lad what's interested in things."

"Ye're on report, Murphy," said Cameron. "Get that lad topside and report to the first mate."

"Ye're an arse, Cameron," said Murphy.

"An arse is it," said Cameron. "Ye're a troublesome sort, Murphy. Ye fancy getting clapped in irons?"

"Come, lad," said Murphy, touching Jimmy Delaney's shoulder. They turned around on the fireman's walk.

"Report to the first mate, Murphy, or it's the irons," shouted Cameron.

"Filthy Scot," said Murphy.

"I am not in peril," said Jimmy Delaney.

"No bother, lad," said Murphy.

"But I am not in peril...can he not see that?"

"He's a filthy Scot," said Murphy.

"What will happen?" said Jimmy Delaney.

"It's no bother, lad."

"What will happen?"

"It's a lecture, lad...nothing else."

"I will go to this first mate and say I am not in peril," said Jimmy Delaney.

Murphy laughed. "Ah, Jimmy...Jimmy, lad," he said.

"But, I am not in peril."

"Go," said Murphy, pointing toward the bow. "We'll get topside into the light. Go ahead of me and mind the troughs."

Murphy boosted Jimmy Delaney through the opening to the fore deck, then pulled himself through and closed the hatch behind them. He looked at the sky and sniffed the air.

"Breeze up and colder," he said. "Bit of weather comin' in. Back to yer cabin now, lad."

"I'll not be bolting, Murphy" said Jimmy Delaney. "That Cameron...he's glocky."

"He's cooling me, lad...I don't chat him up," said Murphy. "It's back to yer cabin now. I must clear this

31

with the first mate. He's a Scot, but he won't make it a hangin' matter."

"I'll not be bolting," said Jimmy Delaney.

"Ye can't go, Jimmy," said Murphy.

Jimmy Delaney took off Murphy's coat and held it out. "Then I'll not be needing this," he said.

"Ye'll not be scampering about in the weather at sea without a proper coat," said Murphy.

"Beggin' your pardon, Murphy, but I'll be doing as I please," said Jimmy Delaney.

Murphy looked at the coat and narrowed his eyes and opened the gate. He pursed his lips, shook his head and motioned Jimmy Delaney through.

"Aye," said Jimmy Delaney, sliding his arm into the sleeve of the coat.

Murphy and Jimmy Delaney crossed the barrier. Murphy called to the first mate, who was about to climb the stairway to the bridge. The first mate was forty-five or so with a chiseled face and a dark beard streaked with gray. He wore a great coat with three gold stripes on the sleeves and a seaman's cap. The ship's crew had heard that he would soon get another stripe and become master of a ship. Most would be sorry to see him go.

"Aye, Murphy...it's a mascot, is it?" said the first mate.

"Reporting for the discipline," said Murphy.

"Aye, what else would it be?" said the first mate. "Cameron, I'll wager. Well, speak up, man."

"Cameron's an arse," said Murphy.

"You vex Cameron deliberate, Murphy."

"It's a toe in the hole he needs."

"I'm obliged to dock you one day," said the first mate.

"Aye," said Murphy.

"Dock?" said Jimmy Delaney.

"It's no bother, lad," said Murphy.

"This Cameron, he's glocky," said Jimmy Delaney.

"Were you in the engine room?" said the first mate.

"Aye, on the fireman's walk...and in no peril," said Jimmy Delaney. "Murphy is telling about the engine when this Cameron..."

"You took this lad through the forward hatch?" said the first mate.

"Aye," said Murphy, bowing his head.

"I was in no peril," said Jimmy Delaney. "This Cameron..."

"He's a lad what's interested in things," said Murphy. "He said a wire makes the bulbs glow...and he picks up quick. He can make fast to a cleat with a bowline and ye can see he's a strapping lad."

The first mate's eyes moved back and forth between Murphy and Jimmy Delaney. He took a deep breath and his face assumed a look of resignation.

"All right, Murphy," he said. "But it's with the understanding..."

"Aye," said Murphy.

"All right, go on then," said the first mate. He turned toward the stairway to the bridge.

"Beggin' yer pardon, sir," said Murphy.

"Aye, speak up."

"Beggin' yer pardon...would ye be supposin' the lad might see the bridge?"

"Murphy..."

"As long as he's here..."

"You fancy seeing the bridge, do you?" said the first mate.

"Aye, I might be after doin' that," said Jimmy Delaney.

"The captain is up there," said the first mate. "He will challenge you...as he would anyone who is on his bridge who shouldn't be. What will you say?"

"I'll be saying I can make fast to a cleat and I can tie bowlines, sheepshanks and hitches and stoppers," said Jimmy Delaney. "And I'll be thanking him for having me on his bridge."

The first mate laughed. "Where did you find this, Murphy?" he said.

"Ran into me chest in the fog, he did," said Murphy.

"What's your name, lad?" said the first mate.

"Jimmy Delaney...bound for America."

"Well, Jimmy Delaney, able seaman's mate...put your brogan up here on this stairway and let's go to the bridge," said the first mate.

The bridge spanned the breadth of the ship and the upper half of the forward bulkhead was made of glass panes. The master's hand rested on top of a large wooden wheel.

"I have eleven knots, Cameron," he said into a tube. "Keep the pressure up...there's weather in the air." Sensing someone behind him, the master turned. "McEwan, I suppose you have an explanation," he said.

"Aye, Captain," said the first mate. "This lad is an able seaman's mate with Murphy here."

"Aye," said Murphy.

"An able seaman's mate is it," said the master. He picked up a length of rope and tossed it to Jimmy Delaney. "Tie a bowline, lad, and bring it here," he said.

Jimmy Delaney tied a bowline knot in the rope while walking toward the master. He stopped and held out the knotted rope.

"Aye, a bowline," he said.

The master took the rope and threw it on the counter.

"Take the helm," he said. "Watch the compass... steady as she goes."

Jimmy Delaney stepped forward and grasped the large wooden wheel with both hands. He looked at the compass card balanced in a round bowl resting on a pedestal.

"West-souwest...steady as she goes," said the master.

As Jimmy Delaney bent over to watch the compass card, the master wrenched the wheel from his grip and pulled it through three turns. The bow of the ship began to slide to port and the compass card passed through south-southwest toward south.

"Captain," said Cameron's voice through the tube. "The ship is lurching. Are you there?"

The master spoke into the tube: "It's an exercise, Cameron. Keep the pressure up for eleven knots."

"Aye, Captain," said Cameron.

"Steady as she goes, I say," the master said to Jimmy Delaney.

Jimmy Delaney decided quickly that the master meant for him to come back to the previous course. He turned the wheel to the right in increments, watching the compass card, which began to move toward west and then settled on west-southwest.

"Steady as she goes," he said.

"Delaney, I believe...the only Delaneys on this crossing, as I recollect," said the master.

"Aye, Jimmy Delaney...bound for America."

"Roache is my name," said the master. "If memory serves, it was overthrowing the authority that vexed you."

"My ma and pa, they do not know those words," said Jimmy Delaney.'

"And how is it that you do?" said Roache.

"Schooling," said Jimmy Delaney.

"And your mother and father have not?"

"Aye, they have...but only writing and some reading and ciphers."

"So you speak for your family?"

"Aye...when it is comfortable for my ma and pa," said Jimmy Delaney.

"Well, Delaney, it's back to my duties," said Roache.

"Aye, I'm thanking you," said Jimmy Delaney.

Roache nodded toward McEwan, who came forward. Murphy did not move.

"See that this lad stays out of trouble," said Roache, turning away.

Jimmy Delaney, Murphy and then McEwan descended the stairway. McEwan straightened his great coat and adjusted his seaman's cap.

"Well, it's off to my duties," he said.

"It's not trouble I'm after," said Jimmy Delaney.

"The captain says many things," said McEwan. "I should not fret about it. Mind your duties now with Seaman Murphy. I'm off to my own." After a few steps, he stopped and turned. A stern expression came to his face. "Murphy..."

"Aye," said Murphy, nodding.

McEwan returned the nod and walked away.

"McEwan's not a bad sort," said Murphy.

"It's not trouble I'm after, Murphy," said Jimmy Delaney.

They passed through the gate in the railing to the fore deck and paused at the top of the stairs to the steerage deck below.

"Trouble is a ghost about the place, Jimmy," said Murphy. "And it might as not look for a fellow. It's not to be gimped...just dander a bit when the trouble is about."

"I'm no gimp, Murphy...cannot be," said Jimmy Delaney.

"It's just dandering a bit, lad," said Murphy. "Ye'll know...a laudy daw, a peeler or just an arse. There's men what has the authority given them or taken by right or just taken. I should not fret...ye're the sort of lad...well, a lad what finds his way."

"Men such as Cameron," said Jimmy Delaney.

"Aye, men such as Cameron...and men such as McEwan," said Murphy. "Some are fit to wear the authority and some for a toe in the hole."

"On the fireman's walk I saw no dandering about by such as yourself," said Jimmy Delaney.

"Dandering about is a splendid trait...especially for lads," said Murphy.

"Aye, Murphy," said Jimmy Delaney.

"Aye, Jimmy," said Murphy. "And while ye're thinkin' on that, ye might have yer supper. Yer ma, she'll be worried."

"Ma doesn't worry," said Jimmy Delaney.

"Well, to yer supper just the same," said Murphy. "Put yer nose in the air, yer eye and yer ear to the sea...what say ye?" He waited, staring intently into Jimmy Delaney's face. "Look at the bow, lad...what do ye see?" he said.

"I do not understand," said Jimmy Delaney.

"It's a bit of weather out of souwest, Jimmy," said Murphy. "The wind is freshening and the ship, it pitches by the head. The cap'n has come about to the wind... takes out the roll."

The sea raised and lowered the bow in a steady oscillating movement and the prow riding up on a wave crashed into the next and displaced the water over the deck in a fine spray.

"Aye, I see it," said Jimmy Delaney.

"Now, off with ye, lad," said Murphy. "Tomorrow morning we start again...aweather as well, if I'm not off me nut."

"Aye, Murphy," said Jimmy Delaney.

Murphy nodded and went through the gate. He walked past the stairway to the bridge, turned again, waved and disappeared through a door.

At his place near the bowsprit, Jimmy Delaney could not keep the setting sun in sight through thickening clouds. The ship pitched hard and the fore deck was awash in the breaking waves. Jimmy Delaney turned his back to the spray and came face to face with a crewman bracing himself against the mast.

"Get below, lad," said the crewman, shouting against the wind. "Ye've not proper clothing or a lashing strap. The storm, it's to be a kicker with the rain and wind."

"I had a slicker," said Jimmy Delaney.

"Well, ye've no slicker now and no lashing strap," said the crewman. "Come, I will get ye to the stairs. Ye cannot stay out here."

Water cascaded down the stairway into the corridor on the steerage deck. The crewman pushed Jimmy Delaney into the doorway.

"I'm closing the hatch, lad, to stop the water," he said. "Ye can still open it from the inside if need be."

Jimmy Delaney raised his arm in reply as the iron door slammed against the bulkhead, cutting off the water and silencing the wind. Pummeled from wall to wall, Jimmy Delaney made his way down the stairs and along the corridor to the cabin. Big Jimmy Delaney and Mary Delaney were in their bunks, staring into shadows cast by the oil lantern.

"Jimmy," said Mary Delaney.

Jimmy Delaney knelt on the floor and held on to the frame of his mother's bunk.

"Aye, Ma, it is a rough sea," he said.

"It will be all right?" said Mary Delaney.

"Aye, Ma, the captain, he has the ship turned into the wind. You're not to worry."

"Try to get some rest, Jimmy," said Mary Delaney.

Jimmy Delaney squeezed his mother's hand and, bracing himself against the wall, stripped off his wet clothing and blew out the lantern. In his bunk he pulled the blanket up around his neck and defied waves of nausea until exhaustion turned off his consciousness.

Six

"It is just something you say."

Light from the porthole filled the cabin and there was a sound of running water. Jimmy Delaney looked at the upper bunk, saw that his father was asleep, and then across the aisle to the other lower bunk.

"Ma, are you all right?" he said.

"Is it over?" said Mary Delaney.

"Aye, I think it is over," said Jimmy Delaney.

"I hear water," said Mary Delaney.

"Aye, it is coming under the door," said Jimmy Delaney.

"Under the door?" said Mary Delaney.

"Stay where you are, Ma," said Jimmy Delaney.

"See what is happening, Jimmy," said Mary Delaney.

Jimmy Delaney threw the blanket around his shoulders and opened the cabin door. Cold water carrying debris and partially digested food rushed in over his bare feet. He leaned forward, looked along the corridor and then closed the door, reducing the flow of water to a trickle.

"It's the crew, Ma," he said. "They have hoses in the corridor. It is many people, I venture, who have the seasickness."

"I thought we were going to die," said Mary Delaney. "And then I remembered that going to America is a sign."

"Aye, Ma," we're still here," said Jimmy Delaney. "I'll get on clothes and get our bearings."

"Is it over?" said Big Jimmy Delaney.

"Aye, Pa, but I do not think we'll be hearing the breakfast bell for a time," said Jimmy Delaney.

"Oh, it is not food I need," said Big Jimmy Delaney.

Jimmy Delaney opened the door. Two men with hoses were washing everything through the open bulkhead at the end of corridor and down the stairs into the engine room. Jimmy Delaney knew that the bilge pump was pushing the water through the troughs along the fireman's walk and then into the sea through ports in the hull.

"We'll be doing the cabins when we clear a place to walk and get everyone to the dining room," said one of the men.

Jimmy Delaney nodded, buttoned Murphy's coat and moved toward the stairway. He pushed open the door to the fore deck. Standing in front of him were Roache and McEwan and three other men wearing great coats with brass buttons and stripes on the sleeves.

Roache broke away from the group. He took Jimmy Delaney's arm and led him to a spot near the railing.

"Delaney, I'm afraid it is bad news," he said. "Seaman Murphy has been lost in the storm."

Jimmy Delaney did not respond.

"Did you hear me, lad?" said Roache.

"Lost in the storm?" said Jimmy Delaney.

"Aye, lad...securing the long boat," said Roache. "His lashing strap let go. There was nothing anyone could do. You may continue your training with another seaman. We can find someone for you."

"Training?" said Jimmy Delaney.

"Aye, your seaman's training," said Roache.

Jimmy Delaney blinked and looked at Roache for the first time. Then he gathered the collar of Murphy's coat tightly around his neck and looked away.

"No one can call Murphy back, lad," said Roache. "It is just bad luck...the fate of some to die young."

"There is no fate, Captain," said Jimmy Delaney. "It is just something you say."

At the railing near the bowsprit Jimmy Delaney held Murphy's coat out over the water. The sun was low in the eastern sky and the cold wind cut through his denim shirt.

"Blarney, we'll roll up the sleeves," he said. "Ye'll not

be treading this deck with Murphy without a proper coat."

Jimmy Delaney pulled the coat back and draped it over his shoulders.

"I'm thanking you, Murphy," he said.

Seven

Roache

" Jimmy, are you awake?" said Mary Delaney. "Someone is at the door."

Jimmy Delaney gathered the blanket from the bunk around his shoulders. He sensed that the ship was not moving.

"Aye, Ma," he said. He pulled open the door. "Captain Roache," he said.

"Good morning, Delaney," said Roache. "It's a calm day and we are anchored in the lower bay. Our destination is at hand. I should think you might want to take a look at Brooklyn. Step out if you please...we have business, you and I."

"Jimmy," said Mary Delaney.

"It's nothing, Ma...don't worry," said Jimmy Delaney.

"Are you in trouble, boy?" said Big Jimmy Delaney. "I have told you..."

"Sir, your son is not in trouble," said Roache. "Get into your clothes, lad, and come along. We shan't be long."

Two uniformed men were waiting near the door at the top of the stairs. Jimmy Delaney recognized the ship's medical officer. The other man, who wore a different uniform, examined a sheet of paper and regarded Jimmy Delaney with a stern expression.

"We don't burn peat, boy...we burn coal," he said. "What else can you do?"

"What is that paper you have?" said Jimmy Delaney.

"This is a manifest sheet," said the man. "And I am asking the questions."

Jimmy Delaney looked at Roache. "What is this, Captain?" he said.

"You might have given me the chance to explain," Roache said to the man. He turned toward Jimmy

42

Delaney. "This man is an American immigration official, Delaney," he said. "His name is Johnson. He is aboard to examine the passengers in second cabin for landing. Normally, our passengers in steerage are not cleared for landing aboard ship. However, since we have attested to your good health and character, you and your parents may be spared further examination at the inspection station on Ellis Island."

"Ellis Island?" said Jimmy Delaney.

"The immigration station in New York harbor," said Johnson. "In the harbor you will be put on a barge and taken there for further interrogation."

"Really, Johnson," said Roache.

"I don't have to do this, boy," said Johnson. "You should be going to the island with the rest of your kind."

"My kind?" said Jimmy Delaney.

"Really, Johnson, stop this," said Roache. "Anyone can see..."

"He's a smart aleck with a smart mouth," said Johnson.

"Can we just get on with it," said Roache.

"A smart aleck," said Johnson.

"Delaney, I gave my word that you and your family would not go to Ellis Island," said Roache. "Murphy was a troublesome sort, but that was talk and bluster. He was a good able seaman who never shirked his duty. You will please cooperate with Officer Johnson."

"Why am I talking to you, boy?" said Johnson. "Where is your father?"

"I can speak for my family," said Jimmy Delaney.

Johnson glanced at Roache, who nodded. "All right," said Johnson. "As I was saying, we burn coal..."

"I'll not be digging peat," said Jimmy Delaney.

"Well, that's a cinch, boy, since we don't have any peat," said Johnson. "What else can you do? Everyone here earns his keep."

"My pa's brother-in-law will teach him the boilermaker

trade," said Jimmy Delaney. "I will help out...and when my pa is set up as a boilermaker, I will continue my schooling."

"Schooling, huh," said Johnson. "What sort of schooling?"

"I don't know," said Jimmy Delaney. "What I know is that I will have more schooling."

"I suppose you know how much is two and one," said Johnson.

"Two and one is three," said Jimmy Delaney. "How much is thirty-six and forty-two?"

"Delaney," said Roache.

"I'm asking the questions," said Johnson.

"Seventy-eight," said Jimmy Delaney.

"Do you wash stairs from the top or the bottom?" said Johnson.

"Really, Johnson, is this necessary?" said Roache.

"From the top so as not to soil what you have already done," said Jimmy Delaney.

"Do you have someone meeting you when the ship docks?" said Johnson.

"Aye, we sent a letter to my ma's brother," said Jimmy Delaney.

"He will help you find a place to live, I take it," said Johnson.

"Aye, he will," said Jimmy Delaney.

"This manifest says you have fifty-eight dollars," said Johnson.

"Aye, it is in our cabin," said Jimmy Delaney.

"It says here you have no medical condition to report," said Johnson. "Is that right?"

"We are all able," said Jimmy Delaney.

"Very well," said Johnson. "You and your family are free to go when the ship docks." He marked three cards and held them out. "These are your immigrant cards," he said. "Show these and your medical certificates to the officer on the pier when the ship docks. Welcome to New York."

Jimmy Delaney took the cards and examined them. He put them away in the inside pocket of Murphy's coat.

"I'm thanking you," he said.

Johnson departed by launch.

"What is this Ellis Island?" said Jimmy Delaney.

"It is the immigration station in the upper bay," said Roache. "This afternoon we shall enter the upper bay and dock in the North River in Manhattan. After the liberty statue, look aport for a large building with four round towers and three archways. This building and several others are on a small island...as I said, just after the liberty statue on the port side. There will be many barges and ferries tied up at the docks and more in the river between the island and the pier line in Manhattan."

"And Murphy...why would he..."

"Assumptions are made regarding steerage immigrants," said Roache. "You heard it in Officer Johnson's tone. It is the way of things."

"They go to this place on barges?" said Jimmy Delaney.

"Aye, all the immigrant ships," said Roache. "When the ship docks, take your family through the gate and wait at the base of the stairway to the bridge. My Number One, McEwan, will be assisting the debarkation of passengers in second cabin. You will go with him."

"Aye, I understand," said Jimmy Delaney.

"I wonder if you do," said Roache. "A lad of your temperament...you must be careful."

"It's not trouble I'm after," said Jimmy Delaney.

"Well, trouble has a way of finding some lads, Delaney," said Roache. "Just take care. It's a rugged world and your fuse is short."

"Murphy said that."

"Just take care," said Roache. "Speaking of Murphy, he hoped you would be a seaman."

"I cannot," said Jimmy Delaney. "I must do my part for my family...at least until Pa is set up as a boilermaker."

"The pay is good, Delaney...better, I'm expecting, than you can do ashore."

"It is more involved than just the pay," said Jimmy Delaney.

"I see," said Roache. "Well, Delaney, it's back to my duties. I shall soon begin gathering the steerage passengers in the dining room for landing instructions. You needn't worry yourself with that. There is one last thing...your valuables. The dockside is alive with scoundrels of the most brazen sort. Do not carry your money or your cards in a suitcase. Split your valuables and carry them on your person in the inside of your coat and do not become distracted. There will be much to distract you and the thieves are depending on your carelessness. Every day brings immigrants wandering the ferry terminals in West Street with nothing left."

"What happens to them?"

Roache hesitated. "Take care of your valuables, lad," he said.

"Aye, I'm thanking you," said Jimmy Delaney.

Roache nodded, went through the gate and walked at a steady pace toward the stairway to the bridge. Jimmy Delaney watched Roache until he disappeared through a doorway and then went to the cabin.

"What did that Scotsman want?" said Mary Delaney.

"To give me these," said Jimmy Delaney, holding out the immigration cards. "It is American immigrants we are, Ma. The ship will dock in the afternoon today and we'll be meeting Tim at the dock."

Mary Delaney's eyes narrowed. "The Burkes in the cabin next door do not have cards, Jimmy," she said. "We have all heard that everyone will be examined."

"What have you done?" said Big Jimmy Delaney. "If we have trouble..."

"There's not to be trouble, Pa," said Jimmy Delaney.

"Well, how did you come about the cards?" said Mary Delaney.

"Ma, it's a long story...not worth telling," said Jimmy Delaney. "We have our cards and..."

"It is not so long you cannot tell it," said Mary Delaney.

"Some are examined on the ship," said Jimmy Delaney.

"Who is examined?" said Mary Delaney. "We have not been examined."

"It is not required, Ma...the captain, he attested for us."

"Attested for us?" said Mary Delaney. "He does not even know us."

"What have you done, boy?" said Big Jimmy Delaney.

"I've done nothing, Pa," said Jimmy Delaney. "The American official, he comes to the ship to examine the passengers in second cabin. The others, those in steerage, go to an immigration station on an island...Ellis Island, in the harbor. Captain Roache..."

"Captain Roache, is it," said Mary Delaney.

"Ma, there is nothing wrong with the cards," said Jimmy Delaney.

"We'll not be using the cards, Jimmy," said Mary Delaney. "Not until I hear how you came about them."

"I've been trying to tell you, Ma...you keep interrupting."

"Jimmy..."

"Aye, Ma. The captain asked the American official to clear us on the ship. We need not go to this Ellis Island. They crowd you together on the barges like cattle, Ma. We should be..."

"Cattle, is it," said Mary Delaney. "The Burkes and the others...cattle, are they?"

"Ma..."

"And why would that Scotsman do this for us?"

"It was a favor to my friend, Murphy," said Jimmy Delaney.

"Murphy...the man who gave you the coat," said Mary

Delaney. "Who is this Murphy and why would he give you a coat and why would he ask a favor for you? You've been gone the whole journey, Jimmy. You have not come to any of the functions in the evening. You have hardly spoken..."

"You have not associated with anyone your own age," said Big Jimmy Delaney. "And now we find this Murphy..."

"Well, we're waiting," said Mary Delaney.

"Murphy was lost in the storm, Ma," said Jimmy Delaney. "He was my friend and Captain Roache..."

"Lost in the storm?"

"Aye, Ma...he was securing the long boat in the storm and his lashing strap gave way. He was my friend... teaching me seamanship...and he made it so we would not have to go to the immigration station and maybe be sent back."

"Why would they send us back?" said Mary Delaney.

"I don't know, Ma," said Jimmy Delaney. "Why do those who have the authority do anything?"

"You'll keep a civil tongue in your head, Jimmy," said Mary Delaney.

"I've done nothing wrong, Ma, and you and Pa..."

"You have too many secrets, Jimmy," said Mary Delaney.

"How are we to know?" said Big Jimmy Delaney. "You are gone all hours of the day and night and no one knows where you are or what..."

"I'm not to find my own way, Pa?" said Jimmy Delaney.

"That schoolmaster, O'Donnell, has filled your head with malarkey," said Big Jimmy Delaney. "You have not any respect for Father Callaghan and you do not know your place."

"Father Callaghan is against learning, Pa," said Jimmy Delaney. "It's not the priests I'll be listening to and my place is not in a peat bog."

"Jimmy," said Mary Delaney. "You will apologize to your father."

"It's no disrespect, Ma," said Jimmy Delaney. "The elders say the priest spread poison that Tim was no good...going to sea when Grandpa O'Brien was down with a sickness, but he was right to find his way just as Pa was and I am. That priest, Callaghan..."

"Tim should have waited," said Big Jimmy Delaney.

"Let's not argue," said Mary Delaney. "Soon we'll be meeting Tim."

"Pa, we must split the money and carry it in our pockets," said Jimmy Delaney. "I am told that thieves stalk the dockside. It is many people milling around. We must take care and not be distracted."

"Thieves on the dock?" said Big Jimmy Delaney.

"Thieves are everywhere, Pa," said Jimmy Delaney. "In Castlerea they steal the alms from the church."

"The lads do not steal from the church," said Big Jimmy Delaney.

"We should divide the money," said Mary Delaney.

"Aye," said Big Jimmy Delaney. "But it seems to me..."

"We'll divide the money," said Mary Delaney.

Big Jimmy Delaney took the money from the suitcase. Jimmy Delaney consigned eight five-dollar notes and the coins to the inside pocket of Murphy's coat.

"Carry this in the pocket of your coat, Pa," he said, holding out the remaining bills.

"Aye," said Big Jimmy Delaney. "But it still seems to me..."

"Everyone to the dining room," said a voice from the corridor. "Attention, everyone to the dining room for docking instructions."

"It's the instructions for Ellis Island," said Jimmy Delaney.

"We do not need these instructions?" said Mary Delaney.

"We have our cards, Ma," said Jimmy Delaney.

"We should ask the Burkes," said Big Jimmy Delaney.

"The Burkes are going to Ellis Island, Pa," said Jimmy Delaney.

"Are you sure about this, Jimmy?" said Mary Delaney.

"Aye, Ma..."

"The Burkes will think something is wrong," said Mary Delaney.

"Aye, we should go for the meeting," said Big Jimmy Delaney.

"Pa..."

"We will go for the meeting," said Mary Delaney.

The Delaneys merged into the crowd in the corridor just behind John Burke, a large man who had gathered his wife and their four children into his arms and guided them into the line. The crowd flowed steadily through the double doors into the dining room.

Roache stood inside the doors. Seeing Jimmy Delaney, he appeared puzzled, then nodded. When everyone was in the dining room he climbed onto a table and surveyed the crowd.

""Good morning," said Roache. "Soon we will dock in New York and everyone seeking residence in America will disembark and board launches for the immigration station at Ellis Island. As you leave the ship, a member of the crew will attach a tag to your clothing. The tag is of no concern...it allows the American authorities to identify the passengers from this ship as opposed to other ships in the harbor. When you arrive at Ellis Island, you will check your luggage in the baggage room and proceed to a set of stairs. At the top of the stairs is the registry room, a very large hall where you will form into queues for examination by the authorities. Certain questions will be put to you. Answer as honestly as you can. Some of you may receive a chalk mark on your clothing and some may be detained for a few hours or a few days. After examination, you will proceed to another set of stairs down to the baggage room where you will collect your luggage and queue up for the ferry to the city. Those who have destinations other than New York may purchase railroad tickets before boarding the ferry. Please check your cabin thoroughly for all of your belongings before leaving the ship. Good luck and I wish you all the best."

Roache scanned the room. The Delaney family stood near the door. Roache worked his way through the crowd, answering questions. He approached Big Jimmy Delaney.

"You have your cards," he said. "When the ship docks, simply show the cards to the American official and go about your business."

"Aye," said Big Jimmy Delaney.

"This meeting is for passengers taking the launch to Ellis Island," said Roache. "Has your son not explained this?"

"Aye," said Big Jimmy Delaney.

"This special treatment," said Mary Delaney. "How is it that..."

"Madam, please accept this gesture in a spirit of goodwill," said Roache. "It was the wish of one of my best crewmen. It is not generally known, of course, but we lost a crewman in the storm. His name was Murphy. As you may know, he befriended your son. They were friends."

"Murphy, who gave my Jimmy the coat," said Mary Delaney.

"Aye, Murphy," said Roache.

"Very well," said Mary Delaney. "We will use the cards. We are thanking you."

Roache nodded formally and backed away, turned and left the room.

In the afternoon the *Edinburgh* weighed anchor and fell into a line of ships crossing the Narrows. Jimmy Delaney stood on a step at the base of the bowsprit. Big Jimmy Delaney and Mary Delaney and the suitcases stood beside him. Jimmy Delaney had explained Roache's instructions.

"Almost there, Ma," said Jimmy Delaney.

"Aye, Jimmy, almost there," said Mary Delaney.

The ship cleared the Bay Ridge bulge, which carried Brooklyn into the Narrows, and the cavernous glacial hole forming the upper bay opened like a panorama. The collective gasp of passengers pressed against the railings was audible. A maelstrom of maritime commerce churned the gray water into foam and looming in the distance, blurred by a haze of smoke, was the skyline of Manhattan. Jimmy Delaney's startled gaze was drawn to an ocean liner crossing the bow of the *Edinburgh*. The liner, attended by tugboats pushing against the hull, was an iron colossus with two rows of portholes and a superstructure of more decks than Jimmy Delaney could count at a distance. Three masts and two stacks reached into the sky. The name *Oceanic* emblazoned the rounded stern high above the water and the union jack, hoisted to the top of the fore mast, telegraphed Britannia to the world.

The *Edinburgh* and other ships in line for docks steamed out of the Narrows into the center of the harbor. The *Oceanic* had crossed the starboard bow and was well aport, close to the piers jutting into the bay from the Jersey City waterfront. Jimmy Delaney studied the chaos and realized that the line of ships from the lower bay steered a straight inbound course and vessels crossing the bay timed their approaches to slip through the line under full steam.

"Aye," he said. "I see how it is done."

"Are you speaking to me, Jimmy?" said Mary Delaney.

"Just mumbling, Ma...it's nothing," said Jimmy Delaney.

"The liberty statue...America," shouted a boy.

A crowd rushed to the port railing. Several men hoisted the boy onto their shoulders and cheered. Jimmy

Delaney studied the statue; that it would be pale green had not occurred to him. He turned away toward the starboard side and the stone towers of a bridge came into view. He knew the bridge from photographs. Staring at the bridge, he wondered why the liberty statue was so much smaller than he had imagined and the bridge so much larger. The bridge, suspended from the massive stone towers, was the purest grandeur, something that did not seem to belong in the world.

The wakes spreading out from the ships broke over the low concrete foundation which sculpted Ellis Island into two squares separated by a narrow harbor. The harbor was lined with barges which stirred the foam and debris into eddies. The barges discharged streams of people and their possessions onto scaffolding made of rough hewn boards nailed to stubby pilings and steadied by poles extending into the water. The people were moving toward a metal and glass awning over the central arch of the large building Roache had described. All were dressed in homespun worsted or denim. Jimmy Delaney could see their faces beneath the hats or bandanas tied into scarves. He could almost hear the clopping sound of brogans against the boards.

"Aye, Ellis Island," he said.

Jimmy Delaney looked again toward the *Oceanic* and his gaze swung around through the skyline of steel and masonry to the great bridge, now close enough to engulf him.

"What manner of men can build such things?" he said.

The *Edinburgh* steamed past the Battery into the river separating Manhattan from New Jersey. The river, almost a mile wide, had been known to mariners as the North River for as long as any sailor could remember and anyone in the ferry terminals or warehouses along West Street who said the river was called Hudson was known to be landlubber or an outsider. Atlantic brine pushed inland for miles and ebbed, allowing cold Adirondack water to vortex into the upper bay and those who made their way on the river obliged its every nuance. The vessels plying the choppy gray water were fast sloops and side-wheelers, plodding schooners, flat scows bearing rail cars and tugboats towing barges strung out behind them and bludgeoning their way through the traffic were the railroad ferries, kings of the river. A deep-throated steam whistle announced a ferry painted Tuscan red with yellow piping. The ferry crossed the port bow of the *Edinburgh*, splitting the line of ships from the bay. Horses and freight wagons packed the lower deck at the waterline and hundreds of commuters and rail travelers pushed against the railing on the passenger deck just below the wheelhouse. The vibration in the deck of the *Edinburgh* waned as Roache slowed and turned aport to pass behind the ferry. Jimmy Delaney was amazed by the chaotic flow of traffic on the river. He was unaware that a steamer had rammed a ferry the previous night and that collective memory of the collision had been lost with the dawn.

The *Edinburgh* shuddered in protest as the engine was pressed into reverse. Jimmy Delaney looked for the *Oceanic*, far ahead of them now, still pushed along by tugboats near the New Jersey shore. As the *Edinburgh* began a turn to starboard toward the pier line, so did the *Oceanic* begin a sweeping motion into the center of the river. Jimmy Delaney felt another shudder as Roache worked the *Edinburgh* expertly into a slip at the foot of Cedar Street. Jimmy Delaney felt the ship brush against the bumpers along the pier and heard the venting steam as the engine was shut down. The steady vibration under his feet faded.

"We're here, Ma," he said. "It's through the gate behind us."

McEwan stood with a group of second class passengers near the stairway to the bridge. A section of the railing had been removed and a gangway spanned the gap to the pier. Two men wearing dark blue uniforms stood on the pier at the end of the gangway.

"Delaney, you and your family...this way," said McEwan.

Jimmy Delaney lifted one of the suitcases and took his mother's arm with his free hand and moved toward McEwan. Big Jimmy Delaney, carrying the other two suitcases, followed.

A man wearing a topcoat and bowler hat stepped in front of the Delaneys, blocking their way.

"What are these steerage people doing here?" he said.

"Jimmy," said Mary Delaney, as her hand swept across her breast and clamped Jimmy Delaney's forearm.

"I didn't pay good money..."

"You'll mind your mouth," said McEwan, stepping forward and nudging the man to the side. "The captain decides what is done here. I require no assistance from you. Is that quite clear?"

The man blanched and backed away. McEwan guided the Delaneys across the gangway. Jimmy Delaney held out the cards toward one of the men in uniform. The man examined the cards and looked up.

"Where did you steal these cards, boy?" he said.

"The cards for this family were issued this morning aboard ship by Officer Johnson," said McEwan.

"This is Johnson's signature right enough," said the man. "Why would he issue these cards? This is irregular."

"The cards are legitimate," said McEwan. "You have my word."

"We should check with Johnson," said the other man in uniform.

"I can't," said the first man. "He's on duty out at the island."

"McEwan's mouth tightened. "I assure you..."

"All right," said the first man, handing the cards to Jimmy Delaney. "You're passed."

The Delaneys walked past the two men and started toward the terminal, joining a steady stream of second class passengers from another steamer docked in the adjacent slip. Jimmy Delaney stopped and turned. People walked around him. He raised his arm.

"Good luck, lad," called McEwan.

Jimmy Delaney looked up toward the bridge. Roache, standing behind the windows, tipped his cap. Jimmy Delaney waved and turned away.

Eight

73 Ludlow Street

The Delaneys made their way along the pier and passed through an iron gate into the terminal. Passengers waiting to board ships and ferries pressed against the gate; guards worked them toward the walls to provide a path for arriving passengers. The Delaneys pushed their way into the terminal.

"Where is Tim?" said Mary Delaney.

"Do you see him, Pa?" said Jimmy Delaney.

"It is so many people," said Big Jimmy Delaney.

"If our letter did not reach him, he would not know we are here," said Mary Delaney.

"Aye, what are we to do?" said Big Jimmy Delaney.

"I wonder if he is waiting for us outside," said Mary Delaney.

"Aye, he is waiting outside, watching the door," said Big Jimmy Delaney.

The Delaneys moved through the crowd toward one of the exit doors. Above the door was a sign: *Please use spittoons. Gentleman must not spit on the sidewalk.* The Delaneys went through the door and emerged from the terminal under a shed covering the sidewalk. They were engulfed by a blast of warm air carrying the smell of horses at close quarter. The iron wheels of horse-drawn freight wagons and ice trucks ground into the cobblestone street. The teamsters pulled up abruptly, shouting obscenities, and then urged the horses forward around pushcarts, trolleys with clanging bells, pedestrians and knots of men conducting business. The Delaneys backed away from the edge of the sidewalk, inched their way along the terminal wall and stopped just short of an alley lined with wagons waiting for the ferry.

"Where is Tim?" said Mary Delaney.

"I did not dream America would be like this," said Big Jimmy Delaney. "What are we to do?"

Jimmy Delaney glanced toward his mother. The expectation he had first seen in her eyes as they settled into the ox cart was there now. He lifted the suitcase he had been carrying.

"Pick up the suitcases, Pa," he said.

"We have no place to go...where are we to go?" said Big Jimmy Delaney. "Tim is not here. What are we to do?"

"Back inside," said Jimmy Delaney. "We will find a quiet corner away from the rush and decide what we are to do."

Jimmy Delaney guided his parents to a row of benches inside the terminal. They sat in the last spaces where the bench ended at a wall. Jimmy Delaney pushed his suitcase under his father's feet.

"Pa, it is either that Tim did not receive our letter or he thinks our ship is docking later," he said. "We cannot stay here. I will find someone who knows directions for Ludlow Street. You must watch the suitcases and look after Ma." He engaged his mother's eyes. "Ma, you and Pa must stay where you are," he said. "I must know where you are while I'm getting the directions. If Tim comes, you must tell him to wait here."

"What are we to do?" said Big Jimmy Delaney.

"We will wait here, Jimmy," said Mary Delaney.

Jimmy Delaney nodded. "Don't worry, Ma," he said.

Emerging into West Street, Jimmy Delaney looked along the sidewalk in both directions and into the traffic. He saw a man standing on the corner across the street from the terminal. The man wore dark blue trousers and a dark blue coat with two rows of brass buttons and a helmet similar to those worn by policemen in Galway. He swung a short wooden club on a leather strap.

"Aye, a peeler," said Jimmy Delaney, stepping off the sidewalk into West Street. He made his way through the traffic, dodging horses and fending off the shouts of pushcart vendors. He approached the policeman.

"And what have we here?" said the policeman.

"Ludlow Street," said Jimmy Delaney, relieved to hear a thick Irish brogue. "Do you know Ludlow Street?"

"Aye, I know it...some way from here," said the policeman. "There's nothing much but haythen now, least on the bottom end. The lads have been moving north for some years...other side of Delancey, all the way to Fourteenth. Me, I come of age up on Eighth...way over near the river. How are ye called, lad?"

"Jimmy Delaney...hailing from County Roscommon," said Jimmy Delaney. "My uncle lives in Ludlow Street."

"Name's Callaghan," said the policeman. "Just off the boat, are ye?"

"Aye, the Edinburgh from Galway...just an hour ago," said Jimmy Delaney. "My ma and pa are in the terminal. I know a Callaghan."

"Priest or copper?" said Callaghan.

"Priest...back in Ireland," said Jimmy Delaney.

"Figured," said Callaghan. "Priests and coppers, lad... priests and coppers and a dash of thieving politician, that's us Callaghans. All but my pa...he was a bartender... didn't fancy priests and coppers or politicians either. My ma and pa, they come over in the great hunger. Pa was a big, strapping fellow...got three hundred dollars from a laudy daw in Gramercy Park to fight in that war...the civil war, they call it. Lived through it, too, he did. Yer uncle...he is not here to meet ye?"

"I wrote to him, but sure we have no way to know..."

"Ludlow is a long hike, lad. Ye're a little pasty, to know the truth. The crossing, I expect. How much ye loaded with?"

"It's just three suitcases...but my ma and pa need a place to ease up," said Jimmy Delaney.

"Ye've money for the trolley?"

"Aye, I've money."

"Are ye a quick lad with a clear head?"

"Aye," said Jimmy Delaney. "I won't be forgetting."

"This here where we're standing is the corner of Cedar and West," said Callaghan. "Walk along Cedar to Broadway...yer ma and pa can make five blocks?"

"Aye, this way," said Jimmy Delaney, pointing east along Cedar.

"Aye, five blocks to Broadway," said Callaghan.

"Five blocks," said Jimmy Delaney.

"Now, I'm giving ye the trolley, lad," said Callaghan. "Go all the way to Broadway. Ye'll get to two Els on the way...Greenwich and Church...but ye don't get to Ludlow on the El. Just walk under the tracks and keep on Cedar 'til ye come to Broadway."

"Under the tracks?" said Jimmy Delaney. "The tracks are on a bridge?"

"Aye, Els...elevated trains," said Callaghan. "Ye climb the stairs to the platforms. Just walk under the tracks and keep on Cedar."

"Aye, under the tracks," said Jimmy Delaney. "Cedar to Broadway...five blocks."

"Now, get on the Broadway trolley," said Callaghan. "Be sure ye get the northbound. The southbound goes to the Bowling Green and ye'll be obliged to start over. Coming out of Cedar, the northbound will be from yer right and going up Broadway. Ye know left from right?"

"Aye, the Broadway trolley coming from the right," said Jimmy Delaney.

"Good, lad," said Callaghan. "Now, minding yer step, ye cross Broadway to the other side and take the northbound. Stay on the trolley 'til it stops at Park Row and get off. The conductor will be calling the stops."

"Aye, off at Park Row," said Jimmy Delaney.

"Now, on Park Row, ye'll see a head end stop...that's the Bowery line and the Centre line. Take the Bowery line...it goes under the El at the Brooklyn Bridge to Chatham Square and from there ye'll veer into Bowery. Ye got that?"

"Head end?" said Jimmy Delaney.

"The Park Row track ends at Broadway," said Callaghan. "The trolley comes down Park Row and makes a circle just at Broadway...it's a head end loop...and goes back up Park Row. That's yer car...the Bowery line."

"Aye, the Bowery line," said Jimmy Delaney.

"Aye, now stay on that car 'til it stops at Delancey and get off...ye're almost there," said Callaghan. "Just cross under the El on Bowery and walk down Delancey toward the river. That's to yer right."

"Aye, under the El and Delancey to the right," said Jimmy Delaney.

"Aye...off the trolley, ye'll be on the right side for Delancey," said Callaghan. "Just walk under the El. There's another car eastbound along Delancey, but ye have...let's see...just about six blocks to Ludlow. If ye walk it, ye'll not have another fare. Have ye the address?"

"Seventy-three," said Jimmy Delaney. "Seventy-three Ludlow Street."

"That's close in on Delancey...to yer right off Delancey a block or so, I'm thinking," said Callaghan. "Now, it's a jungle in there, lad...ye may have to ask again to check what I said and find the right building."

"Aye," said Jimmy Delaney.

"Can ye say all that back to me now?" said Callaghan.

"I'm thanking you, Callaghan," said Jimmy Delaney. "I'll not be forgetting...I make pictures."

"As ye say, lad," said Callaghan, touching his helmet lightly with the night stick. "Good luck to ye."

Callaghan crossed Cedar and ambled along West Street, greeting one merchant and then another. Jimmy Delaney watched Callaghan until he disappeared into the crowd.

"Not so bad, Murphy," he said. "He's fit to wear the authority."

Jimmy Delaney returned to the terminal. His parents were sitting on the isolated bench where he had left them.

Vulnerability was in their posture and their faces, even from a distance.

"We worried you were lost," said Mary Delaney.

"Just outside, Ma," said Jimmy Delaney. "A policeman, Callaghan by name, gave me the directions for Ludlow Street and the history of his life as well."

Mary Delaney smiled. "It is good to keep your humor in times like these, Jimmy," she said.

"We must go back home," said Big Jimmy Delaney.

"There is nothing for us there, Pa," said Jimmy Delaney. "Do you not see that?"

"There is nothing for us here," said Big Jimmy Delaney. "Tim is not here. We know no one and no one knows us. What are we to do?"

"Tim could not have known the hour the ship would dock, Pa," said Jimmy Delaney. "Even Captain Roache could not say our time at sea or the time for a dock to open. It is many crossings he has been late by a day or more."

"Should we wait for Tim?" said Mary Delaney.

"We have no lodging, Ma, and we cannot stay here in this place," said Jimmy Delaney. "We must go along to Ludlow Street. It is strange to us, I know, but I have the directions. With darkness coming soon, Tim will be home."

Mary Delaney nodded.

Attuned to the chaos, Jimmy Delaney guided his parents easily through the traffic in West Street. With directions to Ludlow Street and his parents in tow, he allowed himself a beginning of acquaintance with his new home. Cedar Street teemed with activity and yet east of Washington, only steps from West Street, the city began to shed the waterfront and east of the elevated railway on Greenwich the temper of the city was smoother, its pace more ordered. Passing under the railway on Church and crossing Temple, Jimmy Delaney led his parents into a canyon formed by buildings and from the front of the American Bank Exchange Building at the corner of Broadway he met another of the city's many identities.

The Delaneys beheld a thoroughfare of smooth brick accommodating a carriage lane and two trolley tracks on its east side and a second venue for carriages on its west side. The avenue was bounded by wide sidewalks and an uninterrupted line of hansom cabs and broughams tethered to horses that were sleeker and less muscled than those on the waterfront. The people in this new world, if they had been on the waterfront, had crossed the river on the ferries and fanned out of West Street on Cortlandt, Liberty, Cedar, Albany, Carlisle and Rector for Broadway. The men wore gray trousers and frock coats or morning suits with dark waistcoats and top hats or bowlers rather than the hard denim and wool caps of West Street. The women were daintier and their faces seemed smoother and their hair was gathered under broad-brimmed hats and their long dark dresses seemed to glide along the sidewalks.

"They're all laudy daws, Ma," said Jimmy Delaney.

"You musn't say that, Jimmy," said Mary Delaney. "It is unkind."

"Unkind?"

"Jimmy..."

"Aye, Ma," said Jimmy Delaney.

"Where should we go from here?" said Mary Delaney.

"Aye, Ma, the trolley," said Jimmy Delaney.

The trolley cars were bright yellow or orange with green metal roofs. The motorman, in a blue uniform, stood on an open platform behind a white panel across the front of the car bearing four numbers and a headlight. Jimmy Delaney had unobstructed views from the large side windows that dropped into the body of the car. He was aware that the other passengers did not talk; they sat on the wooden slat benches or stood holding leather straps attached to the roof and most were reading newspapers. At Park Row the Delaneys stepped into the street with two men wearing suits and bowler hats.

"Well, there's Mullet's monstrosity," said one of the men.

Jimmy Delaney followed the man's line of sight. Directly in front of him was a building with four stories of multiple colonnades in receding set-backs and an exaggerated mansard roof as the fifth story.

"A monument to Victorian excess and a disgrace for a post office," said the other man.

The two men crossed in front of the trolley car to the other side of Broadway and merged into the crowd on Vesey Street.

Jimmy Delaney regarded Mullet's monstrosity. Even without an understanding of Victorian excess, he agreed that the post office building was ugly. His gaze swung across Broadway to a stone church behind a wrought iron fence and then back toward the two buildings behind him that rose majestically out of the corner of Broadway and Park Row. He regarded Callaghan's head end loop and sighted along the four trolley tracks set in the brick surface of Park Row.

"Just here where the trolley turns around," he said. "We go this way."

Clearing Mullet's monstrosity, the trolley car window framed a building of white marble with a domed clock tower set behind a pedestrian mall which defined the boundary of a large park with sapling trees and a circular fountain. Jimmy Delaney willed himself to look ahead toward an enclosed elevated railway, which he took to be Callaghan's approach to the Brooklyn Bridge. The trolley car swayed ahead, bell clanging. Freight wagons, hansom cabs, pushcarts and pedestrians and flat-bottomed drays with slatted sides carrying stacks of newspapers abandoned the tracks for a moment and then closed in again behind the passing trolley car. Even graced by greenery and white marble, Park Row did not have the breadth and feel of Broadway and its pace could not match the temper of the waterfront. Park Row was yet another city, a tamer account of both Broadway and

West. Remembering the stark sameness of the stone buildings lining cobblestone streets in Castlerea and Galway, Jimmy Delaney was amazed that a place could be transformed by turning a corner.

As the trolley car passed the marble building, many people were streaming into a barn-shaped building of stone and glass which anchored the enclosed elevated railway extending over the street. Snapping his head forward, Jimmy Delaney realized that two tracks in Park Row turned sharply to the left into another street just before reaching the elevated railway. He could see that their car would pass under the railway, just as it did in his picture, and yet, not expecting any of the tracks to turn, he felt a surge of panic. The trolley car passed another car turning off Park Row and stopped next to the stairway from the street to the railway platform. Admonishing himself for a lapse of attention, Jimmy Delaney pulled Murphy's coat close to his body and stood.

"Do we get off, Jimmy?" said Mary Delaney.

"Just stay where you are, Ma," said Jimmy Delaney, willing himself to stay calm. "I'll just get a better view." He worked his way to the front of the car. "This is the Bowery line?" he said to the motorman.

"Chatham Square, Bowery, Cooper Square, Third Avenue and uptown," said the motorman. "Was yesterday, still is today and will be tomorrow."

Jimmy Delaney returned to his seat.

"It's just a short way now, Ma," he said. "We get off soon."

Mary Delaney nodded. Big Jimmy clutched the suitcases between his knees and stared straight ahead.

The trolley car swung out of Chatham Square into Bowery. Almost as wide as Broadway, the Bowery bricks encased two trolley tracks in the center of the street and two thoroughfares for carriages. The street was bounded by elevated railways covering the sidewalks. The bridges carrying the tracks passed within a few feet of the third floor windows of plain brick buildings, interrupted occasionally by a more ornate structure or a Victorian frame house.

"Delancey next," called the trolley car operator.

Jimmy Delaney's attention automatically shifted away from an ornate marble arcade which reminded him of a tomb in the midst of gravestones.

"We get off here, Ma," he said. "We're almost there now."

"It is all so confusing and tiring, Jimmy," said Mary Delaney.

"I know, Ma...it's not long now," said Jimmy Delaney.

The Delaneys stepped off the trolley car into Bowery Street. Looking along Delancey, they saw a boulevard with a wide promenade in the center lined with streetlights and wrought iron benches with wooden-slatted seats and backs. The boulevard teemed with traffic and pedestrians. Big Jimmy Delaney dropped the two suitcases under his charge; they thudded against the bricks.

"Tim, he could not live in a place like this," he said. "Are we lost, Jimmy?"

"It's just along here, Pa," said Jimmy Delaney. "It is not far now."

"Are you sure?" said Big Jimmy Delaney.

"Aye, Pa...I have the directions."

The Delaneys walked under the railway bridge on the east side of Bowery and merged into the crowd on the Delancey promenade. Men in work clothes or well-worn suits and women wearing long dark skirts and white blouses and hats with crepe flowers made their way around tables set up for checkers or dominoes. Boys in knickers chased girls in print dresses, scattering flocks of pigeons eating peanuts thrown from the benches. The spires and monuments of Broadway and Park Row had given way to nondescript brick buildings with shops that spilled out into stalls on the sidewalks. The suits and buttoned waistcoats were ill-fitting and frayed and the hats were sweat-stained. The same suits hung from racks on the sidewalks.

The Delaneys crossed Allen Street under the elevated railway. Jimmy Delaney overheard men sitting on the benches talking about the new Williamsburg Bridge. The construction site near the end of Delancey Street had come into view. The steel towers dominating the skyline bestowed distinction and east of Orchard Street the second bridge across the East River was the talk of the neighborhood. The approach, rising steeply out of Delancey Street, would provide a majestic climb to the bridge by railway, carriageway or promenade.

The Delaneys stared along Ludlow Street from the corner of Delancey. Jimmy Delaney had not imagined the scene confronting him. No wider than West Street, Ludlow was lined with tenement buildings and awning-covered store fronts. Men in white shirts and suspenders sat on stools behind stalls which extended the stores into the sidewalk. The stalls in front of markets displayed fruit and vegetables and fish laying on chipped ice in partitioned bins and plucked chickens and ducks, hams and sausages hung from hooks. There was no distinction between the sidewalks and the street; both were jammed with people and wagons and peddlers with pushcarts. The sound of the street was a steady din of iron wheels grinding against the cobblestones and the echoes of myriad voices contending for notice. The smell blended humanity, horses, fish and meat-flavored coal smoke.

"We must try to find Tim," said Jimmy Delaney.

"It is possible that he lives here?" said Mary Delaney.

"Aye, Ma, this is Ludlow Street," said Jimmy Delaney.

"Is there a different Ludlow Street?" said Mary Delaney.

"Jimmy, you have brought us to the wrong place," said Big Jimmy Delaney. "Tim, he would not..."

"Sit here on the bench," said Jimmy Delaney. "Sit

here and rest and I will find number seventy-three and then we will know for sure."

"You will get lost, Jimmy," said Mary Delaney. "This place..."

"You must not leave this bench, Ma," said Jimmy Delaney. "We must find out if Tim is here or on a different Ludlow Street. It is much faster if I go alone, but you must stay here so I will know..."

"All right, Jimmy," said Mary Delaney.

Wrapping himself in Murphy's coat, Jimmy Delaney merged into the crowd and began looking for numbers on the buildings. He walked one block, crossed Broome Street and found a building with 73 engraved on a brass plate over the entrance to a shop with used furniture, coal stoves and oil lanterns behind the display windows. Above the shop was a brick building of six floors with iron fire escapes on each floor and several ladders extending to the sidewalk. An iron stairway passed over the entrance to the shop, connecting the sidewalk to a stoop on the second floor.

Jimmy Delaney considered going into the shop, then climbed the stairway and opened the door on the second floor. Straight ahead of him was a narrow hallway leading to a wooden door. To his right was a dark, narrow stairway to the upper floors. A man stood before a row of mail boxes on the wall at the bottom of the stairway.

"Sir, do you know Tim O'Brien?" said Jimmy Delaney.

The man turned. He regarded Jimmy Delaney cautiously.

"Used to, before he got killed," he said.

"Killed?" said Jimmy Delaney. "Tim O'Brien is dead?"

"Boiler he was working on blew up...gone, just like that," said the man, snapping his fingers. "O'brien and a slew of others...never knew what hit them. You a relative?"

Jimmy Delaney nodded. "Nephew," he said.

"Nephew, huh," said the man. "Well, sorry to be the one has to tell you."

"What do I tell Ma?" said Jimmy Delaney.

Nine

Holding On

Jimmy Delaney had been reluctant to leave the grocery store in Hester Street for the job at the stove factory in Peck Slip. Solomon Weiss, an elderly man who could not lift heavy boxes, said that other boys needed work and besides, a man could not settle for eight dollars a week if he had another honest job for twelve dollars a week. Solomon Weiss hired a new boy who sat on a crate when not being watched. Solomon Weiss hired another boy who came to work late on the second day of his employment and then a third boy. Jimmy Delaney watched the new boy for three days before taking the job in Peck Slip.

In the neighborhood it was said that Jimmy Delaney had not turned his back to Solomon Weiss, who had rescued him, passing over industrious and thrifty Jewish boys. In the neighborhood it was said that Jimmy Delaney got the job at the stove factory because Chisel Bill Bannister knew a man who knew Tommy Monaghan, the dock foreman, and even without an inside track, Tommy Monaghan had come across from Ballymoe, a stone's throw across the river from County Roscommon. Jimmy Delaney was lucky. Everyone said so.

"Jaysus, Jimmy, what'd ye do?" said Tommy Monaghan.

"I went back and told them, Tommy...what else could I do?" said Jimmy Delaney.

"Well, after that."

"On the way back I remembered the forty dollars in the inside pocket of my coat," said Jimmy Delaney. "I did not know what we were to do, but I did know that the forty dollars would answer many questions."

"Aye, that it does," said Tommy Monaghan.

"We had two nights with board at the settlement house for a donation of five dollars," said Jimmy Delaney.

"Up on Eldridge at Rivington?" said Tommy Monaghan.

"Aye, that's the one," said Jimmy Delaney.

"Jaysus, Jimmy...nerves of iron, lad," said Tommy Monaghan. "Just off the boat, fourteen years old, yer ma's brother deader'n a cold mackerel...how'd ye find the settlement house?"

"Copper...just like before," said Jimmy Delaney. "There he is, standing on the corner of Broome and Ludlow. Dark's coming on, I tell him. I'm after lodging for my ma and pa and myself...I can pay, I tell him. The settlement house, he says...a nice room with meals for a donation. Just temporary, though, he says. Two nights... that's what we got."

Tommy Monaghan's face relaxed into a blank stare. He drew on his clay pipe and blew out the smoke.

"I come over on my own," he said. "Nothing in Ballymoe but raw weather an' I ain't workin' in no bog in raw weather or no kind of weather, I tell 'em."

"It's the bogs for most lads around there, Tommy," said Jimmy Delaney.

"Not me, Jimmy," said Tommy Monaghan. "Jaysus, there I am, just off the barge from the island...standin' in West Street with fifty cents. Wound up in a flophouse on Bayard...a mattress in a corner for ten cents a day. Ye had to stoop over to get through the door...just like them beer cellars."

"I've seen them," said Jimmy Delaney. "I think my ma might have lost herself in one of those. Sure there are things she need not know."

"Aye, Jimmy, they ain't no place for decent women," said Tommy Monaghan. He withdrew a knife from his pocket and opened the four-inch blade. It was honed to a fine edge. "Right after I got outa there's when I got this," he said.

"You've got to persevere, Tommy," said Jimmy Delaney.

"Persevere...like keep on it?" said Tommy Monaghan.

"Like keep on it," said Jimmy Delaney.

At the settlement house Jimmy Delaney met a man who knew a man who managed a tenement in Eldridge Street for his brother. He had a vacancy. Jimmy Delaney went to the tenement and asked the owner's brother about the vacancy. They climbed the narrow stairway to the third floor, walked along a hallway toward the rear of the building and entered the kitchen of a three-room apartment. The kitchen was the center of the apartment, separating a bedroom from a larger living room with two windows overlooking a fire escape which dropped into a yard. The view across the ten-foot yard was the rear apartment of a tenement facing Allen Street.

"It's a back apartment away from the noise," said the brother. "The privies are in the hall, just across from the stairway...two privies and another sink in addition to the sink here in the kitchen. I get twenty a month...one month in advance."

"It's a lot," said Jimmy Delaney.

"This is nineteen and two, boy...but I'll make it fifteen if you know a janitor," said the brother. "The janitor quit. It's worth five to take it off my hands."

"Five dollars a month and my pa will take on the janitor job," said Jimmy Delaney, holding out a five-dollar bill.

"Fifteen dollars a month for a janitor?" said the brother.

"As you say, it's nineteen and two," said Jimmy Delaney.

"You're just a kid," said the brother. "How do I know he'll take the job?"

"If my pa does not take the job, it's twenty a month for the lodging," said Jimmy Delaney.

"All right, kid, but them privies better stay clean," said

the brother, accepting the five-dollar bill. "The janitor in this block..."

"Block?" said Jimmy Delaney.

"This building is five stories and four blocks...eighty apartments in all. We're on the third floor in the block on the north end. There's a janitor for each block, which means climbing the stairs every day. Does your old man have the stamina?"

"Twenty apartments for each janitor," said Jimmy Delaney. "Four apartments on each floor, five floors, one block."

The brother's eyes narrowed. "As I was sayin', the janitor sweeps up the foyer downstairs by the mail boxes," he said. "And he keeps the hallways clean and picks up the crap in his piece of the yard out back. In the morning he delivers a daily allotment of coal to each apartment from the basement...five floors, twenty apartments. And one other thing...we don't carry deadbeats. When there's an eviction, the janitor takes all the belongings and whatnot down to the street. Now, most important, he keeps the privies clean...and I mean clean. Times ain't what they used to be. I got them health hounds on Park Row sniffin' around like buzzards and if they get on me with their drawers in a wad, I'm holdin' you responsible."

Chisel Bill Bannister was named for the sharp cheek bones and hooked nose which dictated his face. He was in a street gang by age twelve, fought the Italians in Five Points and escaped to the east side of Bowery at eighteen. Time had given a humorous bent to the flashing knives and chains of Chisel Bill Bannister's youth. He regaled Jimmy Delaney with stories of the turf wars and hearing about Ireland, he imagined a quiet life in the countryside of that place. He wondered how Big Jimmy Delaney could have sired the boy with red hair and steel blue eyes who had fixed him in a steady gaze and said, "Five dollars a month and my pa will take on the janitor job."

Ten

Hell's Kitchen

At seventeen, Jimmy Delaney was six feet tall and his build foretold the muscular bulk of the Delaney men. His arms were wrapped around a crate when Tommy Monaghan came out of the warehouse onto the loading dock, which spanned the back end of an alley between the stove factory and the adjacent building. Tommy Monaghan took the clay pipe out of this mouth and quelled his hacking cough with a fist beating against his chest. He launched a wad of phlegm laden with coal dust into the alley. Even on a warm day in June, Tommy Monaghan wore a wool hat pulled down over his ears. The muddy brown threads were permeated with coal dust. Tommy Monaghan took off the hat several times a day and rapped it against the wall. He pointed the clay pipe toward Jimmy Delaney.

"Off with ye, lad," he said. "It's dark soon."

"Not afraid of the dark, Tommy," said Jimmy Delaney.

"Ye go, lad...an' stay out of the old neighborhood," said Tommy Monaghan. "Ye cross the Bowery on this side of Bayard. Better, ye take the Park Row streetcar an' ye stay on Jewtown side of the Bowery."

"You tell me that every day, Tommy," said Jimmy Delaney.

"Well, there's hardly any micks left in the old neighborhood, Jimmy," said Tommy Monaghan. "The chinks is all right, as haythen go, but the wops an' niggers are batty. Now, ye listen to Tommy, lad."

"Aye, Tommy, I'll take the streetcar," said Jimmy Delaney.

"An' ye'll stay on Jewtown side of the Bowery."

"Aye, Tommy," said Jimmy Delaney.

"There's a good lad," said Tommy Monaghan.

"I'm after washing and I'll be on my way," said Jimmy Delaney.

Washing his face, hands and arms up to the elbows was the last thing Jimmy Delaney did at the end of the day. Warm water was pleasurable and heating the water in the tenement wasted coal.

Jimmy Delaney draped the towel over the nail in the bathroom and went out onto the dock. He was not yet in the shadows. He jumped into the bed of a wagon and onto the cobblestones of Peck Slip.

"I'm going, Tommy," he called, waving to Tommy Monaghan. "I forgot my gloves in the privy. Will you put them away for me?"

"Aye, lad," said Tommy Monaghan. "Don't forget...ye stay out of the old neighborhood."

"Aye, Tommy," said Jimmy Delaney.

Jimmy Delaney made his way through the wagons and carts in Peck Slip toward the docks along the East River. Pausing at South Street, he caught the smell of fish from the Fulton Market and realized he had gone the wrong way on Peck Slip. He looked toward the stone tower of the Brooklyn Bridge. Deciding not to turn around, he continued on South Street toward the bridge. He would sometimes walk along South Street under the bridge and out to end of Pier 29, as close as he could get to the tower. Tommy Monaghan had told him that the cables holding up the bridge were made of fourteen thousand miles of wire. He would stand on the end of Pier 29 and look at the tower, listening to the trains rumble overhead, fascinated still that such a thing could be built. On this unseasonably muggy day in June he turned into Dover Street. Remembering his promise to Tommy Monaghan, he crossed Pearl Street next to the anchorage for the bridge cables and continued along New Frankfort Street toward Park Row.

Winter had lingered into March and Jimmy Delaney had fallen into a brooding silence. Chisel Bill Bannister had coaxed him to speak of it and Jimmy Delaney said that Mary Delaney was pregnant again after a miscarriage in December.

"This time I'm sure it will be all right," said Chisel Bill Bannister.

"It's a bad time she's having...sickness and tiring by midmorning...a bad time," said Jimmy Delaney. "The midwife warned against more children. Pa, drunken sot...

"Um, Jimmy, a man and his wife...there's not much you can do," said Chisel Bill Bannister.

"A man can do no less than decency," said Jimmy Delaney. "The midwife has warned him and the selfish drunken sot..."

"Be careful, Jimmy," said Chisel Bill Bannister. "You don't want to do anything you can't take back."

"He'll not be touching Ma again," said Jimmy Delaney.

"It's not your affair," said Chisel Bill Bannister. "A man and his wife..."

"There's a runaway horse in the street and I do nothing...oh well, today must be her time."

"It's not the same thing, Jimmy," said Chisel Bill Bannister.

""He'll not be touching Ma again," said Jimmy Delaney.

Jimmy Delaney had come in from the hallway. He hung his wool cap and Murphy's coat on their usual pegs next to the door and seated himself at the kitchen table. Big Jimmy Delaney was sitting on the other side of the table thumbing a deck of cards. At forty-six, he was an old man.

"Yeah?" he said.

"The midwife warned against Ma having more children," said Jimmy Delaney. "It's a bad time she's having."

Big Jimmy Delaney laughed. "You're a nervy one, boy...always was," he said. "It's a big shot you are on the street, eh...in my house, you're a muzzy what keeps out of my business."

"A muzzy is it," said Jimmy Delaney. "You'll not be touching Ma again."

Big Jimmy Delaney bounded from the chair and leaned into Jimmy Delaney's face, his massive arms supporting his weight against the table.

"Get out of my house, boy, and don't come back," he said. "We'll see how far you get off yer ma's tit."

"Go to a whore house, Pa, if you can scrounge two nickels," said Jimmy Delaney. "Aye, I tell you true...I will have it in the street you are the one violating the little girls in the neighborhood. You'll not be touching Ma again."

Big Jimmy Delaney sank slowly into the chair. Even numbed by stale beer, he knew that an accusation like this need not be true. He would die in an alley.

"You would not do this," he said.

Jimmy Delaney crossed the room toward the door and took his cap and coat from the pegs. He turned toward Big Jimmy Delaney.

"Remember, you'll not be touching Ma again," he said.

He was careful not to slam the door.

Jimmy Delaney emerged into the noisy haste of Park Row from a narrow alley between the Brooklyn Bridge terminal and Pulitzer's skyscraper. He went into the terminal and looked at the clock set on a pedestal at the base of a ramp with ornate stone banisters. The ramp rose gradually out of the cavernous terminal and merged with the promenade in the center of the bridge. Jimmy Delaney had walked across the bridge many times, fascinated by the new skyscrapers which seemed to rise overnight and ever higher. City Hall was not yet in shadow and Jimmy Delaney knew that he would spend the trolley fare for an egg roll at Wo Kee's grocery.

Crossing Park Row, Jimmy Delaney walked under the elevated railway, continued along Park Row past Pearl,

Baxter and Mulberry and turned left into Mott Street at Chatham Square.

Tommy Monaghan's old neighborhood was drenched in the pungent sweet smell of opium and egg rolls. Jimmy Delaney went into Wo Kee's grocery and paid two pennies for an egg roll and a cup of tea. Wo Kee had lately made subtle allusions to the fan tan parlor in the back; Jimmy Delaney, who was comfortable with the Chinese way, declined by not responding. He took the egg roll and tea outside and sat on a bench across the street from the Transfiguration Church. He smiled, thinking of Tommy Monaghan's story about the old priest who finally died.

"The priest...him an' the hierarchy...they was fretting about the Chinamen takin' over the neighborhood," said Tommy Monaghan. "Here's the flock makin' their way through an army of haythen on Sunday, an' naturally they're after gettin' rid of the chinks."

"Always there is somebody after getting rid of somebody," said Jimmy Delaney.

"Well, the church...somehow they buy up the tenements in Mott Street between Park an' Pell...an' naturally they commence expelling the chinks," said Tommy Monaghan. "They couldn't do that acourse with Most Precious Blood up on Baxter. Up there, the ones runnin' off the micks was wops, an' all of 'em was Catholics."

Tommy Monaghan chuckled to himself, knocked his clay pipe against his leg and went through the ritual of packing and lighting the pipe.

"The chinks, though, they was smart...always was," he said. "They stayed in the neighborhood...just moved around the corner and set up shop on Park and Pell. Well, by an' by the micks, they start fightin' among themselves, just like ye'd figure, an' the chinks, they was right back on Mott Street."

Jimmy Delaney gulped the last of the tea and left the small cup on the bench. He continued along Mott Street past Fatty Walsh's old place and turned right into Pell

Street. He passed Nigger Mike's Saloon, which featured singing waiters, and turned into Bowery.

"See, Tommy, I'm south of Bayard," he said.

The sun was dropping out of sight when Jimmy Delaney went through the front door of his building. He bounded the stairs and turned into the hallway on the third floor and his momentum almost carried him into the small knot of tenants standing in his kitchen door. Pushing his way into the kitchen, Jimmy Delaney's sweeping gaze took in Chisel Bill Bannister and a priest standing near the bedroom door and Big Jimmy Delaney sitting at the table. Big Jimmy Delaney's hands were folded in front of him; he gave no sign of recognizing that Jimmy Delaney had entered the room.

Chisel Bill Bannister walked toward Jimmy Delaney.

"It's your ma, Jimmy," he said.

"What?" said Jimmy Delaney.

"It's your ma," said Chisel Bill Bannister. "I got here soon as I heard, but it was too late. There wasn't anything I could do but send for the priest."

"Where is she?" said Jimmy Delaney.

"In the bedroom, Jimmy...but look, you don't need to..."

Jimmy Delaney walked around Chisel Bill Bannister. The priest moved in front of him, blocking the doorway.

"She's with God now," said the priest.

Jimmy Delaney eyes moved over the priest, coldly eyeing his vestments of the last rites.

"Out of my way," he said.

"My son..."

Jimmy Delaney pushed his way past the priest. Mary Delaney was on the bed. The lower half of the sheet covering her body was soaked with blood. He turned to the priest.

"Was it a miscarriage?" he said.

"My son..."

"Was it a miscarriage?" shouted Jimmy Delaney.

"Yes, it was God's will," said the priest. "She was a

good woman. It's only a short time she'll be spending in purgatory."

Jimmy Delaney went into the kitchen and stood before Big Jimmy Delaney.

"Why aren't you dead, you drunken sot?" he said.

"Oh, Christ," said Chisel Bill Bannister, taking Jimmy Delaney's arm and exerting a slight but steady pressure to pull him away from the table.

The priest moved between Jimmy Delaney and the table.

"My son, you must honor your father," he said. "God has relieved your mother of her burdens and..."

"God has relieved my mother of her burdens?" said Jimmy Delaney. "You gammy ball bag...it's your stupid superstition that killed her."

"My son, naturally you are upset and..."

Pulling himself free of Chisel Bill Bannister's grip, Jimmy Delaney lunged forward, grasped the priest around the throat and drove him into the kitchen wall.

"I'll send you to purgatory, you ball bag," he said.

"Jimmy," said Chisel Bill Bannister, pulling Jimmy Delaney's hand away from the priest's throat.

At the same time, Big Jimmy Delaney stumbled toward them and tried to push Jimmy Delaney away. Jimmy Delaney wrenched himself free and flung Big Jimmy Delaney into the table.

"You'll not be touching me," he shouted.

Big Jimmy Delaney careened off the table and fell to the floor, tried to get up and fell back.

"Look at you...you can't even stand, you drunken sot," said Jimmy Delaney.

Chisel Bill Bannister recovered his balance and pushed Jimmy Delaney against the wall.

"All right, all right," said Jimmy Delaney.

"Jimmy, your ma lies dead in the other room," said Chisel Bill Bannister. "You cannot deny her the mass and a proper burial. Do you hear me?"

Jimmy Delaney nodded.

Chisel Bill Bannister turned to the priest, whose face was ashen.

"Get out of here, Father," said Chisel Bill Bannister. "The widow Malone will prepare the body for burial and I will have it brought to the church."

Eleven

A Letter for Chisel Bill

Jimmy Delaney came out of the front room carrying the rucksack. He walked across the kitchen to the door, took Murphy's coat from the peg, slid his arms into the sleeves and put on his cap. He hung the rucksack over his shoulder, regarded the kitchen for a long moment and went through the door, closing it behind him. At the bottom of the stairs he took an envelope from the rucksack and dropped it through the slot in Chisel Bill Bannister's mail box and walked out of the building into Eldridge Street. Chisel Bill Bannister would return from the burial of Mary Delaney and tear away the end of a sealed envelope and find a letter folded into a second sheet of paper with two twenty-dollar silver certificates.

June, 1905. Bill, I'm thanking you for taking up the collection for Ma's service. I could not go to the church. I don't know that I can explain, just leave it that I could not. I'll be going now, looking for something that suits me. Murphy once told me to look out for peelers needing a toe in the hole. I was thinking once that you were one of those fellows sure, but now I'm sure there are none better. Pa is not fit to support himself. He will not survive here, as sure you must know. Please do me the favor of sending him back to Ireland. The other twenty is for hard times. Stay on the east side of Bowery, lad. Jimmy

Twelve

Emma and the Annandale

"My brother, Jacob, is a tailor," said Solomon Weiss. "He will make you a durable and attractive coat for only the cost of materials."

"This is a proper coat," said Jimmy Delaney. "I must keep it."

"It is not a proper coat," said Solomon Weiss. "It is far too large and the salt stains..."

"One can hardly see the salt stains," said Jimmy Delaney.

"It's a stubborn boy you are, Jimmy," said Solomon Weiss. "It is only the cost of cloth...and I will help you with it."

"I'm thanking you, but I cannot discard the coat," said Jimmy Delaney. "It is not a matter of money."

"If you must keep it, Jacob can clean the coat and alter it to fit," said Solomon Weiss. "His shop is only next door...the coat will hardly be out of your sight."

Jimmy Delaney hesitated. "I'm thanking you," he said. "It is not so much the length, but the cuffs are always snagging things."

"I should not wonder," said Solomon Weiss.

The rucksack hung from the shoulder of Murphy's coat. The sleeves stopped smartly at the bottom of Jimmy Delaney's wrists and the collar and lapels were narrower by just the amount needed to cancel the frayed edges. The buttonholes, braced with heavy thread, snuggly accepted the new brass buttons with embossed anchors and the dark blue worsted did not smell of the sea. Walking along Eldridge Street toward Rivington, Jimmy Delaney ran his hand over the sleeve, smoothing the nap of the wool.

Jimmy Delaney made his way through the traffic on Eldridge and went into the settlement house. He nodded to the librarian and laid two books from the rucksack on the counter.

"More Dickens or something else this time?" said the librarian.

"Nothing else just now," said Jimmy Delaney.

"Well, we'll be here," said the librarian.

"Can you put these in the post?" said Jimmy Delaney, handing the librarian two letters addressed to Solomon Weiss in Hester Street and Tommy Monaghan in Peck Slip. Jimmy Delaney had written several drafts of the letters before he was satisfied that they were worthy.

Jimmy Delaney walked along Rivington to Bowery and swung into the door of a moving streetcar. The Els were too fast, he said to Chisel Bill Bannister; you were always backtracking to your destination. Chisel Bill Bannister said that he had seen Jimmy Delaney unnerved only once, when a man sitting in the seat in front of him on the Allen Street El had been killed by a rock thrown from the window of a third floor apartment. Jimmy Delaney admitted that randomness unnerved him.

Settling into a seat on the Bowery streetcar, Jimmy Delaney began to harden his intention to ship out on an upriver steamboat. Planning his route to the pier at the foot of West Twenty-third Street, he felt the streetcar lurch to a stop. Leaning out the window, he saw that several streetcars were backed up by a crowd spilling out of Union Square into Fourteenth Street and Fourth Avenue.

"Look at that," said a man. "The coppers are pushing people out of the street with their horses."

Jimmy Delaney made his way to the front of the streetcar and stepped out into Fourth Avenue. He adjusted the rucksack and decided quickly to go through Union Square to Broadway and then to West Twenty-third at Madison Square. Near the center of Union Square he merged into a dense crowd gathered around a woman speaking from a makeshift platform. Instinctively he buttoned Murphy's coat and held the rucksack close to his body.

The woman was of short stature. She wore a matronly black dress which began in a white lace collar and obscured her shape in a straight line to the platform. Her dark hair was drawn into a bun and covered by a floppy black hat and her round face was accentuated by rimless glasses pinched onto the bridge of her nose. She paced back and forth on the platform, jabbing the air with chopping motions.

"I demand the independence and freedom of woman," she said. "I demand her right to support herself, to live for herself, to love whomever she pleases or as many as she pleases. And I demand free access to information enabling women to escape the tyranny of involuntary pregnancy."

"You tell 'em, Emma," shouted the man standing next to Jimmy Delaney.

"Pregnancy is worse than tyranny," said Jimmy Delaney.

"What was that?" said the man.

"I said pregnancy is worse than tyranny," said Jimmy Delaney.

"What are you...some kind of a nut?" said the man.

"Just a fellow trying to get to Twenty-third Street," said Jimmy Delaney. "Who is that?"

"Why, that's Emma, boy...Emma Goldman," said the man. "This is better than vaudeville. Why, Jesus, boy... this is vaudeville."

Jimmy Delaney sensed the crowd pressing in on him from behind. He turned and saw several mounted policemen. The horses turned toward the platform, moving people aside. Two policemen dismounted, stepped up on the platform and took Emma Goldman by each arm.

"Come along, Emma," said one of the policemen. "That's all for today."

"What is the charge?" said Emma Goldman.

"Inciting to riot," said the policeman.

"Have you nothing original?" said Emma Goldman. "You tried that twelve years ago."

"Come along, Emma," said the policeman. "You are inflaming the crowd with obscene, lewd and lascivious speech."

"Obscene, lewd and what?" said Emma Goldman. "Lascivious," she said to the crowd. "What would they call my homosexual speech?"

Cheers erupted from the crowd and someone shouted, "Leave her alone," as the policemen forced Emma Goldman off the platform. The shouting grew more intense and several additional horses moved into the crowd. The curious began to disperse and lingering protestors could not hold their ground against the horses. Jimmy Delaney moved to the periphery of the thinning crowd and soon found a clear path through the square to Broadway.

Jimmy Delaney passed the new Flatiron Building at the convergence of Broadway and Fifth Avenue and turned into West Twenty-third Street, a bustling expanse of department stores, restaurants and theaters with wide concrete sidewalks the color of gypsum. Two trolley lines in the center of the street joined Madison Square to the Hudson River docks. The tracks were flanked by thoroughfares for hansom cabs, private carriages and motorcars, which added a new voice to the symphony of clanging streetcars and wagon wheels against the bricks.

The summer sun was high in the late afternoon. Jimmy Delaney matched the pace of men with briefcases, passing late shoppers and patrons of the theater crowding into restaurants before the box offices opened. After six blocks he stood in front of the dock spreading along the waterfront from Twenty-second to Twenty-fourth. Hordes of commuters streamed off the ferries from New Jersey and scattered. Jimmy Delaney scanned the piers extending into the river and made his way against the crowd toward the red and green flag of the North River Line. A large sign at the head of the pier proclaimed that the North River Line offered modern steamboats with accommodations and dining for discriminating passengers bound for Albany, calling at Newburgh, Poughkeepsie and Kingston.

Jimmy Delaney walked past the flag and rested one foot on the gangway which crossed a short span of water to the passenger steamer *Annandale,* one of the North River Line's new boats named for small towns and hamlets along the river. The iron hull, two hundred feet long, supported two decks and thirty-foot side wheels amidships. She carried flag masts fore and aft, two banner masts with streamers and a single stack, tall enough to discharge smoke well aft of the passengers on the upper deck. A crewman polishing brass railings regarded Jimmy Delaney.

"Fine looking coat," he said.

"I'm thanking you," said Jimmy Delaney.

"You got business here?" said the crewman.

"Aye," said Jimmy Delaney. "Is the master about?"

"Captain's in the pilot house. You lookin' for a berth?"

"Aye, I am," said Jimmy Delaney.

"Well, that red hair stickin' outa your hat and that ruddy face...I 'spect you'll get one, you got a half a brain in your head," said the crewman. He motioned with his free hand. "Come across," he said.

Jimmy Delaney crossed the gangway. "Haven't been on deck since I came across...three years now," he said. He motioned toward a doorway. "Through here?" he said.

"Through there," said the crewman. "Up the stairs, turn right...all the way to the end. Pilot house is just off the catwalk...last door on the left. Captain's name is Flanagan. Come across just like you...a shade earlier, I guess."

"I guess," said Jimmy Delaney. "I'm thanking you."

Jimmy Delaney walked along the upper deck promenade toward the pilot house, sliding his hand along the cold brass railing. The doors and windows of the passenger cabins were open, revealing thick carpets and heavily upholstered Victorian furniture in a setting of subdued lighting and paneled walls trimmed in dark woods and adorned with prints of Renaissance paintings. The upper deck ended at a gate. Jimmy Delaney went through the gate and walked along the narrow catwalk to the pilot house overlooking the lower deck, which extended another fifty feet to the bow. The door was closed. Jimmy Delaney knocked.

"Come," someone shouted.

Jimmy Delaney opened the door. A man sitting at a table in the middle of the pilot house was writing in a logbook.

"Is it Captain Flanagan?" said Jimmy Delaney.

Flanagan looked up and completed a swift inspection of Jimmy Delaney.

"That's an able seaman's coat," he said. "Are you an able seaman?"

"An able seaman's mate," said Jimmy Delaney.

"Looking for a berth?" said Flanagan.

"Aye," said Jimmy Delaney.

"Running from the coppers?" said Flanagan.

"Just a fellow for a berth," said Jimmy Delaney.

"What are you called?"

"Delaney...Jimmy Delaney."

"When did you come across?"

"It is three years now...from County Roscommon," said Jimmy Delaney.

"Your people?" said Flanagan.

"My mother passed on. My pa is back in Ireland."

"Are you a man what knows his business and tends to it?"

"Aye, I am," said Jimmy Delaney.

"Well, we have a full ship's company," said Flanagan. "But men come and go. I would expect a berth soon. Are you agreeable to work in the galley until a berth is available?"

Jimmy Delaney shifted the rucksack, considering whether he could find a berth before nightfall.

"Aye, I am agreeable," he said.

"Very well," said Flanagan. "Our season is the middle of April to roughly Thanksgiving. After that you can find work cutting ice upriver in the winter...not fit work for an able seaman's mate, but it is always available. We depart in the morning at eight-thirty and dock in Albany at seven. We depart Albany the next morning at eight-thirty and arrive back here at seven. We serve three meals in the dining room on the main deck. This means that your day will start at six-thirty and end sometime after seven in the evening when everything is ready for the next morning. The head chef is in charge of the galley. Your duties will be whatever he says they are. You are an able seaman's mate waiting for a berth. You will be paid accordingly...a dollar and twenty-five per day. You will have a bunk in the ship's dormitory below decks and you are advised to be in the dormitory at midnight. The first mate does not enforce this in the sense of what you would call a bed check. A word to the wise, however... if you are not aboard and fit for duty at six-thirty when the day starts, your only purpose for coming aboard at all will be to collect your final pay. Do you find all of this agreeable?"

"Aye," said Jimmy Delaney.

Flanagan wrote something on a slip of paper and handed it to Jimmy Delaney.

"Take this to the first mate...two doors aft," he said. "He will set you up with a bunk in the dormitory. Welcome aboard."

"I'm thanking you," said Jimmy Delaney.

Flanagan nodded and returned to writing in the logbook.

Jimmy Delaney was assigned a bunk in the dormitory and passed his first evening on the *Annandale* exchanging stories with crewmen. The food was plain and hearty and men older than Jimmy Delaney went out of their way to greet him. Lying awake in the dark, he sensed a cautious serenity.

At six in the morning Jimmy Delaney was shaken awake. He rolled over, dragging the rucksack hooked into a crook in his arm. He focused on the face of the first mate.

"Aye, I'm awake," he said.

"Is this your coat?" said the first mate.

Jimmy Delaney snapped awake, probing the bunk for the familiar feel of Murphy's coat. He swung his legs onto the floor. Before him stood a man he knew vaguely from the mess hall the previous evening. The man was wearing Murphy's coat.

"I say is this your coat?" said the first mate. "One of the fellows says you were wearing this coat last night. This man here says the coat is his. Which is it?"

"Aye, the coat is mine," said Jimmy Delaney. "You fancy another's property, do you?" he said to the crewman.

"The coat is mine," said the crewman. "If you have lost your coat, it is not my fault."

"The coat has a label in the collar," said Jimmy Delaney."

"What say you?" said the first mate to the crewman.

"It's a long time I've had the coat," said the crewman. "I don't remember."

"The label has the name Jacob Weiss, Hester Street," said Jimmy Delaney.

"Hand me the coat," said the first mate. He took Murphy's coat, looked at the label sewn into the inside of the collar and threw the coat on the bunk next to Jimmy Delaney. He turned to face the crewman who had stolen the coat.

"You, you and you," he said, pointing to three other crewman. "Get this thief off my ship."

The three crewmen moved into a tight semi-circle and advanced toward the thief.

A knife appeared in the thief's hand.

"Stay back," he said. "I'm leaving here under my own steam. Stay back...I'll cut you sure."

Another crewman grabbed the thief from behind, pinning his arms to his body. The knife fell to the floor. The first three crewmen moved in quickly and the four men wrestled the thief to the floor and began kicking him.

"Enough," said the first mate. "Get him out of here... you know better than to bring the coppers to the ship."

The four crewmen held the thief upright. The first mate approached him, moving close to the thief's bloody face.

"You're going to wish you'd never signed up on my ship," he said. He turned away, waving his hand.

The crewmen forced the man through the doorway into the hall.

"What's the matter with your face, Jack?" said one of the crewmen. "Maybe you need a little river water to clean it up."

"You will turn him over to the coppers?" said Jimmy Delaney.

"As an able seaman's mate, you should know," said the first mate.

"It's a gate I've not been through," said Jimmy Delaney.

"Well, now you have," said the first mate.

Jimmy Delaney hesitated. "I'm thanking you for saving my coat," he said. "It is a special coat...given to me by an able seaman who lost his life in a storm."

"On the crossing?" said the first mate.

"Aye, on the crossing," said Jimmy Delaney.

"Take the knife," said the first mate, pointing to the knife on the floor. "It's yours."

Jimmy Delaney nodded, picked up the knife and folded the blade into the case.

"We're under way in two hours," said the first mate. "Have your breakfast and get below to the engine room."

"I was told to report to the galley," said Jimmy Delaney.

"No, the engine room," said the first mate.

"Aye," said Jimmy Delaney.

Murphy's coat hung from a bulkhead in the engine room where Jimmy Delaney shoveled anthracite coal. He and two other men had developed a rhythm for transferring coal with large flat shovels from the bin to the stalls; other men stoked the boiler with coal from the stalls.

The master of the engine room made his final inspection. He climbed a short ladder to a landing, examined a gauge while tapping the glass with a knuckle and spoke into a tube to the pilot house.

"Pressure up...ready to engage," he said.

"Delaney," called the first mate from the stair.

"Aye," said Jimmy Delaney.

"Ready to get under way," said the first mate. "You're on the bow line."

"Aye," said Jimmy Delaney. He threw the shovel on top of a pile of coal, grabbed Murphy's coat and slipped it on as he climbed the stair.

The sky was overcast and a raw damp cold enveloped the dock. The wind, having freshened at dawn, stirred the river into whitecaps. Jimmy Delaney crossed the gangway and stood next to the cleat waiting for the signal to cast off the line holding the bow of the *Annandale* against the pier. Another man waited to cast off the stern line.

The ship's deep-throated steam whistle sounded.

"Engaging the screw...quarter speed astern," shouted the first mate. "Cast off the lines."

Jimmy Delaney and the other man released the ropes from the cleats and hurried across the gangway. Another crewman retracted the gangway and other men pulled in the ropes. The *Annandale* backed out of the slip and the bow began to slide to starboard. Jimmy Delaney ran forward to help stow the lines, passing the main dining room where passengers were seated for breakfast. He glanced toward the pier falling away just before the bow had turned enough to point the ship toward the New Jersey shore. The dock appeared again as the bow swung around, pointing the ship upriver. The *Annandale* was poised.

"Side wheels engaging, ahead full," shouted the first mate. "All hands clear."

The whistle discharged a long blast of white steam into the cold air and the transfer of power to the side-wheel paddles sent black smoke pouring from the stack and a cascading vibration through the ship's decks. The side wheels came up to full speed quickly and the ship lurched forward, leaving two trails of churning foam in its wake.

"All hands stand down," said the first mate.

Jimmy Delaney buttoned the collar of Murphy's coat against the wind and leaned into the railing, watching the waterfront docks and warehouses of Hell's Kitchen slide by. Traffic on the river was heavy, even early in the morning on a dreary day.

"First trip, kid?" said a crewman.

"Aye, since crossing over," said Jimmy Delaney. "The big barges...with derricks..."

"Ice barges," said the crewman. "They're heading back upriver to the ice houses to get new loads. They start up about March and go all summer."

"The derricks, they move the ice blocks," said Jimmy Delaney.

"Yeah, and them windmills on deck...you see them canvas blades...well, they run the bilge pumps to get rid of the water from melted ice."

"Where are the ice houses?" said Jimmy Delaney.

"Upriver...north of Poughkeepsie where the salt in the water runs out," said the crewman. "Mainly, they're way up north where the river freezes solid...fifteen inches thick or more. There must be a hundred ice houses between Catskill and Albany. We'll go by 'em...can't miss 'em...huge buildings painted white with elevator chutes ridin' down into the river. They cut the ice into blocks, run the blocks up the chutes into the ice house and store 'em insulated with sawdust and hay. Not that they need much insulation 'til about March and that's when the white paint comes in...reflects the sun away. Anyhow, come spring, they run the ice blocks back down the chutes onto these here barges and run 'em down here. Ice wagons line up at nearly all the piers to take on the blocks. This here's a fast boat. Even with the stops, we'll make Albany by six-thirty tonight. You ever seen the Palisades?"

"Just what you can see from the city," said Jimmy Delaney.

"Let's get over to port," said the crewman. "We'll have a good place aport on the bow. Eerie, they are, the Palisades...supernatural, some say. I never get tired of 'em."

Jimmy Delaney seemed always drawn to the slabs of ancient magma rising out of the river's edge, spires shaped by wind and rain and forested by seeds seeking out every crack. Even after the cliffs flattened and turned away from the river, he lingered for the passing of Haverstraw Bay where the river widened to three miles and factories around the bay fashioned bricks from glacial deposits of blue clay. Smoke from the firing ovens, pouring from tall stacks, was thick and black and smelled of sulfur. The *Annandale* swung wide, yielding the river to barges moving finished bricks downriver from a line of docks below the steep clay banks holding up the village. Hard around the bend after Jones Point and past the highland plain lay open water for ports of call at Newburgh and Poughkeepsie and out of the narrows at Hyde Park the ship swung wide again for the approach to Rondout Creek. Passing the lighthouse in the mouth of the creek, Flanagan called for reverse as if by clockwork and the ship slowed with a shudder for docking at the village of Rondout where carriages conveyed passengers to and from the Oriental Hotel overlooking Kingston Point Park.

Jimmy Delaney shoveled coal from a barge tethered to the dock. The solitary barge was filled from a railroad car and towed past abandoned factories on the rocky slope of Rondout Creek, reminders of a time when the Delaware and Hudson Canal discharged streams of barges, reminders that stimulated talk in the town of guiding tourists up to Eddyville and Creeklocks. Clear of Rondout Creek, Flanagan ordered full power to the side wheels and the *Annandale* pushed against the current past the ice houses clustered along the northern reach of the river between Catskill and Castleton and after Castleton the ship slowed for docking in Albany. A veil of smoke hung over the factories along the riverfront. Jimmy Delaney did not wander far and the next morning he rose early to shovel coal and man the lines.

The heavy air of midsummer was made tedious by the confines of a small space, but not overly so. Jimmy Delaney's duties remained those of an able seaman's mate. Flanagan, retired from the sea, was steeped in the traditions of sea-going vessels; stewards and cooks and waiters and maids served vacationers and politicians and men of business and able seamen and their mates served the ship.

Respect of the men brought with it pride and serenity, sturdy in the daylight, waning in the night. Gradually, sleep did not refresh.

Thirteen

Two Days Liberty

"Delaney, the ship will be removed from service for two days...inspection of the boiler," said the first mate. "You have two days liberty, beginning tomorrow."

"Aye," said Jimmy Delaney. "Is the dormitory closed for the nights?"

"Oh, no," said the first mate. "You have your bunk, but the steam will be down and the coal bin emptied... you'll take your meals ashore."

"Aye," said Jimmy Delaney.

Chisel Bill Bannister was not at home. Jimmy Delaney left a note at the tenement and walked around the city and late in the day he ate ham and eggs at a diner. On the second day he went to the settlement house. Chisel Bill Bannister was waiting on the corner of Eldridge and Rivington.

"Bill, when did you start squandering your time on street corners?" said Jimmy Delaney.

"Jimmy, boy, you're still in one piece," said Chisel Bill Bannister.

"Aye, one piece, let's walk," said Jimmy Delaney.

They sat on a bench along the Delancey promenade. Chisel Bill Bannister loaded his pipe and fired the tobacco using a large kitchen match.

"Your pa went back, Jimmy," he said. "Without your ma he was a lost soul."

"He was always a lost soul," said Jimmy Delaney. "I'm thanking you for seeing to it."

"I don't need the extra twenty," said Chisel Bill Bannister.

"It is not a question of need," said Jimmy Delaney.

Chisel Bill Bannister nodded. "What have you been doing?" he said. "Settled on anything?"

"I have a berth on a passenger steamer...on the river to Albany," said Jimmy Delaney. "I've two days liberty... yesterday and today. Have you ever been without work?"

"Without a job?" said Chisel Bill Bannister.

"Aye, without a job," said Jimmy Delaney.

"Not since I left the west side of the Bowery and quit stealing for a living," said Chisel Bill Bannister. "It is years now I have managed the building."

"You like managing the building, do you?" said Jimmy Delaney.

"It's as good as the next thing," said Chisel Bill Bannister. "I'm not digging ditches and worse."

"These two days are my first days without duties... duties for pay...since coming across," said Jimmy Delaney. "Yesterday I went to Peck Slip and lingered at Water Street...out of sight...and I laughed watching Tommy Monaghan wave his clay pipe and shout orders. The new boy, he is rushing around to move this or move that before Tommy changes his mind."

"Fast enough?" said Chisel Bill Bannister.

"Never fast enough," said Jimmy Delaney. "It is twice a minute Tommy changes his mind. And I went out on the bridge and up to Thirty-first to watch the work on the new railroad station and then to Central Park. I had a fine day."

"Are you staying with the job on the river boat?" said Chisel Bill Bannister.

"When the season ends, I'm expecting to cut the ice up north over the winter," said Jimmy Delaney. "Have you ever thought of leaving the city?"

"Leave the city? Move, you mean?"

"Aye, doing something else," said Jimmy Delaney.

"You won't be staying on the river boat in the spring," said Chisel Bill Bannister.

"It's not long before the river boats will die," said Jimmy Delaney. "The businessmen and politicians are more and more going to the railroad. It is faster, if not the comfort of the river boats. I've heard they are going to build a new railroad...all the way to the Pacific Ocean. Meet me in Albany in the spring...we will go west and build a railroad."

Chisel Bill Bannister looked away for a moment. He rapped the pipe against his shoe.

"I was born in the city, Jimmy, and I'll die here," he said. "I don't have a family, except my brother, but I have a stability I am too old to do without. I suppose you don't understand."

"Aye, I do understand," said Jimmy Delaney. "On the river boat I am comfortable. I am comfortable with sailors, even sailors who do not go to sea. It is a legacy maybe...Ma's older brother, Tim, was a sailor."

"But?" said Chisel Bill Bannister.

Jimmy Delaney shrugged. "I'm thinking it was the sea for Tim," he said. "For me..."

"So, if the river boats were not dying?" said Chisel Bill Bannister.

"I would still go," said Jimmy Delaney.

"Well," said Chisel Bill Bannister, standing.

Jimmy Delaney stood and took Chisel Bill Bannister's extended hand in a firm grip.

"I'll be seeing you, Bill," he said.

"I appreciated your letter," said Chisel Bill Bannister.

Jimmy Delaney nodded, released Chisel Bill Bannister's hand and watched him walk away. He disappeared in the crowd on Eldridge Street and Jimmy Delaney walked along the Delancey promenade toward the trolley line on Bowery.

Fourteen

Willy Gantz

The season was over when frost on the deck had not melted by midmorning. The last sailing of the year began in Albany in near darkness. Jimmy Delaney clapped his gloved hands together against an icy breeze across the bow. He wore a wool hat pulled down over his ears and a heavy slicker over Murphy's coat. The rucksack from County Roscommon lay on the deck. After Castleton, men in every village along the river readied the bright white houses and constructed lean-tos and corrals; soon the local farmers would bring their plow horses to the river for the ice harvest.

Jimmy Delaney took his leave of the *Annandale* in the village of Catskill. He lingered in a light rain on the dock at Dutchmen's Landing and when the ship had passed from sight, he slung the rucksack over his shoulder and walked toward Catskill Creek and turned into Main Street toward the village.

The foreman of an ice company had an office in Broad Street. Jimmy Delaney followed the signs and went in, stomping his feet on the mat. The foreman was sitting behind a desk writing in a ledger.

"You looking for ice work?" he said.

"Aye," said Jimmy Delaney.

"You done any ice harvesting before?" said the foreman.

"I'm just off the river," said Jimmy Delaney. "I worked with Trueblood...he said I'm to see you for the ice work."

"Yeah, I know Trueblood," said the foreman. "Seventy-five cents a day...day is daylight to dark. New guys handle the horses. We got thirty houses to load between here and Athens up the river. That'll take close to two months work, maybe a little longer. We start in two, three weeks...a month at the outside."

"I was watching along the river from Albany," said Jimmy Delaney. "I could start now with sheds and corrals."

"All right, report tomorrow morning. Be here at daybreak. What are you called?"

"Delaney...Jimmy Delaney."

The foreman wrote in the ledger. "You got a place?" he said.

"Trueblood mentioned a boarding house on Greene Street," said Jimmy Delaney.

"Yeah, just down the block...the widow Morse...name's on the mailbox," said the foreman. "You're early, so you won't have no problem. The widow gets three dollars a week...one week in advance. You get a room and two squares...breakfast and supper. She don't give no credit. You got the money?"

"Aye," said Jimmy Delaney. "I'm thanking you."

"One more thing," said the foreman. "It ain't the Irish so much, but union bums was stirring up trouble around here last season and I expect 'em back this season. We don't deal with no unions. I catch you bothering my men, you get canned. You ain't a union plant, are you?"

"I am just a fellow looking for work," said Jimmy Delaney.

"Well, see you keep to that," said the foreman.

Jimmy Delaney's eyes narrowed. He took a deep breath, let it out slowly and left the office.

The boarding house on the corner of Greene and Hill was easy to find. It was a two-story frame house with a broad porch. A black man rocked back and forth in a swing.

"I keeps a garden patch out back," he said. "What you want here?"

Before Jimmy Delaney could answer, the door opened. The widow Morse was a large woman with a flabby face and stern hair drawn into a tight bun.

"Willy Gantz, I've told you about bothering people," she said.

"Yes'm," said the black man.

"Have you a room for the ice season?" said Jimmy Delaney. "It's tomorrow I'll be starting with the corrals. I am just off the river. I worked with Trueblood."

"If you know Trueblood, you ain't a union man," she said. "My late husband, God rest...never mind, I don't rent to union or any other trouble maker."

"What you want here?" said the black man.

"Willy," said the widow Morse.

"Yes'm."

"I'm just a fellow working the ice harvest," said Jimmy Delaney.

The widow Morse regarded Jimmy Delaney for a long moment and motioned him into the foyer. She collected the rent for the first week and walked into the parlor, gesturing again for Jimmy Delaney to follow. She wrote out a receipt and handed it to him and put the money in a safe. Jimmy Delaney expected to cover his expenses over the winter from his wages. He hesitated, wondering if he should keep his stake from the *Annandale* in the safe. He took the room key and listened to the widow's instructions regarding meal times. Heeding a vague sense of unease, he nodded and turned away; Trueblood had not told him anything about the widow except her name.

For three weeks Jimmy Delaney whitewashed ice houses and built lean-tos and corrals. He was the only boarder in the widow Morse's house for two weeks and then three men came into town on the same day and the widow Morse had boarders for all four of the upstairs bedrooms. Jimmy Delaney and the three other men, all much older, ate eggs with bacon or ham, biscuits and coffee at dawn and walked to the line of ice houses, which began at Dutchmen's Landing and extended north along the west bank of the river. The black man known as Willy Gantz lived in the old servant's quarters connected to the boarding house by an arbor covered with vines. He was the only black man working on the lean-tos and corrals. He walked to the ice houses alone and walked back to the widow Morse's house alone and said nothing except "What you want here?" He said this to Jimmy Delaney when the other boarders in the widow Morse's house were out of sight. Jimmy Delaney had never heard him say anything to the other three men.

The ice harvest started in mid-December. The river was frozen to a depth of twelve inches and covered with a thick blanket of snow. During the first week the work settled into a routine. The first ice field was cleared of snow at daybreak and water channels to the ice house elevators were opened using horse-drawn plows and saws. The ice fields were cut along parallel score lines about one yard apart and perpendicular score lines about two feet apart. Men with poles guided the blocks through the open channels toward elevators extending from the top of the ice house into the water. Steam-driven chain belts moved the ice blocks up the elevators and released them onto ramps which carried them by gravity to storage areas where they were stacked and insulated with sawdust and hay. When a house was full, it was sealed and the crews began loading the next house.

Jimmy Delaney was assigned to clear snow from the ice field. He was paired with Willy Gantz, who handled the horses and instructed Jimmy Delaney to walk behind the plow and keep it straight. His instructions were in the form of gestures and nods. Two weeks into the season, just after the Christmas holiday, Jimmy Delaney was transferred to an ice cutting crew, leaving snow removal to teenage boys of slighter build. Each night after work Willy Gantz was in the swing as usual, his dark face highlighted by orange hues from a coal oil lantern. Jimmy Delaney climbed the steps to the porch, stomped the snow off his boots and nodded in Willy Gantz's direction. One night he paused.

"Is it not too cold to sit out here?" said Jimmy Delaney.

"I keeps a garden patch out back and I haves peas and carrots and greens," said Willy Gantz. "Does you like greens with red pepper vinegar?"

"What kind of greens?" said Jimmy Delaney. "Peas are green."

"What...you not a greens eater?" said Willy Gantz. "How does you get along without greens?"

"What are greens?" said Jimmy Delaney.

"Mustard greens," said Willy Gantz. "Ever summer I haves a whole mess of mustard greens...biggest leaves you ever seen. You tenders 'em up in boiling water and then you douses 'em with red pepper vinegar."

"I'm from Ireland," said Jimmy Delaney. "I've never seen mustard greens."

"I knows about Ireland," said Willy Gantz. "You eats potatoes."

"Not as much as in the old days," said Jimmy Delaney.

"I knows about that, too," said Willy Gantz. "A whole mess of you folks done died of the starvation. I hopes none of your folks died of the starvation."

"No," said Jimmy Delaney.

"I is glad to here that," said Willy Gantz.

"Were you born around here?" said Jimmy Delaney.

"Oh, no...I come this way from Ohio," said Willy Gantz. "My peoples, they come up from Tennessee on the underground railway. I goin' up the river here and the widow, she need a hand after Mister Morse done died. So here I is.

"Slaves?" said Jimmy Delaney.

"Say what?"

"The underground railroad," said Jimmy Delaney. "Your people were slaves?"

"How you know that...comin' from Ireland like you done?" said Willy Gantz.

"Books," said Jimmy Delaney.

"Books, you say," said Willy Gantz. "Well, this here how it is...they slaves right enough. My mama a house nigger and my papa, he a field hand, and one day they ups and leave. Old man Gantz, he done lost a hold of 'em. My mama say he busted a gut right enough, only they weren't nothin' he could do...they was gone. And they done had me and my brothers and sisters in Ohio and they passed on and like I say, here I is."

The door opened. The widow Morse came out onto the porch.

"Willy Gantz, I've told you about bothering people," she said.

"Yes'm," said Willy Gantz.

"It's all right," said Jimmy Delaney.

"It's time Willy went in," said the widow Morse.

"Goin' in right away now," said Willy Gantz.

"All right," said the widow Morse. She went into the house and closed the door.

Jimmy Delaney continued to look at the door for a long moment and then turned toward Willy Gantz.

"Well, good night," he said.

Willy Gantz picked up the lantern and walked past Jimmy Delaney and down the steps to the front walkway. He turned.

"Most white peoples, they haves some strange notions about us colored peoples," he said. "I sho hates to give up that garden patch."

Fifteen

The Pinkerton Man

"What they paying you, boy?" said the union man. "He doesn't talk," said Jimmy Delaney. "Deaf and dumb, huh?" said the union man. "Well, what they paying you then?"

Jimmy Delaney took Willy Gantz by the arm and led him along the ice floe. They resumed poling ice blocks through the water channel toward the elevators. The union man followed.

"You like being a slave?" he said. "They not paying you nothin' and they paying the nigger a lot less just 'cause he's a nigger. Daylight to dark they working you just like these horses for slave wages. You don't care? You know how much ice they sell down in the city? You know how much money they raking in? They'll live in style all summer, wearing fine suits, taking the Century Limited to Chicago for the fights, and you'll be sweating at some other slave job."

Another man approached. He was stocky with short, stubby legs. An opening in his overcoat at the neck revealed a starched white collar and tie. He carried a heavy nightstick with the strap wrapped around his wrist. He thrust a gold badge into the face of the union man.

"You're under arrest," he said.

"Kiss my ass, Pinkerton," said the union man.

The Pinkerton man lunged forward and swung the nightstick. The union man moved quickly and the nightstick struck Willy Gantz, knocking him into the water. Ignoring Willy Gantz, the Pinkerton man ran toward the union man, who had fallen, and began beating him.

Jimmy Delaney thrust his pole into the water and shouted, "Take the pole, Willy."

Willy Gantz, thrashing his arms, clamped one hand

around the pole and Jimmy Delaney pulled him toward the ice floe.

"You're at the edge, Willy...steady yourself on the ice," said Jimmy Delaney.

Other ice workers had rushed toward the melee. Several men got on their knees and pulled Willy Gantz out of the water and Jimmy Delaney wrapped him in Murphy's coat. Four ice workers ran toward the Pinkerton man and pushed him away from the fallen union man. The Pinkerton man rolled over on the ice floe, got to his feet and waved the nightstick, warning the ice workers to stay back. They moved forward, forming a phalanx, and pushed him into the water.

"Get him out," a man shouted.

"Let him get hisself out," said another man.

The foreman pushed through a line of men standing on the ice floe.

"I saw that," he said, pointing toward the four ice workers. "You men, get out...you're fired." He motioned to several men. "Get him out of the water," he said. "Get him to shore and find him some dry clothes."

A few men came forward, moving slowly, and pulled the Pinkerton man from the water. They left him standing on the shore and returned to the floe.

"Sombitch can find his own dry clothes," said one the men.

The foreman had turned toward Willy Gantz, who was holding his hand against the side of his face. Blood ran between his fingers.

"Christ, are you all right, Willy?" said the foreman.

"Hit in the eye, I'm thinking," said Jimmy Delaney.

"Get him to the doc," said the foreman.

Jimmy Delaney led Willy Gantz off the ice. They started toward the doctor's examining room in a tent next to an ice house.

The foreman looked around. He pulled one man aside.

"Now listen, this floe is nearly free in the water," he

said. "Get the rest of these blocks to the elevator and then get onto something solid before it separates from the shore. You got that?"

"I got it," said the man.

The foreman nodded and walked along the floe and stood over the union man.

"Two of you, over here," he called.

Two men dropped their ice poles and walked toward the foreman.

"His head's busted in," said the foreman. "I warned 'em...I told 'em last year and I told 'em again this year I was takin' steps to get my ice houses loaded. Get him to the doc and make sure he don't come back here."

Willy Gantz's wet clothes hung in front of the stove. The doctor had returned Murphy's coat to Jimmy Delaney and wrapped Willie Gantz in a blanket and cleaned the blood off his eye. He examined the eye using a magnifying lens.

"Get him home the rest of the day," said the doctor. He gave Jimmy Delaney a small package. "Tell him to wet one of these gauzes with cold water every few hours and hold it on the eye for a few minutes. It'll swell up...can't stop that...but it'll go down in a few days and he'll be able see out of it again." He handed Jimmy Delaney a black patch. "When he goes to work, tell him to wear one of the gauzes and hold it in place with this patch," he said. "Just run the band around his head."

Willy Gantz put on his clothes, which were still damp and cold, and motioned toward Jimmy Delaney. They left the tent.

"I just lays on one of these here gauze and the patch and get on back to the job, said Willy Gantz."

Jimmy Delaney nodded. "Who was that man who hit you?" he said.

"He a Pinkerton man," said Willy Gantz. "They tells me that some kind of a police agency. The boss, he done hired these mens to discourage the union."

"Discourage," said Jimmy Delaney.

"You knows what I mean," said Willy Gantz.

"I have a question for you, Willy," said Jimmy Delaney.

"What question is that?" said Willy Gantz.

"You are like my schoolmaster back in Ireland," said Jimmy Delaney.

"That so?" said Willy Gantz.

"You hold back," said Jimmy Delaney.

"I finds it easier that way," said Willy Gantz. "How does you find it?"

"Easier," said Jimmy Delaney.

"That about how I figured it," said Willy Gantz.

"How much do they pay you?" said Jimmy Delaney.

"I gets forty cents a day," said Willy Gantz.

"The man from the union was right," said Jimmy Delaney.

"Oh yeah, he right and he haves a busted head," said Willy Gantz.

"Some are fit to wear the authority and some for a toe in the hole," said Jimmy Delaney.

"What that?" said Willy Gantz.

"These Pinkerton men," said Jimmy Delaney. "They come all the way from the city and I venture the boss has to pay their room and board in addition to their wages. He would be better off dealing with the union men."

"The boss, he not interested in how to get by the cheapest," said Willy Gantz.

Jimmy Delaney and Willy Gantz walked out onto the ice floe and began poling blocks through the water. Willy Gantz saw the foreman walking toward them and waved him away. The foreman waved and turned around.

"He's not very smart, Willy," said Jimmy Delaney.

"Who?" said Willy Gantz.

"The foreman," said Jimmy Delaney.

"There he is, right over there," said Willy Gantz. "You walk right up and tell him that...I sure he just waiting to get smarter and mend his ways."

Sixteen

Catching Out

Willy Gantz had a way of turning his head to focus his good eye on the floating ice blocks and he did not fall out of the habit after his eye healed. He told Jimmy Delaney that he could see the ice blocks with his good eye and anybody sneaking up on him with the bad eye. Jimmy Delaney said that no one was sneaking up on him and Willy Gantz said he wouldn't know that unless he watched.

The ice floes were separating from the shore when the last ice house was sealed and Catskill reverted to a quiet village. Jimmy Delaney walked around in the morning and went to the lending library in the emporium. He took his meals alone in the widow Morse's dining room and sat on the porch with Willy Gantz. Disagreeable weather lingered into late March past Jimmy Delaney's eighteenth birthday, which he remembered but did not mention.

"What you read down at that emporium?" said Willy Gantz.

"A book about a boy named Huckleberry Finn," said Jimmy Delaney.

"That a strange name," said Willy Gantz.

"The boy goes down a river on a raft with a runaway slave," said Jimmy Delaney.

"They ain't no more slaves," said Willy Gantz.

"This happened a long time ago," said Jimmy Delaney.

"A white boy?" said Willy Gantz.

Jimmy Delaney nodded. "A white boy," he said.

"This here story...it about the white boy or the slave?" said Willy Gantz.

"The white boy," said Jimmy Delaney. "He learns that you can't pray a lie."

"You can't pray nothing," said Willy Gantz. "They ain't nobody listening."

"Cold out here," said Jimmy Delaney, pulling the collar of Murphy's coat close to his neck.

"You looks perplexed," said Willy Gantz. "Colored peoples just like white peoples...some religious, some ain't. Most just say they is."

"Just something you say," said Jimmy Delaney.

"What that?" said Willy Gantz.

"Fate and dying young, Willy...fate and dying young," said Jimmy Delaney.

"Dying young what going to happen to you on the rails, you ain't careful."

"All the way to the Pacific Ocean," said Jimmy Delaney.

Willy Gantz adjusted the flame on the coal oil lantern. He rocked back in the swing.

"I sho would like to see the Pacific Ocean," he said. "I got here back a piece...this place wore out. You reckon those peoples hires colored mens?"

"Why should they not?" said Jimmy Delaney.

Willy Gantz laughed. "They doesn't need no reason," he said.

"Well, I've heard they need able-bodied hands," said Jimmy Delaney. "They'll be hiring everyone who comes along."

"Where you say they starting this here railroad?"

"At the Missouri River in South Dakota," said Jimmy Delaney. "They're building a bridge across the river and going all the way to the Pacific Ocean."

"You ain't never been on the rails," said Willy Gantz.

"And neither had you before you were," said Jimmy Delaney.

"That true enough," said Willy Gantz. "But this here how it is...the high iron, it the most dangerous thing I knows of. Seem like the bulls is everwhere and even when they ain't, you all the time looking for 'em, and you makes a mistake and it your last mistake. When it time to catch out, you has to listen to what I tells you."

One day in April, the only day of that week that did not dawn with rain, Jimmy Delaney packed his rucksack and waited across the street from the widow Morse's rooming house. At about the same time, Willy Gantz left the old servant's quarters carrying a duffle bag. They walked along Water Street away from the rising sun and crossed the bridge over Catskill Creek to the rail yard. They walked between lines of boxcars, flatcars and tankers toward the river where men were putting together a short train. The fire was already up in the locomotive; they could see the flickering glow below the firebox and hear the metal popping from cold to hot.

"This here a local," said Willy Gantz. "Ever morning they hauls a line of cars down to Newburgh and sometime the train go on through down to the main line...just depend. On the main line us can get a red ball and get a long ways away from here. This here a good place to catch out...the train ain't moving and they ain't no bulls."

"Red ball?" said Jimmy Delaney.

"Red ball a fast freight," said Willy Gantz. "Us get the right train, get a long ways from here."

Willy Gantz stopped and bent over. He pointed to the undercarriage of a boxcar.

"Some mens, they lay old boards on these here rods," he said. "This here how it is...you don't never ride the rods. Train speeds up, cinders flying...and the bulls, they ties a pipe on the end of a rope and bounce it along underneath the cars...break you up good. Don't never ride the rods."

Willy Gantz lifted himself into an open boxcar and pulled Jimmy Delaney in behind him. They sat on the floor with their backs to the wall.

"No foot hanging," said Willy Gantz. "I seen three mens got they feet hooked on a bridge. They was all three yanked out and cut in half. No foot hanging."

Willy Gantz took two biscuits from his duffel bag. He gave one to Jimmy Delaney.

"Might as well eat," he said. "Nothing happening now 'til us gets to the main line."

"I'm thinking they could close the door," said Jimmy Delaney.

"That good thinking," said Willy Gantz. "Show you taking this here serious, just like you better. Now, they don't hardly ever close up both doors on the empties. Either they's airing 'em out or they takes too much time since they ain't nothing in 'em anyhow. I only seen 'em closed up once and then they wasn't no padlock on 'em."

The whistle sounded two short blasts and car jolted and started moving. Jimmy Delaney stood by the open doorway. The train cleared the yard and rolled through a switch onto the track to Newburgh. The river, already crowded with ice barges, was orange in the new sun.

Seventeen

High Iron to Lima

The train began to slow. Jimmy Delaney recognized East Kingston.

"Coming into Kingston, Willy," he said.

"How you know that?" said Willy Gantz.

"Many trips on the river," said Jimmy Delaney.

"Train stopping for coal and water...now a good time to talk about that," said Willy Gantz. "When the train stop, you looks out both sides. If the coal bin and water tower on the same side, you gets out to stretch on the other side...that is, if they ain't nobody in the caboose. Back there in the yard...who'd you see in the caboose?"

"The last car was a boxcar," said Jimmy Delaney.

"That good...you got a fine eye," said Willy Gantz. "Just the same, though, you takes a stretch where the mens loading coal and water doesn't see without looking... ain't no use of showing yourself when you doesn't has to. Now when they's a caboose, they got mens looking for everthing. The bulls, they ride in the caboose, and when the train stop for coal and water, they walks the train on the catwalk. Now they ain't hardly ever no bulls on locals, but they will be when us hits the main line...'specially on a red ball."

The train took on another line of cars in Newburgh and then pulled forward for more coal and water. Jimmy Delaney and Willy Gantz ate bread from Jimmy Delaney's rucksack and drank water from a fruit jar in Willy Gantz's duffle bag.

"Look like us going to make the main line," said Willy Gantz. "Be dark time us get there." He pulled a potato from the duffle bag. "These here potatoes I got here in this bag is our ticket to the jungle," he said. "Potato in the stew pot and us got a meal and a place to sleep the night."

"We have means," said Jimmy Delaney. "We can go to a rooming house."

Willy Gantz laughed. "They not going to let Willy Gantz in no rooming house," he said. "Besides, us got to save the money...ain't no telling when us going to need it for sure."

The locomotive whistle sounded twice.

"That us," said Willy Gantz. "When you hears them two short blasts...that the signal to go. When you outside, you gets back in quick or else you has to chase after the car. This here how it is...you always tries to catch out on a train that ain't moving. You tries hard to do that. Chasing after a moving train...it the most dangerous thing I knows of. One mistake and you gets cut in half."

After dark the train passed through a switch on the fly and merged into the main line. Willy Gantz felt the transition to smooth, straight rails. He looked out the doorway and stepped back quickly.

"Get away from the door," he said, grabbing Jimmy Delaney's arm and pulling him away from the open doorway.

A locomotive exploded past the doorway in the opposite direction, filling the boxcar with a deafening noise and a gush of air carrying the acrid smell of a steam engine. In a flash of time the locomotive was gone and the noise settled into a steady din of speeding rail cars and the caboose passed and they were plunged into a sudden quiet.

"When the door on the other side closed like this'n, then the rush of air, it come in, go in a circle and go out," said Willy Gantz.

"And if you are standing in the doorway..." said Jimmy Delaney.

"That right...you gets sucked out," said Willy Gantz.

"We are going faster," said Jimmy Delaney.

"On the main line," said Willy Gantz. "Could get quite

a ways, but I doubts it...this local, it ain't going far on the main line. Good thing this here car ain't a flat."

"A flat?" said Jimmy Delaney.

"Flat place on a wheel," said Willy Gantz. "Train picks up speed...ain't no way to keep from getting pounded down to your bones."

The train slowed, went through several switches and stopped. Willy Gantz peered into the night.

"This a rail yard...Middletown, end of the line," he said. "This good...Middletown a big yard. They's red balls coming through here."

"Hard to see," said Jimmy Delaney. "Are we going out on a train tonight?"

"Hard to tell...need to get off this siding, back to the main line," said Willy Gantz.

They walked back through the switches they had come through. Willy Gantz paused, cupped his hands around his eyes and squinted into the darkness.

"This here the main line," he said. "Quiet...ain't nothing doing. I been out of this a spell now. I knows red balls from the city coming through here...question is, does they stop. Need to start up again in the daylight. Used to be a jungle at the edge of the yard...up a ways. Us gets a meal, some sleep and maybe learns when the red balls come through."

They were drawn by a small fire down an embankment. Peering over the edge into a clearing, they saw a man sitting on a crate. He was alone, stirring stew in a black cast iron pot suspended on a makeshift tripod over the fire. They walked down a trail that had been beaten down. The man turned.

"Welcome lads," he said.

"I peel this, you got a knife," said Willy Gantz, showing the man a potato.

The man held out a hunting knife. Willy Gantz peeled the potato quickly, tossed it into the pot and returned the knife. He and Jimmy Delaney dragged two crates into the fire light and sat.

"Look like you by yourself," said Willy Gantz.

"Some nights are like that," said the man.

"You stay here?" said Willy Gantz.

"I've been here a while," said the man. "Going far?"

"Pretty far," said Willy Gantz.

"When did you come across?" said Jimmy Delaney.

"The man looked up. "Years ago," he said. "And you?"

"It is four years now," said Jimmy Delaney.

"And you are longing to go back," said the man.

"Nothing there for me," said Jimmy Delaney.

"What is there here?" said the man.

"It is more than there," said Jimmy Delaney.

"If you say so," said the man.

"Red balls...does they stop hereabouts?" said Willy Gantz.

"Several times a day, both ways," said the man. "Some go on through, but others stop to drop off or pick up. Catching out here is easy...you won't have any trouble."

"Bulls?" said Willy Gantz.

"On the red balls...but they're pretty lax if you don't cause any trouble," said the man. "Are you going east or west?"

"West," said Willy Gantz.

"Two things," said the man. "First, get a mixed westbound. The coal trains carry the red ball flag, but you won't get any further than Lackawaxen. They turn off to the coal fields toward Scranton."

"I knows about that," said Willy Gantz. "I was through here a piece back."

"Then you know," said the man. "The second thing is there's a bull on this line at Binghamton. He only works the red balls to Buffalo and he carries a rifle. He won't look in the cars...just tries to spot you taking a stretch from the catwalk. Keep it closed up...don't let him see you."

"He got a rifle?" said Willy Gantz. "The law, they lets this bull shoot mens in the yard?"

"Railroad property," said the man. "They won't do anything. Just keep it closed up in the Binghamton yard and all the way to Buffalo if you're going that way."

"Um," said Willy Gantz. "I can't see no use in shooting mens in the yard 'cept meanness."

The man ladled stew into tin pans and laid one in front of Willy Gantz and the other in front of Jimmy Delaney. He offered spoons and cups of water.

"Have something to eat and then take any of these empty lean-tos," he said. "The creek's just through the trees there for washing."

"Mighty thoughtful," said Willy Gantz. "It been a long day...and I ain't been doing this for a spell."

"Let me see your hands," said the man. He took one of Willy Gantz's hands and felt it, turning it over and then back again. "Coal miner," he said.

"Not for a spell," said Willy Gantz. "Not since ought-two."

"Well, things have settled down since then," said the man.

Willy Gantz nodded.

"So, you came across four years back," the man said to Jimmy Delaney. "Where are you from?"

"County Roscommon...just on the road to Castlerea," said Jimmy Delaney.

The man stared into the fire. A distant look crossed his grizzled face.

"County Roscommon...hard hit in the great hunger," he said. "Did you lose anyone?"

"My grandfather was in the work house in Castlerea," said Jimmy Delaney. "I was told that he and my grandmother ran away."

"And he was not brought back?" said the man.

"My grandfather was not like other men," said Jimmy Delaney.

"What would you say if I told you that my father also ran away from a work house...my father, mother and me and my brothers. A British guard killed him and they put us back in the work house."

"I'm sorry...it was a dark time," said Jimmy Delaney.

"I was sorry too," said the man. "That's why I killed the guard."

"You killed the guard?" said Jimmy Delaney.

"I did not even cry for my father," said the man. "I watched the guard and one night there he was, sitting on a rock wall just where he always was, taking his supper. I walked up to him from behind and split his head open with an axe. I was twelve years old...over fifty years ago now."

The man chewed a spoonful of stew and swallowed. The distant look flickered again across his face.

"I'll go to hell, of course," he said.

"They ain't no hell," said Willy Gantz.

"Oh, there is, sir...most assuredly," said the man. "How's your supper?"

"Stew real tasty," said Willy Gantz.

"Good," said the man, nodding. "Have more if you like and take any of these empty lean-tos."

He stirred the stew and rapped the stick against the rim of the pot, laid it down and got up.

"I'm off for my nightly constitution," he said. "If I don't see you again..."

"Us need some sleep," said Willy Gantz.

"Then I'll say good night," said the man.

He turned and made his way up the embankment toward the tracks.

"He's a strange man," said Jimmy Delaney.

"Let's us not talk about that man," said Willy Gantz. "That man the coldest man I b'lieve I ever seen. He doesn't care if he live or die."

"Are you worried?" said Jimmy Delaney.

"Oh, no, he not a danger to us...but mens like that man..."

"What happened in the coal mines?" said Jimmy Delaney.

"Coal strike back in ought-two," said Willy Gantz. "Union, they doesn't budge...mines, they doesn't budge... bosses talk about bringing in scabs and Pinkertons... union say they bust heads if that happen. Somehow they gets it straighten out, but I's gone by then. I can't walk no picket line, black as I is. Pinkertons, they shoot me for the fun of it."

"The Pinkerton man, back on the ice..."

"That a accident," said Willy Gantz. "Still, mens swinging clubs...they doesn't have no notion what they swinging at."

"I know another man who said that," said Jimmy Delaney.

"Well, it true," said Willy Gantz. He ate the last bite of stew and rapped the back of the tin pan with the spoon. "Enough of that," he said. "Us got to get these pans washed up and get some sleep. Now listen, this here how it is...us got to decide what way to go. Does you care how you gets to Chicago?"

"Not through Buffalo," said Jimmy Delaney.

"Then you ain't got any business in Buffalo."

"No business in Buffalo," said Jimmy Delaney.

"I just making sure," said Willy Gantz. "Now, this here how it is...that bull, the one gets on the Buffalo trains at Binghamton...us got to stay away from that man. Now, let's see what you learned. How does us do that? How does us stay away from that bull?"

"Let's go down to the creek and wash out the pans," said Jimmy Delaney.

They walked through the brush to the creek and back to the fire in the clearing. Willy Gantz laid the pans on the ground next to the stew pot.

"Well, what you come up with?" he said.

"Here is what it sounds like," said Jimmy Delaney. "It is two ways to Chicago. Both trains come through here and both go to Binghamton, besides the trains to the coal fields. We catch the train to Chicago that stays on the southern line after Binghamton."

"Tomorrow morning in the yard, how does us decide?" said Willy Gantz.

"Both carrying the red ball flag?" said Jimmy Delaney.

"Both red balls," said Willy Gantz.

"A different track?" said Jimmy Delaney.

"Just one track...one main line," said Willy Gantz.

"I don't know," said Jimmy Delaney.

"Ain't but one thing to do...us has to take a chance and ask," said Willy Gantz. "That a problem...they ain't many mens around here just now...might be in the yard most of the day. That there bring me to one more thing... you doesn't has to do what I does. Buffalo way might be shorter, might not be....I doesn't know."

"It's no business I have there," said Jimmy Delaney.

"Well, whether you does or you doesn't, you has a right to know the rest," said Willy Gantz. "I ain't going all the way to Chicago. My brother, he used to work in the locomotive factory in Lima, Ohio. I getting off there. You a fast learner...I ain't worried about you."

"You won't see the Pacific Ocean, Willy," said Jimmy Delaney.

"I tired, Jimmy," said Willy Gantz. "I doesn't rightly know how old I is, but I has gray on my head, as you can see. It time for me to go home."

The next morning Jimmy Delaney and Willy Gantz climbed the embankment and saw a man inspecting switches in the yard. Willy Gantz stayed below the edge of the embankment. The man turned when he heard the crunch of footsteps on the ballast behind him. He swung the heavy crowbar he was carrying onto his shoulder.

"You looking to catch out?" he said.

"Aye...westbound on the southern line to Chicago," said Jimmy Delaney.

"Mid-afternoon, carrying the red ball flag...track right over there," said the man, pointing. "Fast freight to Chicago...stops just long enough for coal and water and then gets the highball."

"I'm thanking you," said Jimmy Delaney.

The man nodded and turned away. He swung the crowbar against a rail and began working the switch lever.

Jimmy Delaney went to the mercantile and stocked up on food. Willy Gantz filled two fruit jars with water from the creek. In the afternoon they caught out of the Middletown yard on a red ball express. On the second morning Jimmy Delaney awoke at daybreak. There was an eerie silence. He peered into the dim light inside the boxcar. A fruit jar lay on the floor next to the door.

Eighteen

Riding the Cushions

Jimmy Delaney drank water from the fruit jar, poured water over his hands and rubbed his face. He pulled open the boxcar doors a few inches. Each one made a grinding sound that seemed to shatter the pervasive silence. A line of cars on an adjacent track extended as far as he could see and on the other side was a dense cluster of factories behind an iron fence. Black smoke poured from tall brick stacks and the wet smoky air smelled of heavy industry. Two short blasts of a steam whistle broke the silence and the train jolted. Jimmy Delaney grabbed the rucksack, pulled the boxcar door open all the way and jumped out onto the ballast just as the train began to move.

Behind the fence a network of tracks linked the gray brick factory buildings through archways sealed with steel doors. Forged bronze plaques next to the doors spelled out *Lima Locomotive Works*. Jimmy Delaney backed into the fence and waited for the train to pass. The narrow strip of ballast between the track and the fence led to a crossing near the main office building of the locomotive works. Jimmy Delaney walked along South Main Street and stopped in front of a diner. The door was open and the smell of frying bacon drifted onto the sidewalk. Men in work clothes sat on a line of stools in front of a counter. Jimmy Delaney smoothed the nap of Murphy's coat, shifted the weight of the rucksack on his shoulder and went in.

A newspaper lay on the counter in front of the last stool near a wall. The headline read: *San Francisco Leveled by Earthquake and Fire*. The picture showed iron skeletons of buildings and streets littered with masonry against a pall of gray smoke. Jimmy Delaney sat on the stool and picked up the folded newspaper.

"Hell of a mess, huh," said a female voice.

Jimmy Delaney looked up. A large woman resembling the widow Morse with a pencil thrust into her hair stood behind the counter.

"Aye," he said. "When did this happen?"

"Four days ago," said the woman. "They say the quake broke the gas lines and the place burned to the ground. I've heard about that place...Chinamen and bawdyhouses and sins decent people never heard of. God's justice, if you ask me."

"Nobody asked you, Stella," said the man next to Jimmy Delaney. "Just give the young feller some breakfast without the sermon."

"Kiss my arse, Albert," said Stella, not looking at the man. "What'll you have, hon?" she said to Jimmy Delaney.

"Eggs and bacon and coffee," said Jimmy Delaney.

"Coming up," said Stella. "You don't mind me saying so, you look kinda rugged. Are you all right?"

"Road weary a bit, but I'm well," said Jimmy Delaney. "Do you know of a rooming house where I might have a bath and a night's sleep?"

"Right next door...boarding house for railroad men," said Stella. "It's fifty cents for overnight and supper. Tell Old Lady Snodgrass that Stella sent you."

"You tell her that and she'll kick you out," said Albert.

"Kiss my arse, Albert," said Stella.

Albert stood up and threw a quarter on the counter. "See you, Stella," he said.

"Be careful, hon," said Stella. "It's murky out there today."

Jimmy Delaney ate the eggs and bacon quickly and mopped up the plate with bread. Stella reached the end of the counter with the coffee pot.

"Done already?" she said.

"Hungry," said Jimmy Delaney, sipping coffee.

"You sure you're all right, hon?" said Stella.

"Aye, just fine," said Jimmy Delaney. He laid the coffee cup on the counter, slid off the stool and held out a quarter. "I'm thanking you for the information," he said.

"Don't mention it," said Stella. "Come back to see us before you leave. Which way you headed?"

"Chicago for a job," said Jimmy Delaney.

"You been on the rails, ain't you?" said Stella.

"It's a free ride," said Jimmy Delaney.

"If the bulls or thugs don't kill you," said Stella. "You want a job? You can wash dishes for a day or so and buy a ticket and get to Chicago in one piece."

"Oh, I'm a bindle stiff by now," said Jimmy Delaney.

"You ain't old enough to be no bindle stiff," said Stella.

"I'll come in tomorrow morning for breakfast," said Jimmy Delaney.

"Tell Old Lady Snodgrass that Stella sent you."

"I'll do that...and I'm thanking you," said Jimmy Delaney. He tipped his cap and went out.

The large Victorian house next to the diner on West First Street faced the forging and assembly plants of the locomotive works squeezed into a tight triangle between the diverging rail lines of the Nickel Plate Road and the Baltimore and Ohio. Jimmy Delaney knocked on the door and surveyed the factory buildings from the porch and found himself hoping that Willy Gantz could recover some part of the world of his memory.

The door opened. Jimmy Delaney turned away from the factories. He paid for one night's stay, had a bath and left the house in late morning feeling refreshed. With directions from Old Lady Snodgrass, as everyone in the neighborhood called her, he walked toward downtown Lima, first northbound on South Main, then right on West Elm Street and left on South Central Avenue, which became North Central Avenue at Market Street and ended at the railroad station one block north of Wayne Street.

He went into the station and bought a ticket to Chicago for the next day. He smiled, thinking Willy Gantz would approve.

With directions from the ticket master, Jimmy Delaney found the library and read several accounts of the earthquake, perused a table of withdrawn books and bought copies of *Oliver Twist* and *Our Mutual Friend* for a nickel each. The books were tucked away in the rucksack with a leather-bound copy of *Walden and Other Writings* from a shop in Hester Street, the only book Jimmy Delaney owned when he joined the crew of the *Annandale*. Even from another time and place, he sensed a kinship with *Oliver Twist* and the librarian at the settlement house had said that *Our Mutual Friend* was the best of the great works of an age passing away. Jimmy Delaney had not told the librarian that Schoolmaster O'Donnell wondered if any age really passed away.

At the diner the next morning Jimmy Delaney told Stella that he had a ticket for the train to Chicago. Stella smiled broadly, saying that she knew he "weren't no bindle stiff." He walked to the station and boarded the *Erie Limited* at noon. Having treated himself to a first-class ticket, he settled into a plush chair in the parlor car. A black man in a white coat immediately placed a cup of coffee on the table next to the chair.

The *Erie Limited* rolled through the farmland of northwestern Ohio. Jimmy Delaney took his new copy of *Oliver Twist* from the rucksack and sipped coffee from a bone china cup. He read that Oliver Twist had been born in a workhouse.

"Porter."

The black man in the white coat approached the man sitting across the aisle from Jimmy Delaney. The man wore a gray suit with a high stiff collar and black tie.

"Yes sir," said the lounge car attendant.

"That boy there, wearing the dreadful blue coat, is not dressed appropriately," said the man.

The attendant turned, glanced at Jimmy Delaney, who did not look up from *Oliver Twist.*

"Sir, I am only..."

"Don't contradict me, boy," said the man.

"I will bring the conductor," said the attendant.

"I should hope so," said the man. His eyes followed the attendant out of the car.

"I think you are a stowaway," he said to Jimmy Delaney. "And what is that you are reading?"

Jimmy Delaney shifted in his chair. He did not look up.

"I'm speaking to you, boy," said the man.

Jimmy Delaney raised his eyes without moving his head. He saw the conductor and the parlor car attendant coming through the door.

"What is the trouble here?" said the conductor.

"This...whatever he is...has no respect for gentlemen," said the man. "He should be put off the train."

The conductor looked at the attendant. "Has this boy been bothering people?" he said.

"He sit here readin' that book," said the attendant. "This here man..."

"He's right about one thing," said another man, also wearing a suit. The man clipped a cigar and ran it through his lips. "Like the porter said, the boy didn't start it," he said, inspecting the cigar carefully. "But he certainly finished it. Never said a word...effective, I must say."

"I have never been so insulted..."

"Come along with me, sir," said the conductor. "I'm sure you will be more comfortable in the other lounge, two cars ahead."

"You don't intend to do anything about this outrage?" said the man.

"Sir, I cannot permit..."

"Let him stay," said the man with the cigar. "It's entertaining as hell...this idiot doesn't even know what the kid is talking about by not talking about it."

"How dare you, sir, I do not have to sit here..."

"Then pray do not," said the man. He put a match to the cigar, turning it with his other hand to ensure an even burn. He put the match in an ash tray and looked up. "You're still here?" he said.

"Come with me, sir," said the conductor. "We can find you a more comfortable place in the other lounge car."

The man walked ahead of the conductor. "This is an outrage," he said. "Do you know who I am? I'll have your job for this."

After they were gone, the man with the cigar rearranged the newspaper he was reading in a deliberate way.

"Agreeable chap, don't you think?" he said.

"I'm thanking you," said Jimmy Delaney.

The man nodded.

Jimmy Delaney looked at the attendant, who shook his head and walked away. Jimmy Delaney turned his chair toward the window.

"I'm riding the cushions, Willy," he said. "It seems to be faster."

Nineteen

The Elderly Man

The *Erie Limited* slowed in the gray haze near the steel mills on the shore of Lake Michigan, made its way through lines of freight trains laden with iron ore and coal and began a northerly swing through factories and tenements into the city. The conductor came through the parlor car calling the last stop as the train passed under the Roosevelt Road Bridge toward Dearborn Station.

Jimmy Delaney folded the advertisement he had torn from the *New York World* and put it away in the pocket of Murphy's coat.

"Begging your pardon...do you know Union Station?" he said to the man with the cigar.

"Yes," said the man. "Shall I write it down?"

"I won't be forgetting," said Jimmy Delaney.

"Very well, it's not far," said the man. "Just one streetcar will get you there. Outside the station, turn right and walk one block to State and take the Adams streetcar. After a few blocks the car will swing around off State into Adams. You continue on Adams until you come to a bridge across the river. Get off at Canal, the first stop after the bridge. The station is right there on the corner to your right. You can't miss it...red brick, a block and a half long. Are you taking another train?"

"I am looking for an office in Union Station," said Jimmy Delaney. "They are hiring for railroad construction crews."

The man pulled a pocket watch from his waistcoat and looked at it.

"It is late in the day," he said. "If you should need a place to stay, there is a good settlement house on LaSalle between Monroe and Madison. It's the same Adams streetcar you'll be taking to the station. It stops at LaSalle, which crosses Adams. Get off and walk a block and a half north. The settlement house is not that obvious. Once you cross Monroe, just ask someone."

"I'm thanking you," said Jimmy Delaney.

They walked through the ornate lobby of Dearborn Station and out into Polk Street. Jimmy Delaney turned to look at the station, an imposing building of red brick and pink granite dominated by a twelve-story clock tower. The man from the train pointed his cane along Dearborn Street, which flowed toward them, ending at the station.

"Standing in Dearborn Street you can see the clock tower all the way from Water Street about a mile from here," he said, waving the cane toward a hansom cab.

The cab stopped in the wide loading zone in front of the station. The man slid the small suitcase he was carrying into the cab and put his foot on the running board.

"I can drop you off," he said.

"I'm after looking around a bit," said Jimmy Delaney.

"As you wish," said the man. He said something to the coachman and got into the cab. "Good luck with your job," he said, as the cab pulled away and merged into the westbound carriage traffic on Polk Street. The man waved the cane out the window.

State Street looking north was familiar. Masonry buildings of four to ten stories converged to a point in the distance. The store fronts, covered with awnings in bright colors, were served by wide concrete sidewalks merging into carriageways on the hard-packed cobblestone street with two trolley lines in the center. The sidewalks and street were crowded with commuters moving toward the streetcars.

Jimmy Delaney walked about half a mile on State Street, crossed into the Loop under the elevated railway on Van Buren Street and turned west into Adams Street. After two blocks he came to a large granite building with a towering dome on the corner of Adams and Dearborn.

Looking south on Dearborn, he saw the railroad station and another half mile on Adams brought him to a stone bridge over the Chicago River. Union Station, a long thin building of red brick, was sprawled along west side of the river. Looking both ways along the river, Jimmy Delaney saw that stone bridges anchored the east and west sides of every street in his line of sight. Lighted globes on the bridge abutments shone in the fading light. Retreating on Adams, he turned left into LaSalle Street and found the settlement house just after crossing Monroe. He took a room for the night.

The advertisement in the *New York World* for railroad construction crews was a year old when Jimmy Delaney left the settlement house for Union Station early in the morning. He crossed the bridge on Adams Street and walked one block to Canal. The loading area on Canal was crowded with carriages, travelers and men pulling long flat wagons loaded with luggage. Jimmy Delaney made his way through the crowd into the station, looked at the directory and climbed the stairs to the offices of the Chicago, Milwaukee and St. Paul Railway Company on the second floor.

A door with a frosted glass pane in a dimly lighted corridor led to a small waiting room furnished with leather chairs. A bald man dressed formally in a morning suit too large for his thin frame stood behind a heavy wooden counter. He looked over his rimless glasses, then at the advertisement Jimmy Delaney had smoothed out on the counter.

"What is this?" he said.

"Are you hiring for the construction crews?" said Jimmy Delaney.

"This is a corporate office," said the clerk. "We do not hire laborers here. You will have to go to Milwaukee."

"The advertisement indicates that applicants should come here," said Jimmy Delaney.

"I cannot be responsible for what is printed in a newspaper...particularly a newspaper from out of town," said the clerk. "If there is nothing else, I am very busy today."

"Can you say if men are still being hired?" said Jimmy Delaney.

"That is my understanding," said the clerk. "If you wish to pursue this matter, go to the depot in Milwaukee. You may get there on a train from this station. Now, if you will excuse me."

Jimmy Delaney went into a stall in the men's room and counted his money. Soon he would need a job. According to the advertisement, he could expect a wage in the range of a dollar per day working on a railroad construction crew. He bought a second-class ticket to Milwaukee.

The *Fast Mail* consisted of two postal cars, four coaches and a lounge car, an undemanding consignment for a locomotive with six driving wheels taller than a man. The train left the north concourse on schedule and minutes later passed the signal tower at Libertyville Junction at seventy-five miles per hour. An elderly man in the seat facing Jimmy Delaney rubbed his hands together, smoothed out the newspaper he was carrying, wiped his forehead with a handkerchief.

The conductor stopped next to Jimmy Delaney and the elderly man and balanced himself against the sway of a train at speed.

"Tickets, please," he said.

Jimmy Delaney held out his ticket and nodded toward the elderly man.

The conductor punched the ticket and returned it to Jimmy Delaney. The elderly man had made no movement to present a ticket.

"Sir, are you well?" said the conductor. "Do you have a ticket?"

"It's too fast," said the elderly man. "The train is going too fast."

"Sir, I would not..."

The train lurched violently, throwing the conductor into the unoccupied seat across the aisle.

"Goddammit," he shouted, struggling to get up.

The elderly man jumped into the aisle, gripping the backs of seats to steady himself.

"Stop the train, stop the train," he said. "We'll all be killed."

The conductor regained his footing just as the train lurched again, throwing him back into the seat. The elderly man lunged toward the front of the car.

"Madness," he said. "It is madness...stop the train."

"Stop him...somebody stop him," shouted the conductor, struggling to regain his balance. "He's trying to pull the emergency cord."

Jimmy Delaney scrambled to his feet and grabbed the elderly man's coat tail. The elderly man screamed, wrenched himself free and reached the front of the car. He grabbed the emergency cord and pulled, locking the brakes.

Jimmy Delaney tumbled forward into the aisle, coming to rest against a seat brace. He seemed to move in slow motion, aware of bodies and objects being thrown into the rear-facing seats. He could still see the elderly man, who was opening the door into the vestibule between the cars. The train, iron wheels screaming against iron rails, slid to a stop. A smell of burning metal penetrated the silence. Jimmy Delaney rolled over onto his knees facing the rear of the car and saw the conductor coming toward him.

"Oh, Christ," said the conductor. "Are you all right, boy? Where is the old man?"

Jimmy Delaney took the conductor's extended hand and pulled himself up.

"The next car," he said. "I saw him going into the next car."

The conductor began helping people back into their seats. He scrutinized Jimmy Delaney.

"Listen, you seem all right," he said. "Go back to the

lounge car and see what you can do. Tell the attendant I'm going up to the mail cars and the engine. We have to get the train moving again." He looked around. "Help your neighbor, everyone," he called. "It is not a wreck... someone pulled the emergency cord. We'll be going again soon."

The lounge car was strewn with newspapers, books, cups and saucers and glasses. Some of the passengers were still lying or kneeling on the floor. Others were grinding out smoldering fires started by cigars flung onto the floor from overturned ashtrays. Jimmy Delaney saw the attendant, a black man wearing a white coat stained with food and coffee. He shifted the weight of his rucksack and touched the attendant's arm. The man turned.

"The conductor sent me to help," said Jimmy Delaney.

"What happen up there?" said the attendant. "Where the conductor...he ain't hurt, is he?"

"He went to the mail cars and the engine," said Jimmy Delaney.

"We done hit somethin' or somebody done pull the brake?" said the attendant. "Only things I knows of cause this mess."

"The emergency cord," said Jimmy Delaney. "Are there any other attendants on the train?"

"Jus' me," said the attendant. "This here a short run...I don't make no passes through the cars."

"I'll help you get everyone back in their seats," said Jimmy Delaney.

The conductor came in from the observation platform on the rear of the lounge car and the train started moving with a slight jolt.

"The mail cars are a hell of a mess," he said. He looked around the lounge car. "Christ...are you all right, John," he said to the attendant.

"Oh, I's all right," said the attendant. "I don't think they's anything but a few scratches in here. We goin' all the way to Milwaukee or stop and clean up this mess?"

"We'll stop in Sturtevant long enough to send a wire," said the conductor.

"This gent here, he say somebody done pull the brake," said the attendant.

The conductor nodded. "An old man," he said. "We hit that bad rail just north of the Libertyville tower and he panicked...he was already frightened by something. I forgot about the rail and got dumped on my ass. The boy, here, got hold of him...but he broke free and got to the cord. I've been telling those fools in Chicago for weeks to fix that rail."

"Did you find him?" said Jimmy Delaney.

"He's dead...out there beside the track, back a ways," said the conductor. "He's dead all right...looks like he jumped off the train before it stopped. Must have went crazy."

"We leavin' him there?" said the attendant.

"We're not going to make Milwaukee on time as it is, John," said the conductor.

"So, you sendin' a wire from Sturtevant?" said the attendant.

"I'll wire Libertyville and they can see to it," said the conductor. "I know what you're thinking...the crowd will strip him clean by then. An old man like that, though...he's probably not carrying much anyway. Now listen, when we get the highball out of Sturtevant, we'll be pouring it on. With a little luck, we can still make Milwaukee not much behind schedule."

The switchman, not expecting the *Fast Mail* to stop, did not acknowledge the approaching train until he heard the whistle. When he looked through the window of the shack, he saw that the train was slowing and the fireman was waving a flag. He hurried outside and pulled the switch bar and the train rolled onto the siding which led to the station platform in Sturtevant, Wisconsin.

The train stopped in front of the station and the conductor hurried to the telegraph shack and wrote out a message. He drew a watch from his vest pocket, glanced at the time and returned to the platform. Many passengers had gotten off the train; some were walking into the station. The lounge car attendant was stacking luggage on the platform.

"Goddammit, John, what are you doing?" said the conductor. "People aren't supposed to get off here... we'll never get to Milwaukee near on time. Goddammit, John."

"Soon as we stop, why I look out and peoples done open the doors and gettin' out," said the attendant.

"Everyone on this train bought a ticket to Milwaukee, John," said the conductor.

"I 'spect they distressed...need to take stock of things," said the attendant.

"Take stock of what?" said the conductor. "You can't get to Milwaukee by getting off at Sturtevant."

"Well, I 'spect all that's gonna get off has," said the attendant.

"I'll get the porters from the station to move this luggage," said the conductor. "We're not waiting for anyone to get back on. We have to go if we plan to see Milwaukee any time this week."

"They not gonna be pleased...clearin' for an unscheduled train," said the attendant.

The conductor regarded the attendant with an incredulous expression, went into the station and ordered the porters to clear the platform. He pushed the porters out the door, pointed toward the baggage wagons, admonished them to hurry and strode to the head end of the train, looking at the pocket watch repeatedly.

"That man hate to be late worse than any man I ever seen," said the attendant.

"What happens if the train is late?" said Jimmy Delaney.

"Nothin'...nothin' at all," said the attendant. "That what make it so silly. I ain't sayin' it don't matter about runnin' the train on time...I ain't sayin' that...but that man, he don't let nothin' stand in his way. That poor old man back there, layin' in a ditch...no dignity, no nothin'. Who know what demons cause him to do what he done?"

The train crossed the steel bridge over the Menomonee River and coasted into the Milwaukee station just over one hour late. The conductor and lounge car attendant stood on the platform. Jimmy Delaney shifted the weight of the rucksack on his shoulder and shook hands with the two men. He turned to walk away and stopped short; a man dressed in a suit was coming toward them through the crowd.

"I'll do the talking, John," said the conductor. "It's not your responsibility."

"We got a wire from Libertyville," said the man. He grasped the conductor's arm lightly. "Don't worry," he said. "You did the best you could."

Twenty

The Wobbly Man

The railroad office on the second floor of Everett Street Station was trimmed in dark woods and adorned by a sofa upholstered in dark leather. The outline of a man, whose features were blurred against the back light from a large dormer, stood behind a weighty oak counter. Jimmy Delaney approached, holding the advertisement from the *New York World*.

"Yes?" said the clerk.

Jimmy Delaney laid the advertisement on the counter. The clerk's eyes followed the paper.

"Are you hiring for the construction crews?" said Jimmy Delaney.

The clerk pushed the advertisement aside, took out a form and laid it on the counter.

"Can you read and write?" he said.

"Aye," said Jimmy Delaney.

"Fill out this form...you may use the pen and inkwell there next to you."

Jimmy Delaney wrote the answers to several questions and slid the form across the counter.

"An itinerant, I see...no fixed address," said the clerk. "We are building a railroad to the Puget Sound. Do you know where that is?"

"Aye," said Jimmy Delaney.

"Are you willing to work any division?"

"Aye, anywhere," said Jimmy Delaney.

The clerk wrote on a card and then on another slip of paper, which he sealed in an envelope. He handed the card and the envelope to Jimmy Delaney.

"The pay is one dollar a day," he said. "A work train will leave tomorrow morning. Report here at eight and show the card to the foreman at the assembly area at the west end of the station. Please deliver the envelope to him as well, if you don't mind."

"Aye," said Jimmy Delaney.

"The railroad maintains a boarding house at the corner of Fourth and Michigan...a block from here," said the clerk. "Go downstairs and out the front of the depot. You will see a park across the street. Go to the left and take Fourth bordering on the park up to Michigan. It is a large white house on the corner. Show the card to the landlady."

"I'm thanking you," said Jimmy Delaney, tucking the card and the envelope into the inside pocket of Murphy's coat.

The clerk resumed writing in a large ledger. Jimmy Delaney walked across the office and opened the door.

"Delaney...welcome to the employ of the Chicago, Milwaukee and Saint Paul," said the clerk.

Jimmy Delaney turned. The clerk's outline was again blurred by the light streaming in from the dormer behind him. Jimmy Delaney nodded, went into the hall and closed the door.

The boarding house was a two-story Victorian with a broad wrap-around porch bounded by ornate railings. Like the other Victorian boarding houses in Catskill and Lima, a bland white paint concealed the original vibrant colors and the proprietor was a widow. The widow Forrestal employed six maids and two cooks to keep up with the demand of the railroad for construction crews.

"You'll room with two other gentlemen on the second floor," said the widow Forrestal. "Last door on the right... shared bath at the end of the hall. Dinner is at six in the dining room...prompt. Breakfast is also at six...prompt."

"The rent for one night?" said Jimmy Delaney.

"No rent," said the widow Forrestal. "The railroad takes care of the rent. Don't be late for dinner or breakfast...we have to keep a tight ship here."

Fifteen men for the next work train to the west were served the evening meal at a common table in front of a large fireplace. The maids brought in roast beef, potatoes and gravy, green beans and hot coffee. The men passed three wooden bowls of bread around the table.

"Eat hearty, boy," said the man sitting next to Jimmy Delaney. "You get stew, bread and water on the work train. There's plenty of it, but it ain't exactly top drawer like this here."

"You've been on the work train before?" said Jimmy Delaney.

"You betcha, boy," said the man. "I'm the fastest gandy dancer you ever saw. You see these arms on me. I built the line down to Chicago more'n thirty year ago...been gandy dancing ever since. I been waitin' for a chance like this. Now I'm gonna build a line all the way to the big ocean and when I get there I'm gonna retire and lay in the sun."

"Not in the Pacific Northwest," said another man. "It rains all the time."

"Then I'll gandy dance my way to California and lay in the sun there," said the first man.

"Don't you read the papers?" said the other man. "They just had an earthquake in California...it leveled a whole city."

"Well, I'll find the sun somewhere out west," said the first man. "After this here run, I'll be getting too old for gandy dancing and I sure ain't gonna sit around in the gloom."

"You do that, old timer," said the other man.

The maids served apple pie for dessert and Jimmy Delaney, feeling sated and warm, settled into an easy chair in the parlor. He was in a group of four sitting in a circle around the coffee table.

"Do you ever take off that coat?" said one of the men.

"At times," said Jimmy Delaney.

"You were on the train from Chicago this morning," said the man. "I was on that train...saw you on the platform."

"Aye," said Jimmy Delaney.

"I heard somebody pulled the emergency cord," said the man.

"What happened?" said another man.

"Somebody pulled the emergency brake cord in one of the cars," said the first man. "I heard it was an old man...and then they threw him off the train. I heard the conductor threw him off the train without even stopping."

"Without stopping?" said the second man.

"Everybody knows that is what happened," said the first man. "The damn railroad killed him for interfering with their schedule."

"This is not how it was," said Jimmy Delaney.

"I say that is exactly how it was," said the man.

"No," said Jimmy Delaney.

"Why are you sticking up for the railroad?" said the man. "Those bastards killed a man just for delaying them."

"No," said Jimmy Delaney.

"I say they did," said the man.

"The boy has a right to his opinion," said the second man.

"It is not an opinion," said Jimmy Delaney.

"How do you know what he's saying ain't true?" said the second man.

"The man who pulled the cord was sitting across from me," said Jimmy Delaney. "He was elderly and frightened by the speed. The conductor came for the tickets just as the train swerved. The old man was afraid the train would crash because of the speed and in a state of panic he ran to the end of the car and pulled the cord and then ran into the next car. The conductor and I were both thrown to the floor and we could not right ourselves until the train stopped. This is how it was."

"Well, what do you say to that?" said the second man.

The first man stared at Jimmy Delaney. His face was a mask of disdain.

"Do you deny that the railroad left the old man's body by the track?" he said.

"Aye, the conductor wired the details from the next stop," said Jimmy Delaney.

"And you think this was right?" said the man.

"It is not my place to say it is right or wrong," said Jimmy Delaney. "It is not my business."

"It's everybody's business unless you're a railroad plant," said the man.

"I am just a fellow looking for work," said Jimmy Delaney.

"Don't play the innocent with me," said the man. "Do you know what I think? I say you're a railroad plant."

"So, what do you say, kid?" said the second man.

"The last time I heard that word was in the ice fields on the Hudson," said Jimmy Delaney. "The foreman was after warning everyone that union plants would find trouble. There was one and he did...find trouble, that is. Now I hear that word again." Jimmy Delaney shifted his gaze from the second man to the first man. "It does not seem that the railroad needs a plant," he said. "The union fellows I have met might just as well carry signs."

"You're a union man?" said the second man.

"You're on the wrong side, kid," said the union man. "Think about it."

"It is not my business," said Jimmy Delaney. "I am just a fellow looking for work."

"Well, one day you will marry and you'll be shafted just when you have mouths to feed...and to feed your children you'll be scabbing against honest men turned out of their jobs because they stood up for themselves. Don't you know what these people are?"

"There's good and bad...in the union and everywhere else," said Jimmy Delaney. He stood and adjusted the rucksack strap on his shoulder. "A good night to you all," he said and strode toward the door.

"Kid," said the union man.

Jimmy Delaney turned.

"You'll get shafted sooner or later," said the union man. "You have no power and no supporting structure... it's inevitable."

Jimmy Delaney walked in the park, read two chapters of *Oliver Twist* and went to bed. Sleep was fitful, interrupted by an old man suspended in space beside a moving train. The bed clothes, bleached stark white and stiff with starch, were limp and sweaty when the recurring image of the old man's face was shattered by pounding on the bedroom door at dawn.

Jimmy Delaney and his two room mates were startled awake. Jimmy Delaney opened the door. Two men wearing the blue regalia of police were in the hall.

"Get dressed and bring your belongings," said one of the men. "Everyone in this boarding house is being assembled in the parlor."

"What happened?" said one of Jimmy Delaney's room mates.

"To the parlor...and no lollygagging," said the man. "Inspector Hessler is waiting."

Jimmy Delaney dressed and packed the rucksack. He was the first out of the room.

Hessler, a tall man with a distinguished air, wore a well-fitting three-piece suit. He stood next to the fireplace. Jimmy Delaney moved to the other side of the parlor next to a window. He shifted the weight of the rucksack on his shoulder. He watched Hessler, as the men came in and milled around in the center of the room. After a few minutes Hessler tugged his waistcoat straight and nodded toward the widow Forrestal. The widow counted the men by pointing her finger at each one.

"Is this everyone?" said Hessler.

"There are only thirteen," she said. "Besides the poor man on the lawn, one man is missing."

"Which man?" said Hessler. "What is the man's name?"

"I don't know," said the widow. "We don't take the names."

Hessler stared at the widow Forrestal. "Do you mean to say that you rent rooms to people without knowing their names?" he said.

"Names are none of my business," said the widow. "The men get their employment cards at the railroad station and come here for the night and leave on the work trains the next morning. I am only required to look at the cards."

Hessler drew a pocket watch from his waistcoat, rubbed his thumb along the back of the case, returned the watch to his waistcoat pocket.

"It is a daily occurrence?" he said. "That is, do you board a new consignment of employees every night?"

"Yes, almost every day for more than a month now," said the widow. "The railroad has been hiring for construction crews in the west. We receive fifteen new men almost every day."

"Fifteen new men each day," said Hessler.

"Yes, the house has five bedrooms...three men to a room," said the widow Forrestal. "That's fifteen...all we can handle."

"Very well," said Hessler. He motioned to one of the uniformed officers. "Take up all the cards, write down the names and leave the cards here on the table," he said. "Then take the list across the park to the Milwaukee depot and match the names against the list of men hired yesterday and assigned to this house. The office will probably not be open. No matter...have your breakfast if you haven't eaten and go back. The man we seek has certainly left the city and the name he gave will certainly be false. However, he may return, he may believe he can use the name again, he may reveal himself in some innocuous way. If he does..."

The uniformed officers made a list of names and left. Hessler asked the men to stand in circle around him.

"Now, let us see what we can learn about this man," he said.

"What has happened?" said one of the boarders.

"I'm afraid there has been a murder," said Hessler.

"A murder...here?" said one man, and the other men began gesturing and talking to each other.

"Your attention, please," said Hessler, and when the din had died down, he said, "Thank you."

"Who was it?" said a man.

"The victim belonged to a union...the Industrial Workers of the World...a Wobbly," said Hessler. "He was probably here to recruit railroad workers for the union. Is anyone here a union man?"

Some of the men looked at each other. No one spoke.

"Did any of you talk to the victim?" said Hessler. "Does anyone remember the missing man?"

A man stepped forward, nudging Jimmy Delaney's arm. "Last night...after dinner," he said.

"Your name," said Hessler.

"Jones...Jacob Jones," said the man. "There were four of us sitting in the parlor by the fire...the union man and another man, me and the boy here. The other man is not here...he must be the missing man."

"Your name, son," said Hessler.

"Delaney."

"Thank you," said Hessler. He looked around the room. "Did any of the rest of you have anything to do with either of these men?" he said.

A man stepped forward. "When your bobbies come bangin' on the door this mornin', why there was only the two of us...me and this here fellow," he said, pointing to another man. "There was supposed to be three of us, but we never saw the third fellow...and then when I was packin' this mornin', I seen his bed ain't been slept in."

"Who had a similar experience?" said Hessler.

"Same thing here," said another man. "The third guy

was in the room before supper, but he never slept in his bed."

"That would be about right," said Hessler to no one in particular.

The clock on the mantle struck six times. Hessler pulled the pocket watch from his waistcoat, looked at it and began rubbing his thumb against the back of the case.

"Very well, everyone is excused," he said. "You may take your work cards from the table there and have your breakfast." He motioned for Jimmy Delaney and Jacob Jones to remain behind. "Just a few moments," he said.

Hessler rubbed the pocket watch until everyone had gone, then turned his attention to Jimmy Delaney and Jacob Jones.

"Did the Wobbly identify himself?" he said.

"The boy here...he dragged it out of him...pretty clever, too," said Jacob Jones.

Hessler glanced at the pocket watch, looked at Jimmy Delaney. "How was that?" he said.

"I was in the ice fields on the Hudson River last winter," said Jimmy Delaney. "There was a union man there. This man...he spoke against the railroad in the same way."

"I see," said Hessler. "What can you remember about the missing man? Try to picture him...his appearance, his manner, anything out of the ordinary."

"He was just another guy," said Jacob Jones.

"He was short and heavy," said Jimmy Delaney. "And his hair was neat...combed and parted in the middle."

"That's right," said Jacob Jones. "Oh, and he dressed good...his overalls were new."

"Anything else?" said Hessler.

"He did not say anything," said Jimmy Delaney.

"Nothing at all?" said Hessler.

"Come to think of it, no," said Jacob Jones. "Strange... he didn't say a word."

"Did it seem to you that he was listening to the

145

conversation?" said Hessler. "Or perhaps he was just sitting there...looking around the room, for instance...as if distracted or uninterested?"

"He looked at you when you spoke," said Jacob Jones.

"What did you talk about?" said Hessler.

"The union man...he was making accusations against the railroad," said Jacob Jones.

"What kind of accusations?" said Hessler. "Regarding the unions, I assume."

"No, wild accusations, I would say...like throwing people off trains," said Jacob Jones.

"Throwing people off trains?" said Hessler.

"You tell him," said Jacob Jones, nudging Jimmy Delaney. "You were there."

"The train from Chicago yesterday morning," said Jimmy Delaney. "The train was moving very fast and an elderly man, fearful of the speed, pulled the emergency cord and I think jumped from the train before it stopped. He was killed. The union man was after saying the conductor threw the man from the train. This is not how it was. The conductor was in my car...he was thrown to floor."

"You told him this," said Hessler.

"I told him the way it was...that the conductor was thrown to the floor and could not regain his balance until the train stopped," said Jimmy Delaney.

"The Wobbly must have been pleased with you," said Hessler.

"He was angry, but I think not so much after a moment," said Jimmy Delaney. "He realized..."

"Realized what?" said Hessler.

"That he would have to think of something else to say about the railroad," said Jimmy Delaney.

Hessler smiled. "Quite," he said. "The other man...did he follow this exchange closely?"

"I did not notice," said Jimmy Delaney.

The clock struck the half hour past six. Hessler rubbed

the back of the watch and returned it to his waistcoat pocket.

"Well, I think that is about all we can learn for the moment," he said. "You men may go to breakfast now. Don't forget to pick up your work cards."

"That's all?" said Jacob Jones.

"Yes, I think that's all," said Hessler.

The door opened and another man dressed in a suit came in.

"Inspector," he said. "I was told at the precinct that there has been a murder here."

"Good morning, Sergeant," said Hessler. "Good of you to come...I think we have everything we need."

"A union man was killed, I'm told," said the sergeant.

"A Wobbly," said Hessler.

"Wobbly, huh," said the sergeant. "Well, sometimes I think they ask for it. Do we know who did it?"

"Oh, yes," said Hessler. "He is no longer in Milwaukee, but we know who he is...what he is, I should say. He is a Pinkerton or an employee of some other private army out of Chicago. Soon we will know at least one of his aliases. The Wobbly was a trouble maker, of course, but the situation with private armies is getting out of hand. Eventually it will come to a head...one cannot tolerate this kind of thing indefinitely."

"An assassin comes to town and simply kills a man?" said the sergeant.

"Oh, quite so," said Hessler. "The Wobbly was undoubtedly followed here. We will discover that he was quite high in the union...a Russian or Pole or some other East European...most likely with connections to the anarchists." He turned toward Jimmy Delaney and Jacob Jones. "It so happens that the union man's name was also Jones," he said. "I suspect that is an alias. Did he speak with an accent?"

"Not that I could tell," said Jacob Jones.

"Well, in any case, he was perceived by someone to be a considerable threat...and eliminated," said Hessler.

"But the man was dressed well and quiet," said Jacob Jones. "How could we know he kills people?"

"You couldn't," said Hessler. "You never can."

"So we will not bring the assassin to justice?" said the sergeant.

"No," said Hessler.

"But he was undoubtedly hired by the railroad," said the sergeant. "There will be a record of money changing hands."

"Not necessarily," said Hessler. "In fact, I have not heard of the railroad being involved in this sort of thing. I suspect it was an old score which played out here by coincidence." Hessler looked at his watch. "A perfect situation, actually," he said. "Pose as a railroad worker, but do not draw attention to yourself, eliminate the target quickly and quietly with a dagger on the front lawn after dark, get out of town with a long head start and the investigation will turn up a false name which leads nowhere."

"What is the world coming to?" said Jacob Jones.

"The world is what it always has been, Mister Jones," said Hessler. "You're going to miss your breakfast."

Jimmy Delaney and Jacob Jones accepted Hessler's handshake. They crossed the parlor to the table and picked up their work cards. Jimmy Delaney opened the door to the hall.

"Check with the ticket agents on duty at all the train stations last night, Sergeant," said Hessler. "I'll write out a description for you. Our man was careless, but probably not careless enough. It is doubtful, but someone may remember him."

"Let's get some food," said Jacob Jones. "We can still make the work train and it'll be a long day."

Jimmy Delaney nodded and closed the parlor door. A muffled click sealed the door against the jamb.

Twenty-One

The Air Ye Breathe

The gothic clock tower dominating the skyline along
the Menomonee River and the stone depot spreading
out from its base were deep red in the early morning sun.
Carriages, passengers for the morning trains and porters
heaving against the long iron tongues attached to luggage
wagons had spilled out of the loading area into Everett
Street. Jimmy Delaney and Jacob Jones made their way
through the depot and saw a line of men standing behind
a rope drawn taut across the platform. A man wearing a
dark blue uniform inspected work cards, checked off the
names in a ledger and passed each man under the rope
toward a train. Jimmy Delaney and Jacob Jones took
places in line.

"Reporting for the work train," said Jacob Jones.

The man examined the card and wrote in the ledger.

"You too?" he said to Jimmy Delaney.

"Aye," said Jimmy Delaney. He held out the work card
and the sealed envelope given to him by the clerk. "I was
asked to deliver this envelope to the foreman," he said.

"I'm the foreman," said the man. He examined the
work card, wrote in the ledger and then inspected the
envelope, turning it over. "By someone in the office?" he
said.

"Aye," said Jimmy Delaney.

"Tall...full head of hair?" said the foreman.

"He was bald and wearing spectacles," said Jimmy
Delaney.

"That'd be Frank," said the foreman. He opened the
envelope, read the note inside and looked up. "Jones, car
number nine," he said, holding up the rope. "Go along
the platform here until you get to car number nine...
there are signs on the cars and there will be an attendant

at the door." As Jacob Jones stooped under the rope, the foreman held out his arm across Jimmy Delaney's chest. "Wait a moment," he said.

"We're together," said Jacob Jones.

"You're excused," said the foreman. He watched Jacob Jones walk reluctantly into the crowd. "Friend of yours?" he said.

"Just a fellow," said Jimmy Delaney. "Am I not hired for the construction?"

"What wage were you promised?" said the foreman.

"One dollar," said Jimmy Delaney.

"Do you know anything about telegraphy?" said the foreman.

"Aye, it is sending messages through a wire using a code," said Jimmy Delaney.

The foreman nodded. "The Morse code," he said. "This work train arrives at the Missouri River tonight... Mobridge in South Dakota. We are training telegraphers there. The apprentice pay is seventy-five cents a day with room and board. If you're any good, you'll be trained and assigned to a post at twenty-five dollars a week. If not, we always need men for the crews. Are you interested?"

"Aye, sure," said Jimmy Delaney.

The foreman wrote on a card and handed it to Jimmy Delaney.

"Show this to the attendant in car number two at the front of the train," he said. "He will give you further instructions."

Jimmy Delaney shifted the weight of the rucksack on his shoulder and took the card.

"Aye, car number two," he said.

Jimmy Delaney stepped on the stair and lifted himself into the vestibule of car number two. The old passenger car had been scraped and painted many times. He looked into the coach through the glass pane in the door; the seats and carpet were stained and threadbare. The attendant opened the door and extended his hand. Jimmy Delaney gave him the card.

"Telegraph operator, eh," said the attendant. "You don't look old enough to me, but what do I know?" He returned the card. "Take a seat with a table," he said. "I'll get your code book."

Jimmy Delaney looked around. There were eight seats with tables, four on each side of the car. He took a seat facing rearward. The attendant opened a cabinet near the door to the vestibule, took out a leather-bound book and laid it on the table in front of Jimmy Delaney.

"That's your code book," he said. "You know any Morse?"

"I've only seen it," said Jimmy Delaney.

"Well, you best get started," said the attendant. "They'll be expecting you to know at least something. How old are you?"

"Of age," said Jimmy Delaney.

"Well, you must have something they saw," said the attendant. "The first part of the book is the Morse code. Just start memorizing...course when you get started on the key and listening to the sounder, it'll come easier. The second part of the book talks about using the key. That's the official version, but everybody develops his own fist."

"I'm thanking you," said Jimmy Delaney.

"You won't be when you meet those slave drivers in Mobridge," said the attendant. "I guess you can always go back to rail work."

"I will manage," said Jimmy Delaney.

"Whatever you say, but they ain't reached the point yet where they ain't still kicking people out," said the attendant. "You can put your coat and bag up there in the luggage rack. Or you can just throw it there in the other seat...this car won't be crowded. The diner is one car back...I'll announce the meals. You can get out when we stop, but don't get too far away."

"I was told that we will arrive tonight," said Jimmy Delaney.

"That's right...you got all day to learn that code,"

said the attendant. He pulled a watch from his pocket. "It's nearly eight now," he said. "We'll head out past the Thirty-fifth Street overpass, back up to the yard and take on the flatcars with ties and rails and another engine... we'll be so long, we'll be double-heading. That'll be about nine-thirty out of the yard and Mobridge about midnight. Did they tell you what to do when we get there?"

"That I will be trained for telegraphy," said Jimmy Delaney.

"Trained for telegraphy in the middle of the night," said the attendant. "Just like them...leave everything to me. There's a boarding house right next to the depot. Just rap on the door and show the old woman your card. She'll be up...somebody will wire ahead. Get some sleep, have a good breakfast...the old woman is a good cook... and look for the slave drivers in the depot tomorrow morning. Get there about eight...they ain't going to start no sooner than that."

The steam whistle sounded twice and the train began to move. Three men had joined Jimmy Delaney in car number two. They were older, wore suits and carried briefcases. Each one had spoken to the attendant and taken a seat facing a table. Within minutes they were working on papers drawn from the briefcases. None was distracted from his work as the train eased out of the station, creaked through hard turns and backed across the bridge over the Menomonee River into the rail yard. The dance through the switches in the yard merited only a glance and there was no awareness of the slow serpentine passage through the city into the open country.

Jimmy Delaney took in the homesteads blending into the lush countryside and began to learn the code by imagining the sound of the dots and dashes. He lapsed into a relaxed ease and the farms blurred into a steady drizzle over a treeless plain. A man stood stooped in a bog, stacking squares of peat. The man leaned on a wall of rocks and pushed himself erect to ease the pain in his back. Jimmy Delaney saw the hard-edged face and hollow eyes staring over the distance and then a woman lying in a pool of blood. He slammed his fist against the table.

"Are you all right?" said the attendant.

"Aye, sorry," said Jimmy Delaney.

"Coming into La Crosse," said the attendant. "We'll be backing into the station to pick up more men. Get out for a while...take a walk on the platform."

"Aye," said Jimmy Delaney.

Car number two passed a roundhouse and came to a stop on a chain of steel bridges spanning three islands in the Mississippi River. Thirty years old and still considered a marvel, the spans connecting Wisconsin and Minnesota included a draw bridge and a swing bridge allowing passage of steamboats and barges through two river channels. The backing maneuver over the draw bridge took car number two past the roundhouse and along the river bank into the train shed at Second and Vine Streets.

"La Crosse," called the attendant from the end of the car. "We're taking on more men here. You can stay aboard and eat in the dining car or you can stretch your legs or you can eat in the Cameron House dining room there in the depot if you're a mind. It's generally crowded, though, and expensive. In any case, we'll be here an hour or so and the dining car will stay open."

"What is your job with the railroad?" said one of the other men.

"I'm to be a telegrapher," said Jimmy Delaney.

"Ah, Mobridge," said the man. "You'll love it in the winter."

"I have never been there," said Jimmy Delaney.

"There is nothing there except a depot and a boarding house," said the man. "There will be, though...it's the railhead for the western expansion."

"What is your job?" said Jimmy Delaney.

"My companions and I are accountants," said the man. "We will be in South Dakota for a week...Aberdeen, to be exact...to audit the books for the division. Never fear, though, we never have to be in South Dakota in the winter."

"I can manage," said Jimmy Delaney.

"Oh, I'm sure," said the man. "There was a time I might have looked forward to it...but as you can see, I'm not a young man any more."

"I'm sure accounting is important work," said Jimmy Delaney.

"Boring, but important," said the man. "The contractors building the new line would steal us blind if they could get away with it."

Jimmy Delaney packed the code book into the rucksack and slid his arms into Murphy's coat.

"I'll be having a short walk," he said.

"That's a nice seaman's coat," said the man. "Are you a seaman?"

"Seaman's mate," said Jimmy Delaney. "You know seamanship?"

"My brother didn't want to be an accountant," said the man.

Jimmy Delaney nodded. He shouldered the rucksack and walked to the end of the platform, passing a group of men standing behind a rope. He counted fourteen coaches, three diners sandwiched between the coaches and ten flatcars laden with cross ties and rails secured with heavy ropes. Two men dressed in overalls leaned against a caboose behind the last flatcar.

"Long train," said Jimmy Delaney.

"Been that way for a month...been double heading near every day out of Milwaukee," said one of the men. "You headed out west?"

"Aye, I'm to be a telegrapher," said Jimmy Delaney.

"Key tapper, eh," said the man. "Well, it takes all kinds."

"You fellows go all the way to Mobridge?"

"Nah, just Minneapolis, then back to Milwaukee on a regular freight," said the man.

"Jimmy," said a voice.

Jimmy Delaney turned.

"I thought you weren't on the train," said Jacob Jones.

"Aye, I am," said Jimmy Delaney.

"I was looking for you. What happened back there in Milwaukee? Why'd you get held up?"

"It's nothing," said Jimmy Delaney.

"It must have been something," said Jacob Jones.

"Nothing...only a short delay," said Jimmy Delaney.

"Well, I'm glad you made the train," said Jacob Jones. "I was about to find the dining car. Let's eat."

Jimmy Delaney laughed. "Are you always hungry, Jacob?" he said.

"Always, Jimmy...and even hungrier when the food is free," said Jacob Jones.

"Good luck," said Jimmy Delaney to the men standing beside the caboose.

"You too, lad," said one of the men.

"When did you come across?" said Jimmy Delaney.

"Years ago," said the man.

"Your accent is scarcely detectable," said Jimmy Delaney.

"It's living with all those Germans in Milwaukee," said the man.

"Aye, that must be it," said Jimmy Delaney, nodding and turning away.

Jimmy Delaney and Jacob Jones walked past the flatcars toward the front of the train. Jacob Jones suddenly stopped, grasping Jimmy Delaney's arm. His face was ashen.

"Jacob, are you ill?" said Jimmy Delaney.

"It's him, Jimmy," said Jacob Jones.

"Who?" said Jimmy Delaney.

"The man in the parlor...the one back there in Milwaukee...it's him," said Jacob Jones, nodding toward the men behind the rope.

"Here?" said Jimmy Delaney, looking toward the men waiting to board the train.

"He's right there in front," said Jacob Jones. "He ain't even changed them new work clothes."

Jimmy Delaney's eyes swept over the men waiting behind the rope and settled on a man wearing a stained fedora and new overalls over a red checkered shirt.

"I see him," he said.

The man passed under the rope and walked toward them. His eyes registered recognition.

"Jesus Christ, Jimmy, he sees us," said Jacob Jones.

"*Dry yer arse, lad.*"

"Murphy?"

"What?" said Jacob Jones.

Jimmy Delaney thrust his hand into the pocket of Murphy's coat, touched the knife given to him by the first mate on the *Annandale.* He turned toward the approaching man.

"Stand still, Jacob," he said.

"What?"

Jimmy Delaney studied the face and paused, struck by an odd sense that he was not in danger. His grip on the knife relaxed.

"Hello again," said the man.

Jacob Jones backed away, bowing. "Well, I'm off," he said.

"You're not going any further?" said the man.

"I'm taking another job here," said Jacob Jones. "I was just leaving."

Jacob Jones turned and walked quickly into the crowd.

"Your friend is in a hurry," said the man.

"You are boarding the train?" said Jimmy Delaney.

"Yes," said the man. "After our lively encounter last night, I took the night train. I almost missed it...just as well things broke up when they did and it was only a block to the station."

"You left last night," said Jimmy Delaney.

"Yes, I have a sister here in La Crosse," said the man. "Since I'll be away for some time, I thought I might visit her. I trust the journey from Milwaukee was a pleasant one."

"Aye, well enough," said Jimmy Delaney. "You are assigned to the construction crew?"

"Yes," said the man. He held up a card. "Car number eleven," he said. "Is that toward the front from here?"

Jimmy Delaney looked around. "I think we are almost even with car number eleven," he said.

"Come, walk with me," said the man. "Where is your car?"

"Toward the front," said Jimmy Delaney.

"You acquitted yourself very well last night."

"Are you against the unions?" said Jimmy Delaney.

"No, not especially," said the man. "To borrow a quote...I'm just a fellow looking for work."

"It is not my business, but you do not look like a fellow for the construction crews," said Jimmy Delaney.

The man stopped beside car number eleven.

"No?" he said. "What should I look like?"

"Excuse me, it is not my business," said Jimmy Delaney.

"Join me for a late lunch," said the man. "The diner is just here...one car back."

"The diner for my car is toward the front," said Jimmy Delaney.

"You have to eat in your own diner?"

"That is what I am told," said Jimmy Delaney.

The man sighed. "Very well," he said. "Perhaps we can talk another time."

The whistle sounded and attendants moved into the crowd, looking at cards and directing men toward the train. Jimmy Delaney nodded curtly and turned away. He looked back after walking the length of one car. The man matched his card with the sign on the rail car and stepped into the vestibule. He did not look toward Jimmy Delaney.

The work train moved easily out the station and onto the steel bridges over the river. Jimmy Delaney stared vacantly at the barge traffic and his focus shifted to the reflection of his face in the glass. He closed his eyes. He was on the deck of the *Edinburgh*. Murphy walked beside him. They stopped and Murphy said, *"Ye stand for yerself, lad. If it's a legger ye be now, ye'll always be and ye won't be worth the air ye breathe."* Jimmy Delaney smiled.

Twenty-Two

Mobridge

Harry Archer, the engineering supervisor, came through the door of the Mobridge depot. He had just arrived on a work train from McLaughlin, little more than a siding on a wind-swept plain. The brim of his floppy fedora hat fell over the top of his brow. Sweat caked the dust to his face and arms. He rapped the hat against the door jamb.

"Thumper, I'll never get used to this place," he said. "I'm a hell of a long way from the Rensselaer and God knows I'm not getting any closer or younger. Did you get the order I sent from McLaughlin about the bridge girders?"

"Aye, I sent it on to Aberdeen," said Jimmy Delaney. "The girders should be here tonight."

"Well, hell," said Harry Archer. "Get back to Aberdeen... tell 'em to put the girders in the hole. God knows how long we're going to have to put up with that wooden bridge... two or three trains for every one because of the load limit. God knows how much coal we're going through. Listen, the work train with bunk cars, kitchen cars and cooks...I need it out there in Standing Rock tonight if possible. The men out there aren't getting enough to eat and they're sleeping too many to a bunk car. You'd think there'd be a road out there, but God knows what Sitting Bull needs with a road. Tell 'em to highball the work train through Aberdeen and then release the girders. Got that?"

"Aye," said Jimmy Delaney.

"I'm going to the boarding house to get cleaned up," said Harry Archer. "I'll be back shortly."

Jimmy Delaney sent the message: *Aberdeen. Disregard last transmission MSP girder train. Hold girder train for priority work train following. Mobridge.*

Ten minutes later, Light Finger replied from Aberdeen: *Mobridge. Girder train scrubbed MSP. Long truss train through here west-bound twenty minutes ago. Aberdeen.*

"Tapper, cover the incoming," said Jimmy Delaney, tearing the sheet from his pad.

"Yeah, I got it," said Calvin Livermore, as Jimmy Delaney went out the door.

A year had passed, almost to the day, since the work train had lumbered heavily out of Aberdeen into a dark plain broken only by dim lights set on poles at the sidings. Two hours ahead lay the far western outpost of the rails against the Missouri River. The first flurry of snow at Roscoe Siding grew into a blizzard and the depot and boarding house in Mobridge were blurred images in blowing snow. Jimmy Delaney stepped out onto the platform at one in the morning and buttoned the collar of Murphy's coat around his neck. He watched the work train pull away toward the railhead at Moreau Junction on the other side of the river and went to the boarding house. Hattie Johnson was awake; she was waiting for him, just as the attendant had said.

Through the summer of Jimmy Delaney's training, telegraph messages fed a steady flow of men and supplies into the expanding railhead west of the river. Other trainees arrived and in the autumn they were re-assigned. Jimmy Delaney stayed in Mobridge, taking over the telegraphy desk for the Dakota section of Lines West, the name given to expansion of the railroad to the Puget Sound. His fist was heavy and fast; he was Thumper from Aberdeen to Miles City.

The railhead, demanding without remorse, brought Calvin Livermore to the depot in late autumn. He was an older man with a telegrapher's ear for subtlety. He was known as Tapper in places further away than Aberdeen or Miles City. Calvin Livermore complained about dust and smoke and wind and snow in the slow drawl of his native Alabama and at the same time he was thankful that he did not eat and sleep in a boxcar tethered to the telegraph line on a siding.

The snow was gone, leaving early that year, and a hot, dry wind pushed Jimmy Delaney along the platform in front of the depot. He stretched a bandana over his nose and mouth against swirling dust and hurried toward the boarding house.

"Aye, Missus Johnson...a message for Mister Archer," said Jimmy Delaney, stamping his feet in the foyer.

"Go on up, Jimmy," said Hattie Johnson. "He's washing up in this room. By the way, those books of yours are getting out of hand. It's getting so I can hardly clean your room. Where do you get all those books?"

"I have a shelf coming from Aberdeen," said Jimmy Delaney. "I will straighten everything up."

"Well, where do you get all those books?" said Hattie Johnson.

"They come on the work trains from Minneapolis," said Jimmy Delaney.

"I never heard of mail-order books," said Hattie Johnson.

"I send the money with the conductors," said Jimmy Delaney.

"One day they're going to transfer you out," said Hattie Johnson. "What then?"

"I'm thinking a trunk," said Jimmy Delaney. "What do you think?"

"You're going to need it," said Hattie Johnson. "You read all that stuff?"

"Oh, yes ma'am, I do," said Jimmy Delaney, walking away toward the stairs.

"Come," shouted Harry Archer in response to the knock on his door.

Jimmy Delaney opened the door and held out the message from Light Finger.

"First girders, now trusses...for the Cedar River in Iowa, no doubt," said Harry Archer. "All right, try to get the truss train in the hole at Roscoe. If not, just let it through and we can stop it here and let the work train have the bridge."

"Aye," said Jimmy Delaney.

"Is your shift about over?"

"Is there something?"

"Get the message off to Roscoe and hang around for a few minutes. I need to do a few calculations and then I'll have some other things to go over with you and Tapper for the morning."

Jimmy Delaney returned to the depot and closed the door quickly against the blowing dust. He sent Harry Archer's message without writing it out: *Roscoe. Hold truss train from Aberdeen for priority work train following. Mobridge.*

"Incoming quiet," said Calvin Livermore.

Jimmy Delaney's sounder started clicking.

"Until now," said Calvin Livermore.

Mobridge. Message received. Truss train in the hole. Highball work train. Roscoe.

Jimmy Delaney laid the message aside for Harry Archer. He and Calvin Livermore took the sporadic messages coming in at dusk and sorted the messages to be sent the next day.

"Jimmy," said Calvin Livermore, holding out a sheet torn from his pad.

Jimmy Delaney took the sheet and read aloud: "Station Master Mobridge. Telegrapher James Delaney transferred Northern Pacific depot Wallace Idaho. Expect new man two days to assist telegrapher Calvin Livermore. Dispatch James Delaney day after via McLaughlin, branch line New England, overland Dickinson. Deadhead tickets waiting Northern Pacific depot Dickinson...Northern Pacific train one Missoula, Northern Pacific work train six-eight Wallace. Report Station Master."

"So, you're going to Idaho," said Calvin Livermore.

"Aye, so it seems," said Jimmy Delaney.

"And I'm staying here in all this dust," said Calvin Livermore. "It's a wonder I don't..."

"Now, you know..."

"Don't say it," said Calvin Livermore. "Things could be worse...and have been."

"Aye," said Jimmy Delaney. "The message...was it Light Finger?"

"Yeah, it was him...smooth as silk," said Calvin Livermore.

Jimmy Delaney hunched over his key and sent the following: *LF. Wallace Idaho message received. Needing my trunk from the freight house. T.*

Five minutes later, Jimmy Delaney's sounder began clicking. After a few characters he knew it was Light Finger: *T. Way ahead of you. Trunk out early am. Good luck Idaho. LF.*

The door opened. Harry Archer came in.

"God knows when this dust will stop blowing, if ever," he said.

"Not until winter and then we can enjoy blowing snow," said Calvin Livermore.

"Very funny," said Harry Archer.

"Jimmy's going to Idaho," said Calvin Livermore, handing the message to Harry Archer.

Harry Archer read the message. "Well," he said, returning the paper to the station master's basket. "Not much time...two days, three...and you'll be the man in Wallace."

"Am I to work for the Northern Pacific now?" said Jimmy Delaney.

"Oh, no," said Harry Archer. "We're putting in a new tunnel in the mountains on the border of Montana and Idaho. Until the rails catch up, everything we use is on freight contracts with the Northern Pacific. They've had a branch line in there for several years to service the silver mines. We unload just east of Wallace and haul it four miles up to the construction site at East Portal and it's fed into the tunnel from there. They're also drilling from the west side. I'm not sure where those supplies are unloaded. Being in Wallace, I expect you'll be handling the telegraphy for East Portal."

"The messages," said Jimmy Delaney.

"What?" said Harry Archer.

"Your calculations," said Jimmy Delaney. "The messages you mentioned...for the morning."

"Oh, this message," said Harry Archer, holding up a scrap of paper.

"Aye," said Jimmy Delaney.

"Just the one at the moment," said Harry Archer. "Do we have anything on the trusses coming in? How many trusses? What section of the bridge? Rivets? Do we have anything?"

"Nothing," said Jimmy Delaney. "Aberdeen said the train is long."

"Long," said Harry Archer. "God knows what that means. Is anyone still there in Aberdeen?"

"Aye, Light Finger was there a few minutes ago," said Jimmy Delaney.

"All right, get hold of him," said Harry Archer. He waived the scrap of paper in Jimmy Delaney's direction. "No use asking about this," he said. "If Minneapolis doesn't know anything, God knows how we can expect Aberdeen to know anything. God knows how they expect me to build a truss bridge over the river. They don't tell me a damn thing. They just send trusses when they damn please and somehow the cranes, rivets and men are supposed to appear out of thin air. Do you suppose any of those Indians across the river can set rivets?"

Jimmy Delaney's expression did not change.

"What?" said Harry Archer.

"You wanted me to contact Aberdeen?" said Jimmy Delaney.

Harry Archer laughed. "Never mind," he said. "The damn train will be here later tonight...even holding it at Roscoe, it'll be here by morning. We'll figure it out then. I promise you, though...those idiots in Minneapolis couldn't build an outhouse."

"The messages for tomorrow are sorted," said Jimmy Delaney.

"All right, we'll deal with that and the train tomorrow, but I'm telling you...they won't send rivets with the trusses. You mark my word...no rivets. Shut it down. Hattie's got supper ready. Let's eat."

"The work train," said Jimmy Delaney. "It's to take on coal and water and go on to McLaughlin tonight? And the truss train...it has an open siding?"

"Yes, thanks for reminding me, said Harry Archer. "I saw Michaels...he's already passed it on to the yard."

"Aye," said Jimmy Delaney.

"All right, shut it down and let's eat," said Harry Archer.

Jimmy Delaney and Calvin Livermore tied down the telegraph keys and sounders. Jimmy Delaney made a last inspection of the room and switched off the light. They stood on the platform in front of the depot.

"Well, the damn wind is finally dying down, said Harry Archer.

"Don't worry, not for long," said Calvin Livermore.

They were joined in the dining room of the boarding house by Michaels, the station master. As was his habit, Michaels had changed into a suit for dinner. Hattie Johnson set out the food and took her place at the head of the table. Everyone began passing the dishes around.

"Jimmy is going to Wallace," said Harry Archer to Michaels. "There's a message in your basket."

"Is the new man any good?" said Michaels.

"This is a railhead, John," said Harry Archer. "They can't build a snowman but they've never sent us a bad telegrapher."

"When does he get here?" said Michaels.

"In two days, maybe three," said Harry Archer.

Michaels turned toward Calvin Livermore. "You're staying on?" he said.

"Looks like it," said Calvin Livermore. "With the traffic what it is, I hope the new man knows what he's doing."

"So do I...it's all we need," said Michaels. "Everything for the first two hundred miles of rail is going west from here. That's not counting the new bridge. Can't build eastbound from anywhere...can't get supplies into that wilderness before we hit the Northern Pacific in Montana."

"The new man will be fine," said Harry Archer.

"Good luck, boy," said Michaels to Jimmy Delaney. "You'll be busy...I hear things are hopping out there, what with all the tunnels and trestles."

Jimmy Delaney nodded.

"What did I tell you?" said Hattie Johnson. "Now what do you do with all those books?"

"I am happy to say that my trunk will be here tomorrow," said Jimmy Delaney.

"Well, you're a lucky boy," said Hattie Johnson. "I thought I'd have to be shipping those books to you."

"You would have?" said Jimmy Delaney.

"Certainly," said Hattie Johnson.

Harry Archer, standing by the window, shook out the match he had just touched to the end of a cigar. He blew gray smoke toward the ceiling.

"The work train is coming in," he said. "You would have thought it could wait until I finished my cigar. God knows how bad these things are when you have to light 'em twice. I'll just end up wasting it."

"Have you ever finished a cigar?" said Hattie Johnson.

"I don't remember," said Harry Archer. He crushed out the cigar in the ash tray on the window sill and turned toward the door. "I'll stay on the train out at McLaughlin tonight," he said. "I'll catch a ride back tomorrow morning after I get things organized out there."

"The yard men know what to do," said Michaels.

"I know," said Harry Archer. "We'll just take coal and water and keep moving."

"Have your pie and coffee, Harry," said Hattie Johnson. "They won't be ready to go for some time yet."

Harry Archer hesitated. "Harry, have some pie and coffee...I believe I will," he said.

The front door opened and the floor in the hallway creaked. Everyone looked toward the dining room door. The man standing in the doorway wore a three-piece suit and a bowler hat. He held a small valise. He removed the hat and his eyes examined the room in a slow arc.

Jimmy Delaney leaned back in his chair. Everyone else at the table glanced at each other. Michaels approached the stranger.

"Did you come in on the work train?" he said. "I have had no message to expect anyone."

"I am aware that you have received no message," said the man, lowering the valise to the floor. He took a watch from his waistcoat, inspected it and returned it to the waistcoat pocket. He approached the table.

"It has taken me quite some time to find you, Mister Delaney," he said.

"What is this?" said Harry Archer. "Who the devil are you?"

"My name is Hessler," said the man. "I represent the Milwaukee police. Mister Delaney and I have unfinished business."

"Mister Delaney is a railroad telegrapher," said Harry Archer. "This is not Milwaukee and whatever you think he has done, you're mistaken."

"Oh, he hasn't done anything except disappear," said Hessler. "I am looking for a criminal and Mister Delaney is a material witness. He is my only link to this criminal...a man I mean to have in a Milwaukee jail."

"It would seem so if you are willing to come here," said Harry Archer. "Do you know where you are? Do you know that there are no passenger trains back to civilization?"

"I am aware," said Hessler. "The railroad has been very cooperative. May I sit down?"

Harry Archer gestured toward a chair. "Please do and have some supper and spend the night, since you have nowhere else to go," he said. "I have to go out to the railhead, but I'll be back tomorrow. I still haven't decided about you, but I will."

"Are you threatening me, sir?" said Hessler.

Harry Archer walked to the door, took his hat from the peg and turned. He ran his finger along the crease in the crown, an old habit.

"I am only an engineer trying to build a railroad," he said. "Why would I threaten an officer of the law?"

Harry Archer put the hat on his head and disappeared through the doorway. Everyone heard the front door open and close.

"Quite an intense man," said Hessler.

"I should not take him lightly," said Michaels.

"Oh, I do not take lightly anything that is said to me," said Hessler.

Hattie Johnson placed a plate and silverware before Hessler and took his hat. She hung the hat on a peg near the door and returned to the table.

"Eat," she said.

"Thank you," said Hessler. He spread a cloth on his lap and took a slice of roast beef and helpings of mashed potatoes and green beans.

"I have told you everything I know," said Jimmy Delaney.

"Not quite," said Hessler. "You saw the man again."

"Aye, I did...in La Crosse that same afternoon, saying that he had left Milwaukee the night before," said Jimmy Delaney.

"And you did not think I would wish to know that," said Hessler.

"But you do know," said Jimmy Delaney.

Hessler stared at Jimmy Delaney. "Quite right," he said. "If the ticket agent at the depot had been more observant when he sold our man a ticket to La Crosse, we might have known it sooner. As it happened, Mister Jacob Jones returned to Milwaukee...quite shaken, I might add. Now, it is curious that you did not think it necessary to report what Jacob Jones could not...namely, where did the man go after leaving La Crosse?"

"I did not see him again," said Jimmy Delaney.

"You were on the same train," said Hessler.

"Aye, in separate cars," said Jimmy Delaney.

"You just said that you did not see him again," said Hessler.

"I saw him board the train several cars behind mine," said Jimmy Delaney. "After that, I did not see him again."

"Then you don't know if he got off somewhere," said Hessler.

"I cannot say," said Jimmy Delaney. "I did not see him again."

Hessler laid his knife and fork in the plate in front of him. He leaned back in his chair.

"Understand my point of view, Mister Delaney," he said. "Here is a man who murdered another man by stabbing him with a large knife."

"You saw a murder?" said Hattie Johnson.

"I did not see a murder," said Jimmy Delaney.

"As I was saying," said Hessler. "Pardon my confusion, Mister Delaney, but you do not seem very concerned... and what is more, you rode the same train with this man and do not give the impression that you were concerned even for your own safety."

"I did not think I was in peril," said Jimmy Delaney.

"And how was that?" said Hessler.

"The man was riding the same train as the rest of us, had not even changed his clothes," said Jimmy Delaney. "He did not seem concerned or cautious or fearful."

"Then, as I understand it, you do not think he committed the murder," said Hessler.

"He did not act like a man who had just killed someone," said Jimmy Delaney.

"And how would you know the behavior of a murderer?" said Hessler. "How many professional killers have you met?"

"I have met none," said Jimmy Delaney.

"Actually, you have," said Hessler. "You have met at least one."

"How are you so sure?" said Jimmy Delaney.

"I'm sure," said Hessler.

"Why would this man...why did I sense no danger?" said Jimmy Delaney. "I am not innocent."

"I did not say you were," said Hessler. "Perhaps it is because you were right...you were not in danger. The man is a paid assassin. Most assassins do not kill for pleasure...it is business. He does not consider you or Jacob Jones a danger to him, although you are the only two in that boarding house who had more than a passing contact with him. Consider...you do not know his name... even his false name, if I understand you...and you do not know where he got off the train or if he got off. It is obvious that he meant for you not to see him again after the chance encounter. Still, it was worth the trip. I had an outside chance to pick up his trail again."

"I told him nothing about myself and I was content to remain hidden," said Jimmy Delaney.

"No danger, eh?" said Hessler.

"I did not sense it, but a friend once told me I should not kick sleeping dogs," said Jimmy Delaney.

"A wise choice," said Hessler. "Perhaps we can still learn something. Assume he stayed on the train...where would that take him?"

"Here," said Jimmy Delaney. "The men on the train were hired for the construction crews."

"Here?" said Hessler. "He would have come here?"

"Just across the river at the railhead," said Michaels. "But that was more than a year ago."

"I find this hard to believe, but if the man is still working for the railroad..."

"I know what you're thinking," said Michaels. "Forget it...he could be anywhere."

"There is no record of work crews?" said Hessler. "I have at least the false name he used in Milwaukee to obtain the work card. He is compelled to keep that name as long as he is associated with the railroad."

"You must be kidding," said Michaels.

"Why?" said Hessler. "How are the men paid?"

"By head count," said Michaels. "The foreman of each crew does a head count and wages are shipped out and dispersed every week. There are hundreds of crews stretched from here to the coast and the turnover is high. There are no names. You have no chance of finding your man in a construction crew."

Hessler sighed and turned to Hattie Johnson. "I thank you for the delicious meal," he said. "Are you the proprietor of this establishment?"

"This is a railroad boarding house," said Hattie Johnson. "I am the manager."

"Might I have a room until I can arrange transportation back to Milwaukee?" said Hessler. "I have a voucher of five dollars per day. Will that suffice?"

"You are our guest," said Michaels. "A work train is being assembled for the east tomorrow morning. The eastbound trains are mostly empty, but a diner will be available for the crew. We can get you back to Milwaukee by tomorrow night. Will that be satisfactory?"

Hessler nodded. "Quite satisfactory," he said. "Thank you."

"If it is not being too forward, do you think you will ever capture this man?" said Michaels.

"No, I suspect not, unless he blunders badly," said Hessler. "I thought he might have made a mistake in La Crosse, but he rectified that mistake quickly and disappeared. He is probably out of Chicago. He works clandestinely for people who wish to destroy labor unions. He will probably not be found out except by accident. Unfortunately, the incident in La Crosse will make him more careful."

"He works against the unions, you say," said Michaels.

"Among other things, undoubtedly," said Hessler.

171

"Well, I don't see why he would be in a construction crew," said Michaels. "There aren't any unions outside of the trains and the yards. The railroad expansion is spread all across the country among many contractors and subcontractors. The labor force is completely unorganized and the turnover is high. It's not worth the effort."

"I see," said Hessler. "Perhaps my theory of the crime and its aftermath is incomplete. Perhaps obtaining a work card at the depot was nothing more than a ploy to gain access to the boarding house. Perhaps, perhaps..."

"I think your man is back in Chicago," said Michaels.

"I wonder if I might go to my room now," said Hessler, turning toward Hattie Johnson. "I would like to make some notes for my report before retiring."

"Of course," said Hattie Johnson.

Hessler pushed back his chair and stood. Jimmy Delaney, Michaels and Calvin Livermore followed his lead.

"Mister Delaney, I dare say you will probably not see this man again," said Hessler. "Nevertheless, if you do, be careful and try to contact me by telegraph."

"Aye," said Jimmy Delaney.

Hessler nodded and followed Hattie Johnson into the hall. Jimmy Delaney, Michaels and Calvin Livermore heard the stairs creak under his footsteps and lowered themselves again into the dining room chairs.

"A man with burdens," said Michaels.

"I don't think he's ever gonna catch that fellow," said Calvin Livermore.

"I wonder...hard to know," said Michaels. "He's on a wild goose chase, but he knows it. I'll bet he starts looking in Chicago."

Jimmy Delaney pushed back his chair. "I'll be turning in," he said.

"How'd you run into this fellow, Jimmy?" said Calvin Livermore. "Weren't you scared?"

"He was at the boarding house in Milwaukee where a man was killed...a union man...during the night," said Jimmy Delaney. "The next day I saw him again when the train stopped in La Crosse. He had gotten there the night before. He seemed to me a regular fellow. I have not seen him since then."

"You weren't scared?" said Calvin Livermore. "Something like that would sure scare me."

"I was cautious," said Jimmy Delaney.

"Well, I hope you never see him again," said Calvin Livermore.

"It is not likely," said Jimmy Delaney.

"Well, are you ready to take over in Wallace?" said Calvin Livermore.

"Aye," said Jimmy Delaney. "I seem to be always moving west."

Twenty-Three

Wallace

"I just don't like coppers," said Harry Archer above the noise of the train.

"It is doubtful you will see Inspector Hessler again," said Jimmy Delaney. "I think he would rather be in Milwaukee."

"Well, they're nosy...always looking under rocks and nosing in things that are none of their business."

"There are good coppers and bad, peelers and not," said Jimmy Delaney.

"We're coming into McLaughlin," said Harry Archer.

"Aye, I'll get my trunk," said Jimmy Delaney.

"Many more books and you won't be able to carry that thing," said Harry Archer.

"I was about to begin trading them, but now...maybe I should settle down."

Harry Archer laughed. "I doubt you want to settle down in Wallace," he said.

"Do you know Wallace?"

"No, but I'm sure the winters are at least as bad as Mobridge and you weren't too pleased with that."

"I will manage," said Jimmy Delaney.

"Oh, I know," said Harry Archer.

Jimmy Delaney and Harry Archer walked along the siding to the end of a supply train of empty flatcars. Harry Archer swung the trunk onto the rear platform of the caboose.

"The cushions," said Jimmy Delaney.

"The cushions?" said Harry Archer.

"An old saying from riding the freights," said Jimmy Delaney.

"You rode the freights?" said Harry Archer.

"Not for some time," said Jimmy Delaney.

"How much more do I not know about you?" said Harry Archer.

"There is little to tell," said Jimmy Delaney.

"Well, it was once my privilege to come out here from Mobridge on a flatcar," said Harry Archer. "You'll like the caboose better, I promise you."

A man holding a lantern stepped down from the caboose. He waved the lantern toward the front of the train in wide arcs.

"You Delaney?" he said.

"Aye," said Jimmy Delaney.

"Well, let's get to it," said the man.

"Good luck in Wallace, boy," said Harry Archer, offering his hand.

Jimmy Delaney clasped Harry Archer's hand in a firm grip and nodded. He grabbed the rail and pulled himself onto the platform in response to two short blasts of the steam whistle. The train jolted forward.

"Maybe when we're done here, I'll be building bridges in Idaho," called Harry Archer.

Jimmy Delaney waved and watched Harry Archer until the train swung away from the main line to the north. The train passed quickly into the barren plain. Jimmy Delaney scanned the horizon; a hawk soared overhead, watching for movement in the cool of mid-morning.

The conductor hung out the window until the train passed the last frame shack at the edge of town. A Sioux woman and several children on the porch waved. The conductor turned away from the window and settled in a chair behind the overturned shipping crate he used as a desk. He opened a ledger and dipped a pen into an inkwell.

"They tell me you're a tapper," he said.

"Aye," said Jimmy Delaney.

"Hunh," said the conductor, turning his attention to the ledger.

The branch line crossed into North Dakota nine miles from McLaughlin and followed the Cannonball River to the freight depot in the village of New England. A wagon and a driver named Pop were waiting at the loading dock.

Jimmy Delaney moved his trunk to the wagon and sat on the spring-loaded seat. Pop nodded, snapped the reins and two horses pulled the wagon away from the dock onto the road, which had been cut into the plain by heavy wagon wheels.

Pop was a weathered Scandinavian born in Dakota Territory. He told Jimmy Delaney that the Dakota plain was not for everyone. He listened carefully to Jimmy Delaney's telling of the Irish potato famine, stared ahead for a moment and allowed that life seemed to be brittle everywhere.

They ate and rested the two horses at a way station in mid-afternoon and crossed the Northern Pacific main line through Dickinson late in the day. Pop guided his team along the hard-packed dirt of Villard Street to the depot and Jimmy Delaney slid his trunk off the back of the wagon. Pop nodded and turned the horses into the fading sun toward the livery stable.

Jimmy Delaney collected his ticket, paying extra for a berth, had dinner at a diner on the corner of Villard and Sims and spent a fitful night on a cot in the freight house. In the morning he went to the same diner for breakfast and waited in the freight house, not able to concentrate on any of several books from the trunk. He was standing on the platform when train number one arrived from the east just after noon. He hoisted the trunk into the baggage car and settled into a sleeping car for the overnight trip to Missoula.

Steam shovels and graders grooming the new rail bed along the Yellowstone River came into view in the late afternoon. Jimmy Delaney followed the work through Rosebud County until the new line diverged at Forsyth, following Big Porcupine Creek to the north, turning west along Musselshell Creek, descending through the canyon of Sixteenmile Creek and emerging at the headwaters of the Missouri River near the Continental Divide.

Work train number 68 sat on a siding at the Northern Pacific depot in Missoula, well away from passengers waiting for the *North Coast Limited* to Chicago. Jimmy Delaney had awakened refreshed, taken breakfast in the dining car and followed construction of the new railroad along the Clark Fork River into Missoula. He reclaimed the trunk and found his way to the work train. A lone coach behind three locomotives was followed by a long line of flatcars laden with construction supplies. Jimmy Delaney stepped into the vestibule of the coach and pulled the trunk in behind him.

"You Delaney?" said the attendant.

"Aye," said Jimmy Delaney.

"We got the wire on you," said the attendant. "Just take any seat you like...nobody else on the up trip. There's time for breakfast in the depot if you ain't had any."

"I ate on the train coming in," said Jimmy Delaney. "I'm on the train since yesterday...I'll be walking around in the yard until it is time to go."

"Well, we'll be away in about an hour...soon as they coal and water the three beasts up front. Just leave the trunk here in the vestibule if you're a mind. Like I say, just you on the up trip. We'll be stopping at Taft near the top of the pass to drop off the flatcars and two engines, but even with that, Wallace ain't but about three hours from here. After your walk, just take any seat you like, if you like any of 'em. If you don't, take one anyway."

"Aye," said Jimmy Delaney.

The work train threaded its way along the Clark Fork River, climbing steadily to Regis, where the Clark Fork turned away to the north and the track followed another canyon formed by another river cascading off the spine of the Bitterroot Range. West of Regis, Haugan and Saltese, Bryson Siding marked the beginning of the battle of the hill. The coach shuttered as the three locomotives strained against the grade, enveloping Bryson in a pall of black smoke.

The supply train stopped in Taft, five miles east of the highest point on the line at Lookout Pass. The map Jimmy Delaney had seen in Mobridge came into focus. The new rail bed had diverted south at Bryson and followed the long loop of Dominion Creek before settling into the climb along Rainy Creek to the summit of St. Paul Pass. Jimmy Delaney stood on a loading dock of weathered planks separating two parallel rail lines from a construction town of wooden buildings and tents obscured by dust and smoke. Heavy wagons drawn by teams of four horses stood on the approaches to the loading dock. Dozens of men with grappling hooks moved cross ties, rails, crates of spikes, boring tools and dynamite from the flatcars across the dock to each wagon in the line and the wagon pulled away for the four-mile climb to the tunnel at the end of Rainy Creek Road.

"You need work?" said the dock foreman. "There's plenty of work here and booze and women as well."

"The supplies for the new Milwaukee line go up from here?" said Jimmy Delaney.

"That's it...the land of tunnels and trestles and cuts and another two or three years of work with good pay," said the dock foreman. "After that, this place'll dry up and blow away, what with all the silver down on the west side of the pass. But in the meantime..."

"I have a job," said Jimmy Delaney. "I'm just waiting for the train."

"Well, if you see anybody needs work..."

"Aye," said Jimmy Delaney.

The rump work train, consisting of the coach and caboose drawn by one locomotive, made the slow, winding climb to the crest of Lookout Pass. Topping the pass, the train plunged downward through a narrow corridor in the mountains which carried the south fork of the Coeur d'Alene River into a glacial lake. Jimmy Delaney lowered the window and peered over the edge of the rock shelf carrying the track. The plains had given way to steep canyons which always took a ransom before yielding.

The railroad depot was a two-story compact structure of Roman buff bricks and stucco built in the style of a chateau with a turret on one corner and a steep roof. Jimmy Delaney swung the trunk out of the vestibule of the old rail coach and stepped down onto the platform, which followed the north bank of the river to a bridge separating the depot from a compact settlement of brick buildings pushed against a steep wooded slope.

A man was waiting on the platform. He was heavy set with thinning hair, a broad neck and muscular arms and wore loose-fitting work clothes.

"Delaney, I presume," he said.

"Aye," said Jimmy Delaney.

"Welcome to Wallace," said the man. "Floyd is my name. I'm the station master. There's not much to master around here, but I'm the station master just the same."

"Mister Floyd," said Jimmy Delaney, taking Floyd's extended hand.

"Let's get inside," said Floyd, lifting the trunk with one hand. "I'll get you squared away and you can get settled. They tell me you're to start handling the wire the day after tomorrow. Pardon my saying, but you seem very young for this job."

"I am able enough," said Jimmy Delaney.

Floyd nodded.

A large framed photograph inside the door portrayed a man sitting in an open carriage. He wore a tightly drawn cape and a top hat and stared through rimless glasses directly into the camera lens. The carriage and several men on foot were crossing the track in front of the depot toward the bridge into town.

"Is this Mister Roosevelt?" said Jimmy Delaney.

"Indeed it is," said Floyd. "He came here some time back...three or four years ago...and gave a speech right out there on the platform and then took the carriage over to the park and gave another speech from the gazebo.

Damn dreary day, too...overcast, cold drizzle...didn't faze him. See that bunting on the station there in the picture... the town paid five thousand bucks for flags and bunting draped all over everything. You can still see some of it around town."

"I saw Mister Roosevelt in New York," said Jimmy Delaney. "He is shorter than I thought."

"Yeah, he's kind of a runt," said Floyd. "Maybe that's why he's all the time spoiling for a fight...shaking his fist in the air and the like. You from New York, are you?"

"Aye, it's five years since I came across from Ireland," said Jimmy Delaney.

"Wales for me...long time ago," said Floyd. "When I first got here, my name was Lloyd. My father was Lloyd Lloyd. He thought that was goofy, so he changed it to Lloyd Floyd. Beats me...one sounds just as goofy as the other."

"Your family...they settled in New York?" said Jimmy Delaney.

"Nah, Boston," said Floyd. "I left there years ago...I like the west. Looks like you didn't wanna stay in New York any more'n I wanted to stay in Boston."

"I am seeing the country," said Jimmy Delaney.

Floyd nodded. "There's not much to see in Wallace," he said.

"I will manage," said Jimmy Delaney.

"Well, let's get you settled," said Floyd. "The ladies waiting room is there in the turret and we're standing in the general waiting room. That's the ticket cage across the room there. We don't have an agent...not enough traffic...I just handle it myself. People just come in and look at the board there and when it's near time for the train, I open up the cage. The station master's quarters...like I said, that's me...are on the second floor. The telegraph shack is next door. You'll be handling the Milwaukee wires, of course. John Sluman, the other operator, handles the Northern Pacific and public traffic. Do you know your hours?"

"Aye, seven to seven, except Sunday," said Jimmy Delaney.

"Standard, same for Sluman," said Floyd. "He's in there now...you can meet him when you come in to work, I guess."

"Aye," said Jimmy Delaney. "Can you recommend a boarding house?"

"The McNair house," said Floyd. "Cross the bridge, go along Sixth...second house on the left after you cross Cedar. Just ask for Missus McNair. I took the liberty."

"Aye, I'm thanking you," said Jimmy Delaney. "Missus McNair is a widow?"

"Belle McNair...oh my, no," said Floyd. "John Henry McNair is very much alive...him and Belle also run a cafe, mostly for the miners. Might also have an interest in the Oasis, our best establishment for ladies of the evening...but that's just a rumor. You thought Belle was a widow?"

"It is only curiosity," said Jimmy Delaney. "I have noticed that the proprietors of many boarding houses are widows."

"Not Belle," said Floyd. "She doesn't look like a widow either. I'd call her Missus McNair, if I were you."

"Aye, that I will," said Jimmy Delaney.

"Can you carry that trunk?" said Floyd. "It's small, but a little heavy. You got all your belongings in there?"

"Just clothes and a few books," said Jimmy Delaney. "I can manage."

"There's a cart out front on the platform," said Floyd. "Just bring it back when you come in to work."

"I'm thanking you," said Jimmy Delaney.

"Well, then, you're off," said Floyd. "Lots of daylight left. You can get settled at Belle's and walk around town...maybe see some of the big guns we got here for the trial."

"The trial?" said Jimmy Delaney.

"You haven't read about it?" said Floyd. "The Adams trial...Steve Adams...they say he killed a claim jumper

181

up at Marble Creek, but it's really revenge...or blackmail, I should say. They're out to get him because he won't help them send Big Bill Haywood to the drop-down in Boise. We got everybody here...that Pinkerton detective, McParland, Darrow, the big time labor lawyer, Senator Borah...they might get him on a timber fraud deal... everybody."

"I have read about the Haywood trial," said Jimmy Delaney. "Haywood and two others in the mining union are accused of killing the governor?"

"Former governor...name of Steunenberg," said Floyd. "He was a friend of the miners and then turned traitor. They say a fellow name of Orchard blew him up with a bomb and I guess Orchard said Haywood hired him. Steve Adams, he was gonna back up Orchard and then reneged, so they brought him up here on a murder charge. Near as anybody can figure, they think if they can get his head in a noose, he'll go back to doing what they want."

"Maybe he will," said Jimmy Delaney.

"Maybe, maybe, but I doubt it," said Floyd. "This town is mining and that jury is miners. Now this Adams is no saint, but everybody knows they're just using him to railroad Haywood and break up the union."

"Is the trial open for visitors?" said Jimmy Delaney. "I have the extra day before starting on the telegraph."

"Sure, if you can get a seat," said Floyd. "Thing is, though, the fireworks are over. Darrow and this other lawyer from Denver, Richardson...they got the Pinkerton detective on the stand and started gigging him about some things he did in Kansas...and McParland got what you might call testy. I think all that's left is Darrow's summation, not that it matters. He's talking tomorrow and everybody that can get off work will go. You better get there early...second floor of the courthouse on the corner of Seventh and Bank. If you want to see him before then, he'll be in the bar at the Sweets Hotel after supper... him and his cronies congregate in the Sweets bar and

McParland and Borah and their cronies congregate in the other hotel bar at the Wallace. They both of 'em hold court every night, you might say...and people in town here, they sort of move around from one revival to the next, hoping that one night everything will come together at the same bar."

"You do not think much of this trial," said Jimmy Delaney.

Floyd shrugged. "I'm only a station master," he said. "But I know they'll never stop trying to break up the union...it's like money and the power to force other men into submission can deliver them from their own mortality."

"Nothing can do that," said Jimmy Delaney.

"Well, when men get caught up in something..."

"I will see you the day after tomorrow," said Jimmy Delaney.

"Don't forget the cart for your trunk," said Floyd. "Just bring it back when you come in to work."

Twenty-Four

The Telegraph Shack

Jimmy Delaney sat in the first row near a skull on the prosecutor's table. The skull, said to be that of the murder victim, was propped upright, staring at the men in the jury box. The lawyer paced in front of the jury. He wore a dark and rumpled three-piece suit with a gravy stain on the waistcoat. He glanced occasionally toward the skull. When he gestured, a lock of hair fell over his forehead, and when he paused, his shoulders slumped and his large head sagged into his chest. The pauses were brief rest periods before the lawyer hurled the next invective. Just before eleven in the morning, the lawyer nodded, backed away from the jury box and settled into his chair at the defense table and the sense of high drama waned and people began to leave the courtroom.

Jimmy Delaney walked north on Seventh to Cedar and turned left in front of the city hall. He passed the white picket fence in front of the Oasis Saloon and Evening House and turned right into Sixth Street and continued across the bridge to the depot.

"You aren't due until tomorrow," said Floyd.

"I'll be organizing my space in the telegraph shack," said Jimmy Delaney. "I'll be needing a rhythm when the wires start coming in."

"I'll walk over with you...introduce you to Sluman," said Floyd.

"This lawyer, Darrow, is very emotional," said Jimmy Delaney.

"So, you went up to the trial," said Floyd.

"Aye...and some fellows belong on the stage, as a friend of mine once said."

Floyd laughed. "It could not have been better than what happened during the jury selection," he said.

"Every banker and mine owner in Shoshone County was on the jury list. Darrow went at them like there was no difference between a banker and any other thief...one works in a suit during the day with interest and stock juggling and the other works in overalls at night with a jimmy and dynamite. He got rid of all of them...like killing snakes. And you wait...the men who are left will never convict Steve Adams."

"I wonder if he believes everything he says," said Jimmy Delaney.

"I think maybe he does," said Floyd. "They say he can tune up and bawl at the drop of a hat. But I've been fooled before...probably will be again. How's your room?"

"It's a nice room," said Jimmy Delaney. "Missus McNair was expecting me. I've returned your cart."

"Fine," said Floyd. "The price is right for the room?"

"Aye, it is what I expected," said Jimmy Delaney. "And the food is good. My fellow boarders are miners working in Burke. Where is that?"

"It's in a canyon north of here," said Floyd. "It can't be but about a hundred yards wide. Nothing up there but the mine...there's no room for anything else. The railroad runs down the street because there's no room to run it anywhere else. All the miners stay down here. Did you wanna see if any of your wires have come in?"

"Aye," said Jimmy Delaney.

Floyd and Jimmy Delaney walked to the telegraph shack. Hearing footsteps, John Sluman turned toward the door.

"Sluman, this is Delaney," said Floyd. "He'll be working the Milwaukee wire."

"Well, hello again," said Sluman.

"You know each other?" said Floyd.

"We stayed in the same rooming house once and rode a train together," said Sluman. He shifted his weight to face Jimmy Delaney. "I didn't know you were a telegraph operator," he said. "What is your handle?"

"Thumper," said Jimmy Delaney.

"I'm Easy Finger," said Sluman.

"A smooth fist?" said Jimmy Delaney.

"That's what they say," said Sluman.

"Well, I'll let you get re-acquainted," said Floyd. "The train from Spokane will be here soon."

After Floyd had gone, Jimmy Delaney took off his cap and Murphy's coat and laid them on the long table which held the telegraph equipment. He took his knife from the pocket of Murphy's coat and slid it into the pocket of his trousers. Sluman did not seem to notice.

"In La Crosse you were after joining a construction crew," said Jimmy Delaney.

"I thought you were as well, but I never saw you again," said Sluman. "What happened?"

"I was on my way for training in the telegraph," said Jimmy Delaney.

"That's odd, I was quitting the telegraph," said Sluman. "After a few weeks of laying rails, I changed my mind."

"How did you get an assignment here?" said Jimmy Delaney.

"I was on the freight detail hauling ties and rails on the reservation," said Sluman. "One day I just stayed up in Dickinson and went back to the telegraph. The Northern Pacific was there and so I signed on and they sent me here. So, you'll be handling the Milwaukee wires for the construction."

"Aye, that's right," said Jimmy Delaney.

"Say, what happened to that other fellow?" said Sluman. "You remember...the little fat guy in such a hurry...he couldn't believe somebody would throw a person off a moving train."

"Did you believe it?" said Jimmy Delaney.

"Hell, I would have," said Sluman. "People will do anything. The union guy...intense fellow...he sure believed it 'til you rained on his parade."

"Why would you believe me and not him?"

"Now that you mention it, I don't know," said Sluman.

"I guess it just seemed to me like you didn't have an axe to grind."

The door opened and a man wearing a three piece suit came in. He closed the door behind him and looked around the telegraph shack suspiciously.

"Help you?" said Sluman.

"You in charge of the telegraph?" said the man.

"I am," said Sluman.

"Who's he?" said the man, nodding toward Jimmy Delaney.

"We have two telegraph operators here," said Sluman.

"All right, I need to send a wire to Boise," said the man.

"Just write it out on the pad there on the table," said Sluman.

The man wrote out a message, tore the sheet off the pad and handed it to Sluman.

"Send this right away," he said.

Sluman sat on the high stool he used for telegraphy and scanned the paper.

"James Hawley, Idanha Hotel, Boise," he said. "Adams case to jury this morning. Will advise verdict, but do not expect conviction. Whitney." He looked up. "Is that right?"

"Yes...how much?" said the man.

Sluman counted the words and said, "That's twenty cents."

The man took two silver dimes from his pocket and laid them on the table.

"Send it now," he said. "I'll wait."

Sluman tapped out the message.

"The boy will take it from the Union Pacific depot to the hotel," he said.

"Give me the message," said the man.

"Right there," said Sluman, gesturing toward the paper lying on the desk.

The man took the paper, folded it and left.

"So, the fix is in," said Sluman.

"Fix?" said Jimmy Delaney.

"That was Eugene Whitney...McParland's flunky," said Sluman. "The guy on the other end...Hawley... is prosecuting Haywood down in Boise. They won't get Adams and that means they won't get him to rat out Orchard and that means they can't use Orchard to get Haywood...no corroboration. Adams is gonna get off and they're gonna have to put in the fix to get him another way. Do you know what I'm talking about?"

"Aye, the trials," said Jimmy Delaney.

"That's right, the trials," said Sluman. "How do you stand?"

"I know little about it," said Jimmy Delaney. "How do you stand?"

"With the union, as always," said Sluman.

"A union man?" said Jimmy Delaney.

"In spirit," said Sluman.

Jimmy Delaney's eyes narrowed. He hesitated. His hand passed over the bulge of the knife in his pocket.

"A policeman in Milwaukee thinks you are a Pinkerton," he said.

"A Pinkerton!" said Sluman. "That's rich. What policeman?"

"You were visiting your sister in La Crosse?" said Jimmy Delaney.

"Yeah, I told you that," said Sluman. "What is this? What policeman?"

"The man in the parlor that night..."

The door opened. The man standing in the doorway was middle-aged, heavy-set with a square jaw and wore work clothes of coarse denim. The man adjusted his weather-beaten hat and glanced toward Jimmy Delaney.

"Who's this?" he said to Sluman.

"Delaney, new telegraph operator," said Sluman.

"Are you leaving?" said the man.

"No...Delaney is handling the Milwaukee construction," said Sluman.

The man regarded Jimmy Delaney. Piercing blue eyes channeled his menacing demeanor toward the red hair, blue denim shirt, coarse worsted trousers and sturdy brogans. The eyes moved back to Jimmy Delaney's face. Their eyes locked for a moment before the man looked away.

"Your coat?" he said, nodding toward the long table.

"Aye," said Jimmy Delaney.

"A seaman's coat," said the man.

"Aye," said Jimmy Delaney.

"I'm Blalock," said the man. "When did you come across?"

"It's five years," said Jimmy Delaney.

"Your people?" said Blalock.

"Passed on," said Jimmy Delaney.

Blalock nodded and turned away.

"I saw Whitney leaving here," he said. "What did he want?"

"He wired Hawley," said Sluman. "They don't expect a conviction."

"What is Hawley going to do?" said Blalock.

"I don't know," said Sluman.

"They'll keep Adams here or possibly take him back to Boise," said Blalock. "They won't let him go...and even if they do, they'll pick him up on something else after Darrow and Richardson are gone."

"That's what I figure, too," said Sluman. "Listen, we were talking before you came in. You're hearing this from me...some copper in Milwaukee is saying I'm a Pinkerton."

"What copper?" said Blalock. "You've never even been to Milwaukee."

"Yes, I have," said Sluman. "I was there back when I was thinking of quitting the telegraph. Me and Delaney here, we stayed in the same boarding house."

"That's all?" said Blalock. "Is something following you?"

""I don't see how," said Sluman. "Nothing happened...I

went to the boarding house, had dinner, talked to some other boarders and then left for La Crosse. I decided to see my sister before heading west."

Blalock turned toward Jimmy Delaney.

"What about this copper?" he said.

"This is not my business," said Jimmy Delaney.

"You brought it up, so let's hear it," said Blalock.

"Begging your pardon, I did not bring it up with you," said Jimmy Delaney.

"Do you know who I am?" said Blalock.

"I have never seen you before," said Jimmy Delaney.

"When you came across...where did you land?" said Blalock.

"New York," said Jimmy Delaney.

"I'm out of West Virginia and the anthracite mines in Pennsylvania...Scotch-Irish, third generation," said Blalock. "You're what we call a hardhead. It's probably a good thing to be in New York. Did you know that we are kinsmen?"

"On this side you are Scotch-Irish...in Ireland you are a Scot among Ulstermen," said Jimmy Delaney. "How is it that we are kinsmen?"

"You split hairs," said Blalock.

Jimmy Delaney shrugged.

"In any case, I meant that all Scots were once Irish," said Blalock.

"Aye, Gaelic tribes moving from Ireland to Scotland and some moving back...after they became Scotsmen," said Jimmy Delaney.

"So, you've had schooling...and by someone knowledgeable," said Blalock. "Are you a separatist?"

"I'm a telegrapher," said Jimmy Delaney.

"See here, Blalock," said Sluman.

"Be quiet, Sluman," said Blalock. "Tell me about the policeman in Milwaukee," he said to Jimmy Delaney.

"Go ahead," said Sluman. "Tell him."

"A man was killed," said Jimmy Delaney. "They are after saying it was you."

"What?" said Sluman. "Why? Who was killed?"

"The union man from the parlor."

"The one talking about throwing the old man from the train...he was killed?"

"Aye, he was," said Jimmy Delaney.

"They're saying that I did it?" said Sluman.

"You left during the night," said Jimmy Delaney. "Your bed had not been slept in when the police came the next morning."

"I told you in La Crosse about my sister," said Sluman. "This is crazy...I take a late train to see my sister and someone gets killed and I must have done it. Do you believe that?"

"Inspector Hessler's belief is more important," said Jimmy Delaney.

"Enough," said Blalock. "When did this happen?"

"Last year...a year ago, at least," said Sluman.

"His name was Jones...Edward Jones," said Blalock. "He came out of the coal mines in West Virginia. He left a wife and three children."

"I had no idea," said Sluman.

"Well, it's a small world," said Blalock. He turned toward Jimmy Delaney. "You must have gleaned by now that I represent the union," he said.

"Aye," said Jimmy Delaney.

"Are you for the union or against it?"

"I am not against the union," said Jimmy Delaney.

"But you are not for it," said Blalock.

"I am not against it," said Jimmy Delaney.

"Do you have money?" said Blalock.

"Not in the sense you mean," said Jimmy Delaney.

"Do you want money?"

"Not in the sense you mean," said Jimmy Delaney.

"What do you want?"

"To organize my space," said Jimmy Delaney. "I am to begin handling the telegraph tomorrow."

Blalock smiled. "All right, just answer me this much...

what is your opinion of this Milwaukee copper?" he said.
"Hessler...Inspector Hessler, I think you said."

"You've a good memory for names," said Jimmy
Delaney.

"I have a good memory for everything that concerns
me," said Blalock.

"Hessler is determined," said Jimmy Delaney.

"Is he looking for a telegrapher?" said Blalock.

"He is looking for a Pinkerton," said Jimmy Delaney.

Blalock turned toward Sluman. He took a cigar from
his shirt pocket, wet it with his tongue and rolled it
between his lips.

"You don't look like a Pinkerton," he said.

"That's not funny, Blalock," said Sluman.

"What is your sister's name?" said Blalock.

"You're checking on me?" said Sluman.

"I'm trying to help you, you fool," said Blalock. "What
is your sister's name?"

"It's Robinson...Clara Robinson," said Sluman.

"Robinson is the husband?"

"Yes...Claude Robinson."

"Clara and Claude, how nice," said Blalock. "Are they
still in La Crosse?"

"As far as I know," said Sluman.

"This Hessler...does he know your name?"

"He might," said Sluman. "I filled out a work card at
the train depot in Milwaukee."

"He probably thinks it's a fake, but he'll figure it out
eventually if he hasn't already," said Blalock. "You had
to give up the telegraph and try manual labor. What were
you trying to do...cleanse your soul?"

"I don't like the telegraph," said Sluman.

"What do you like?"

"I don't know."

"Have you written your sister since you got here?"

"No."

"Well, that's something," said Blalock. "You'll let me

know, of course, if Whitney gets a reply from Boise," said Blalock.

"Of course," said Sluman.

Blalock opened the door, stopped and turned.

"Welcome to Wallace, Delaney," he said.

Jimmy Delaney nodded.

Twenty-Five

Blalock

Gray patches of snow lay on the dirt behind the white picket fence in front of Belle McNair's boarding house. The fence was identical to the one separating the Oasis Saloon and Evening House from the traffic on Cedar Street and both fences were stripped and painted every spring, always white. The air on a Sunday morning in March was clear and crisp with a light cold wind out of the north which carried the voices of churchgoers and the sound of their footsteps on the board sidewalk. Jimmy Delaney waited on the porch. He turned up the collar of Murphy's coat against the chill. The rucksack from County Roscommon hung from his shoulder.

The front door of the boarding house opened. Belle McNair, a sturdy middle-aged woman with the look and manner of self-assurance, came out and closed the door behind her. As always, she wore a long black dress with a lace collar and a broad-brimmed black hat.

"They tell me the tunnel is finished," said Belle McNair.

"Aye, it is," said Jimmy Delaney. "The drillers from each side have met. It is only a matter of days to lay the rails."

"So, your job here is over?" said Belle McNair.

"Aye," said Jimmy Delaney. "The sections here are finished with only sidings and spurs left. They are saying that the railroad is almost ready for opening to the coast."

"When will you be leaving?"

"Soon," said Jimmy Delaney. "The telegraph will move to Avery. It's to be a division point I am told."

"My God, Jimmy, Avery's in the middle of nowhere. Still, it must be better than the other side of the pass at Taft. What a hell hole...not even a pretense of civilization."

"I don't have a new assignment yet," said Jimmy Delaney.

"Well, you've been a good tenant these last two years," said Belle McNair. "People who mind their own business do fine by me. If you need a reference, don't hesitate to ask."

"I'm thanking you," said Jimmy Delaney.

Belle McNair nodded and went through the gate and turned south along the sidewalk toward Bank Street.

Blalock's horse, Charlie, led the buckboard out of Cedar Street into Sixth and stopped in front of the boarding house. Jimmy Delaney went through the gate, threw the rucksack into the buckboard and climbed onto the seat.

"What do you think about the weather?" he said.

"Christ, who knows around here?" said Blalock. "I got a tarp back there and a couple of tents. Was that Belle I just saw?"

"Aye, it is," said Jimmy Delaney.

"Where's she going on a Sunday morning? She hasn't seen a church in years...if ever."

"I knew a man on the ice harvest," said Jimmy Delaney. "His name was Willy. One day I said the foreman did not seem very smart. Willy pointed across the ice and said I should tell him that. Willy was sure the man would be eager to mend his ways."

"Hunh," said Blalock. "So, you want to see the trestles."

"Aye, it is two years I've heard of the trestles and not seen them," said Jimmy Delaney.

"It's no wonder," said Blalock. "There's nothing out there but wilderness. You got your railroad card?"

"Aye, I have it."

"You better, unless you plan to live outdoors for the next few days," said Blalock. "Except for Grand

Forks, there's nothing where we're going but railroad barracks."

"We have tents...and bread, beans and molasses," said Jimmy Delaney.

"That doesn't mean I don't care to have a bath, a decent meal and a bed," said Blalock.

"You're getting soft," said Jimmy Delaney.

"Damn right," said Blalock. "Listen, what are you going to do?"

"I'm going to see the trestles," said Jimmy Delaney.

"The whole world loves a smart ass," said Blalock.

"I have not decided," said Jimmy Delaney.

"Your telegraph job is over and you refused the railroad's offer to go somewhere else," said Blalock, snapping the reins. "You have to do something. This fellow we're meeting in Grand Forks...Archer...you say he's an engineer?"

"Aye, I knew him in Mobridge," said Jimmy Delaney. "He worked on the bridge across the Missouri there and then came here to build trestles."

"Well, I guess that job's almost over as well," said Blalock.

"It's quite a while yet," said Jimmy Delaney. "Some of the trestles are timber. They're going to open the railroad, but replace the wooden trestles with steel."

From Sixth they turned west into Bank Street and then south into King and followed Placer Creek Road through a break in the mountains. Blalock settled Charlie into a steady walk on the trail to Moon Pass. The buckboard passed the turnoff to the Nicholson mine. Jimmy Delaney studied the cascading water of Placer Creek.

"The bridge to the mine washes out nearly every spring," said Blalock. "The creek carries it on into Wallace where folks fish it out and break it up for firewood. They could save themselves a lot of trouble if they just built it higher with some ramps."

"What happened to Sluman?" said Jimmy Delaney.

"Sluman?" said Blalock. "Two years and you've never mentioned that before."

"Did he have a sister in La Crosse?" said Jimmy Delaney.

"Did you ever contact that copper...the one from Milwaukee?"

"No," said Jimmy Delaney.

"Why?"

"There was nothing I could tell him," said Jimmy Delaney.

"You heard anything more from him?"

"No," said Jimmy Delaney.

"You know, I never asked you to intercept messages for the union," said Blalock.

"Aye, I know," said Jimmy Delaney.

"There was no sister in La Crosse," said Blalock, looking straight ahead.

"So, Inspector Hessler was right," said Jimmy Delaney. "He solved the crime in his mind right away... as soon as he learned that Sluman was missing. From that moment, he knew. I have wondered how he could have been so sure."

"Experience, I expect," said Blalock. "All coppers are not stupid...it just seems that way sometimes. Maybe he caught up with Sluman."

"I don't think so," said Jimmy Delaney.

"Were you ever worried?" said Blalock.

"For a time, I suppose," said Jimmy Delaney. "It seems long ago now."

"You were never in danger," said Blalock.

"I know," said Jimmy Delaney.

"Sluman was playing a dangerous game," said Blalock.

"Have I ever told you about my coat?" said Jimmy Delaney.

"You have...a seaman...Murphy by name," said Blalock.

"On the steamboat...the season I worked on the

197

river...the coat was stolen from my bunk during the night," said Jimmy Delaney. "The thief did not know of the label inside the collar and so was found out. Other crewmen overpowered him...and when I asked the first mate if he would turn the thief over to the law, he said that an able seaman's mate should know the answer. I have the thief's knife...given to me by the first mate."

"Eddie Jones was a good man," said Blalock. "He was not a violent man and he believed in what he was doing. As I said, Sluman was playing a dangerous game."

"Why have you not asked me to take messages for the union?" said Jimmy Delaney.

Blalock shrugged. "Henderson was our man long before he replaced Sluman on the key," he said. "And so is Floyd. I thought you knew that."

"I did," said Jimmy Delaney.

"Then why ask?"

"Was there another reason?"

"If there was, I wouldn't tell you," said Blalock.

"You wouldn't have to," said Jimmy Delaney.

"But I do have something to tell you...from when I was out east a few months back," said Blalock.

"Aye, to see your family," said Jimmy Delaney.

"I don't have a family," said Blalock. "They're all dead. That's why I left West Virginia in the first place."

Jimmy Delaney nodded.

"You knew," said Blalock.

"I guessed," said Jimmy Delaney.

"How?" said Blalock.

"Different things," said Jimmy Delaney. "Your father being killed in the mine...other things."

"Well, you might as well know the rest," said Blalock. "After the explosion, my mother and two brothers were in the crowd protesting conditions in the mines. They were shot down by soldiers sent to restore order, they said. After that they sealed the blind passage...they didn't even have the decency to recover the bodies."

"Are you religious, Blalock?" said Jimmy Delaney.

"Hunh, God no," said Blalock. "Why do you ask?"

"The bodies of your father and the others," said Jimmy Delaney.

"It's not the bodies," said Blalock. "It's the reason they weren't recovered."

The switch backs in the road were sharper near Moon Pass. The forest thinned and the snow had not yet receded into islands and the sound of rushing water in the valley far below had faded. The light air was cold and quiet, heightening the sound of the buckboard's wheels against the gravel.

"Where were you?" said Jimmy Delaney.

"What...when the mine caved in?" said Blalock.

"When the soldiers fired into the crowd," said Jimmy Delaney.

"I was in town...at the pool hall."

"And you blame yourself."

"I did, but I don't anymore," said Blalock. "I blame those who did it and their agents. I learned and you will learn that all authority is arbitrary and corrupt."

"I've no need to learn that," said Jimmy Delaney.

Blalock pulled on the reins. He turned and looked at Jimmy Delaney.

"Then why do you work for the railroad?" he said.

"The telegraphy has given me the chance to learn something useful, maintain my library and to save up a stake," said Jimmy Delaney. "And the railroad has asked nothing more of me."

"That's tunnel vision, Jimmy," said Blalock. "It's like the blinders on Charlie out there to keep his eyes on the road."

"Do you say there is no authority in the union?" said Jimmy Delaney.

"It's not the same thing and you know it," said Blalock.

"Let's go," said Jimmy Delaney.

Blalock popped the reins lightly and Charlie resumed walking.

"Some authority is necessary," said Blalock.

"Sure that is what the mine owners think as well," said Jimmy Delaney.

"I think you're an anarchist," said Blalock.

"Why did you go back east?" said Jimmy Delaney.

"Because Haywood is a fool," said Blalock. "He has no discipline. This thing with the Wobblies is nuts. They're trying to organize illiterate foreigners with no skills and the miners are going to pay the price."

Jimmy Delaney said nothing.

"You don't have anything to say?" said Blalock.

"I'm listening," said Jimmy Delaney.

"I'm going to work for the United Mine Workers," said Blalock. "They care about men who work in mines. They got the eight-hour day and the minimum wage and we have Haywood and all his causes. I'm tired of wild-eyed radicals who are determined to fail. I'm looking forward to seeing the trestles. I'll be leaving in three weeks."

"Where?" said Jimmy Delaney.

"Pennsylvania...Scranton, Pennsylvania."

"The anthracite mines," said Jimmy Delaney.

Blalock snapped the reins lightly and said something to Charlie. He glanced briefly at the wall of rock on his left and the chasm on his right.

"This road is getting narrow," he said. "How do you know about the anthracite mines? You're probably not aware of it, but the first day we met...there in the telegraph shack...I looked at your hands...an old habit. You've never been a miner, so how do you know about the anthracite mines?"

"Do you have to do something to know of it?" said Jimmy Delaney.

"That's usually the case, but I guess not," said Blalock. "I forget that you read all those books."

"I once knew an anthracite miner," said Jimmy Delaney. "It is surprising that you would want to see the trestles."

"Why?" said Blalock.

"The engineers belong to no union," said Jimmy Delaney. "The men in the construction crews do not either."

"I have found that college men think they have little need of unions," said Blalock. "And the construction gangs...with many of the men working in the summer and going south for the winter, it is not a stable situation for the union. In any case, I have heard that the trestles are magnificent feats of engineering and I have as much appreciation for that as the next man."

"What is your new job?" said Jimmy Delaney.

"I'll only be in Scranton a short time," said Blalock. "Then I'll be traveling around and organizing in West Virginia. I suppose it's useless to ask you to come along."

"This work is not for me," said Jimmy Delaney. "I'm an anarchist...you said so yourself."

"Hunh," said Blalock.

They stopped at the summit of Moon Pass and held a barrel of water for Charlie. They heaved the barrel back into the buckboard and Blalock ran his hand along Charlie's back.

"Not much of a sweat in this cool air and all downhill to Pearson from here," he said.

"How old is Charlie?" said Jimmy Delaney.

"Oh, Charlie's in his prime," said Blalock. "Let's see... he was five when I got him and that's four years ago. Like I say...in his prime."

"Have you found a place for him?" said Jimmy Delaney.

"Oh, yeah...I sold him to the livery stable back in town. He'll pull light loads and have plenty of oats. What are you going to do...really?"

"I don't know," said Jimmy Delaney. "I'm thinking it is time to continue my schooling."

"I thought that might be it...you've talked about it enough," said Blalock. "Do you mean going to a college or something like that?"

"I'm thinking I will speak to Archer about it," said Jimmy Delaney.

The road fell into the valley of the North Fork of the St. Joe River and followed the river to its junction with Loop Creek flowing off the ridge of the Bitterroot. Blalock pulled up at the junction.

"Just like the fellow at the stable told me," said Blalock. "Off to the left here is Loop Creek Road to Grand Forks. The railroad is across the creek, just around the next bend at Pearson, but I think it just goes through to Avery. There's not much there."

"Aye," said Jimmy Delaney. "There's only a tool shed at Pearson...named for two brothers prospecting the Lucky Swede mine, by the way."

"Gold and some copper, I hear...no silver," said Blalock. "I also hear they won't have much ore to ship even after the railroad gets going. Not much of a mine, I'm afraid. Where are the trestles?"

"The Adair Loop," said Jimmy Delaney. "The track drops about two thousand feet over twelve miles from the west end of the tunnel at Roland to Pearson. Most of that is in the Adair Loop, starting about a mile south of the tunnel. The line runs along the ridges north of Loop Creek to the Adair construction camp and a switch back tunnel turns the track west again along the south side of Loop Creek to Pearson. This road to Grand Forks continues through the valley to Adair. After Grand Forks we'll be at creek level in the middle of the loop. There are three trestles on the upper loop to the north and four trestles on the lower loop to the south."

"This was the only way to manage the grade, I take it," said Blalock.

"Aye, the drop is very steep from Roland to Pearson," said Jimmy Delaney. "The long way around the loop allows a shallow grade...and still, with the cuts and fills, trestles and tunnels, this is the most expensive section of railroad ever built."

"Why did they come through here?" said Blalock. "There must be an easier way."

"Aye," said Jimmy Delaney. "The Northern Pacific and Great Northern surveyors were here first."

"Well, let's get Charlie bedded down in Grand Forks," said Blalock. He snapped the reins and Charlie turned into Loop Creek Road.

"You've been to Grand Forks?" said Jimmy Delaney.

"Nope, heard about it...been to Taft, same thing," said Blalock.

"Did Haywood kill that governor?" said Jimmy Delaney.

"Steunenberg?" said Blalock. "Harry Orchard did it... he got life. Haywood was in Colorado."

"Did Haywood hire Orchard?"

"Not according to the jury in Boise," said Blalock.

"Hunh," said Jimmy Delaney.

"No, seriously, I doubt it," said Blalock. "Steunenberg was old news. If it had been McParland that got blown up, well..."

"Sluman was a Pinkerton?" said Jimmy Delaney.

"Yes," said Blalock.

"So Inspector Hessler was right again," said Jimmy Delaney.

"It would seem so," said Blalock.

Twenty-Six

Meeting in Grand Forks

The buckboard crossed Cliff Creek on thick planks laid over cedar logs and the road narrowed to a dirt trail between the Anheuser Hotel and the North Pole Saloon. The trail led to the crossroads of Grand Forks, marked by a fir tree bearing a sign which advertised midnight lunch at the Bon Ton Restaurant. At the crossroads, Loop Creek Road continued to the right toward the trestles of Adair Loop. To the left, unpainted buildings with steep sheet metal roofs behind flat plank façades were clustered around a muddy lane littered with empty kegs and piles of lumber. A board nailed to a post identified the lane as Cliff Creek Road. Men stood in small gatherings or sat on tree stumps, reminders that the town had been hewn from dense coniferous forest. Others sat on kegs turned upright on the elevated board sidewalk in front of the El Rey Hotel. A woman came out of the Bitter Root Mercantile and crossed to the El Rey on planks laid over the mud. The only other woman visible from the street hung out of a second story window of the Old Crow Saloon.

"Where's the livery stable?" said Blalock to a man standing next to the fir tree.

"Straight through town," said the man. "You got a nickel for a war veteran? I'm awful dry."

"Which war was that?" said Blalock.

"I was a rough rider with Teddy," said the man.

"Where was that again?" said Blalock.

"The Philippines...me and Teddy was in the Philippines."

"Um, used to be Cuba...they must have changed the name," said Blalock, flipping a nickel into the air.

"I wonder how often that works," said Jimmy Delaney.

"Well, at least he knows who Teddy is," said Blalock.

A sharp turn in the lane past the elevated sidewalk brought the livery stable into view. The main barn and the paddocks surrounding it stood on a shoulder of meadow along the bank of Cliff Creek. The lane widened through the meadow and settled into a steep climb through dense forest to the north ridge of Loop Creek Draw.

"The railroad payroll for the Falcon camp comes to the post office here," said Jimmy Delaney. "I wonder how."

"There's another road from Taft," said Blalock. "Bullion Pass...runs into this road north of here at Moss Creek. There are lots of roads in here...old Indian trails graded over, they tell me."

Blalock paid extra for oats and a private stall inside the barn. He wiped Charlie down, brushed him, cleaned the mud and rocks from each hoof and tightened his shoes.

"Comb the knots out of his mane and tail before putting him away," said Blalock to the stable boy, holding out a silver dime. "Put fresh sawdust and hay in the stall and fresh water in the trough and tell your boss that we'll back tomorrow morning. And don't put the fresh bedding in over the old...muck out the stall."

"You take good care of your horse, mister, said the boy.

"Any man who doesn't take care of his horse is a damn fool," said Blalock. He turned. "You ready, Jimmy?" he said.

"Aye, I have my rucksack and your valise," said Jimmy Delaney. "Is it anything else you need from the buckboard?"

"Nope, that'll do it," said Blalock. He stretched a length of canvas over the buckboard and tied it down to stays along the sides. He surveyed the buckboard and turned to the stable boy. "There's no reason for anyone to remove the canvas," he said. "If it rains, the buckboard will be fine where it is."

"Yes sir," said the stable boy.

"And if I like what I see when I pick up my horse tomorrow morning, there's another dime for you," said Blalock.

"Yes sir, you'll like what you see," said the stable boy.

Blalock nodded and he and Jimmy Delaney walked to the lane and back to town. Blalock paused at the mouth of the narrow alley between the Log Cabin Saloon and the El Rey barber shop. He shifted his valise to the other hand.

"Look at this place," he said. "This is what Haywood is trying to organize. They don't even know what he's talking about."

"These are not railroad men," said Jimmy Delaney.

"Bums," said Blalock. "There can't be more than a dozen buildings in this town and half of them are saloons. This place is overrun with gamblers, whores and bums. What the hell was your friend, Archer, thinking?"

"Who wanted a bath, a bed and a meal?" said Jimmy Delaney.

"You think there's any of that here?" said Blalock. "We might as well jump in the creek, eat the beans and molasses and sleep in the buckboard."

"The Anheuser is probably all right," said Jimmy Delaney. "Archer is staying there."

Blalock regarded the Anheuser Hotel at the head of the lane near the crossroads. A large white sign nailed to the plank façade identified the hotel. Two small windows below the sign anchored a banner advertising St. Louis beer and below the banner was a double door in the center of the building flanked by two plate glass windows.

"The Anheuser is probably all right, he says," said Blalock. "There it is, right ahead of us. Look at it...a puff of wind would blow it down and if a fire started, it would go up like kindling."

"It is sturdy enough," said Jimmy Delaney.

Hunh," said Blalock.

"It is hard to understand why you work for the union," said Jimmy Delaney.

"Is it?" said Blalock.

"Aye," said Jimmy Delaney. "Why do you not work on behalf of the horse pulling the coal car?"

Blalock laughed. "Is it that obvious?" he said.

"Aye, I'm thinking you prefer horses to men," said Jimmy Delaney.

"Some men, without a doubt, Jimmy, without a doubt," said Blalock. "And while we're at it, I don't hear any great love of humanity from you."

"I have a list...a short one," said Jimmy Delaney.

"As do I," said Blalock.

"The union work...it is worth the danger?" said Jimmy Delaney.

"It's the bosses," said Blalock. "Diamond stickpins, fat rings on their fat fingers, pot bellies and fat cigars, private rail cars, private armies...we'll bring them down someday."

Jimmy Delaney shifted the weight of the rucksack and gestured toward the Anheuser Hotel. They began walking again.

"As you say, they have private armies," said Jimmy Delaney.

"Eventually the unions will have the power, Jimmy, and corrupt politicians will be living on borrowed time," said Blalock.

"A woman, I think, said if voting changed anything, they would outlaw it," said Jimmy Delaney.

"I've known you two years, Jimmy," said Blalock. "You never forget what you read. Who said that?"

"Emma Goldman."

"I might have known," said Blalock. "Well, it may be... it very well may be."

They went through the double doors of the Anheuser Hotel. Blalock tested the flooring under his weight; the tongue and groove planks were solid. Several men stood at the bar; others played cards at a few scattered tables.

207

A stage across the back of the room was hidden by a heavy maroon curtain. The bartender glanced toward the doorway and approached, wiping his hands on a stained apron.

"Help you?" he said.

"Room for the night and a bath," said Blalock.

"Seventy-five cents each...fifty more for the bath," said the bartender. "No free drinks and no food. There's restaurants in town...the Won Ton is the best."

"We saw them," said Blalock, holding out a quarter eagle gold coin.

"Over this way to the desk and sign the register," said the bartender.

"Just get us a key and point the way," said Blalock.

The bartender shrugged, walked to the reception area and returned with two skeleton keys.

"Makes no never mind to me," he said, handing the keys to Blalock. "Number two, up the stairs to the right. You're in luck...you got a view of Cliff Creek."

"I can't wait," said Blalock, handing one of the keys to Jimmy Delaney. "Where's the bath?"

"Tub's in the room," said the bartender. "Let me know and I'll send a girl with hot water. If you want her, it's another fifty...each."

"No thanks," said Blalock.

"Makes no never mind to me," said the bartender.

"God knows this place is not the Ritz," said a voice.

Blalock and Jimmy Delaney turned. A man stood on the landing at the top of the stairs. He wore a khaki shirt and khaki pants tucked into riding boots. A crumpled fedora was pushed back on his head.

"Archer," said Jimmy Delaney.

"You filled out some, boy," said Harry Archer. "Still got your seaman's coat, I see...fits you just about right now."

"I'm thinking that hat is about done," said Jimmy Delaney.

Harry Archer took off the hat and ran his finger

through the crease in the crown, replaced it on his head and came down the stairs. He grasped Jimmy Delaney's hand.

"Barely broken in, Jimmy, barely broken in," he said. "How are you?"

"I'm well," said Jimmy Delaney. "This is Blalock. He doesn't tell anyone his first name."

"All right...you can call me Harry and I'll call you Blalock," said Harry Archer, taking Blalock's hand. "Listen, you fellows get rid of your grips and clean up a little if you need to and meet me back here. Let's eat. God knows, a man could starve waiting for you two...and we don't want to miss the fight."

"A prize fight?" said Blalock.

"At the El Rey tonight," said Harry Archer. "A local fellow, a lumberjack who thinks he can punch, is going up against Paddy O'Brien. I saw O'Brien in Taft...a big kid and God knows he hits like a freight train. I hear he's trying to get Johnson's attention for the title. Shake a leg...the place will be packed with railroad workers."

"Jeffries is coming out of retirement," said Blalock. "He'll take care of Johnson."

"Maybe, but I doubt it," said Harry Archer. "Jeffries is overweight and out of shape, but even if he can beat Johnson, neither one of them can stand up to this O'Brien kid, if what I saw is any indication. You fellows get ready...I could eat a horse."

"That's what you will be eating in this town," said Blalock.

"Ha," said Harry Archer. "Last night, I had a fried steak and potatoes at the Bon Ton and it was not bad."

"Are you sure it was a beef steak?" said Blalock.

"Now that you mention it..."

"You see," said Blalock.

"Just kidding," said Harry Archer. "You fellows get going...I'll just have a beer while you get straightened around. And shake a leg."

Blalock and Jimmy Delaney climbed the stairs and

found room number two. Blalock opened the door, revealing a large room with a double bed, a couch, a galvanized tub and two windows with broadcloth curtains.

"Well, I guess this is acceptable," said Blalock.

"So, you will have your bath after all," said Jimmy Delaney.

"Later," said Blalock. "Let's just brush the dust off these clothes and go eat. I don't want to miss the fight."

"Boxing?" said Jimmy Delaney. "You surprise me again."

"See that?" said Blalock, touching a scar which followed the line of his left jaw. "I bet you've wondered where that came from."

"I've noticed it," said Jimmy Delaney.

"Boxing...or brawling, I should say," said Blalock. "It pays better than the coal mine and you breathe sweet cigar smoke instead of coal dust. This scar...I walked into a right one night and it damn near took my head off. This guy knocked me cold as a wedge. I'd seen him before...he had a compact style, always coming in out of a crouch with a short, straight right. I was a fool to fight him to begin with. They threw a bucket of water in my face and I still didn't know where I was for twenty minutes."

"It must have been when you decided to go into the union business," said Jimmy Delaney.

"Damn right," said Blalock.

"A wise decision, even considering the Pinkertons," said Jimmy Delaney.

"Well, my fight career was over before the gas explosion and the rest of it," said Blalock. "As for the Pinkertons... you just keep them close and let them hear what you want them to hear."

"If you know who they are," said Jimmy Delaney.

"Oh, it's not as difficult as you might think," said Blalock.

"Well, let's get cleaned up and go to dinner," said Jimmy Delaney.

"You bet," said Blalock. "I have to admit, I still like the fights. I'm like the old dog that can't satisfy the ladies anymore, but his ears perk up just the same."

Harry Archer and Blalock and Jimmy Delaney crossed the lane and went through the wide double doors of the Bon Ton Restaurant, a square one-story building with log walls and a façade of vertical planks facing the crossroads. They had two helpings of a heavy beef stew with potatoes and carrots, hard rye bread and black coffee. Harry Archer ordered whiskeys and prepared his cigar by practiced ritual. He leaned back in his chair and touched a match to the cigar and blew smoke toward the ceiling.

"You fellows don't know what you're missing," said Harry Archer. "There is nothing like a fine cigar after a meal."

"I tried a pipe for a while...too much trouble to keep up with it," said Blalock. "Tried cigars too, but they take too damn long to smoke and I was always leaving it somewhere. Finally, I said the hell with it."

"Well, to each his own," said Harry Archer. "So, what work do you do?"

"I work with the union," said Blalock.

"Oh, the railroad workers?" said Harry Archer.

"Miners," said Blalock.

"Miners," said Harry Archer. "My older brother works for a coal mining firm back in Pennsylvania. He's an accountant...never gone near a mine."

"No offense, but they never do," said Blalock.

"No offense taken," said Harry Archer. "My brother is a nice fellow who wears a nice suit and has no imagination."

Blalock laughed. "Well, maybe I'll run into him," he said. "I'll be going to Scranton shortly to take up a new job."

"I doubt it," said Harry Archer. "My brother is afraid of unions and almost everything else. He's afraid the streetcar will crash taking him home. So, Jimmy, your telegram said you are not staying with the railroad. What's up?"

"I have a stake," said Jimmy Delaney. "I'm thinking it is time to finish my schooling."

"I thought as much," said Harry Archer. "Do you still have the trunk?"

"Aye, and another one," said Jimmy Delaney.

"How are you getting your books now?"

"As before," said Jimmy Delaney. "The Northern Pacific conductors take the money to Missoula and bring the books on their next run."

"How do you know what books to buy?"

"As before...I read the reviews in the newspaper," said Jimmy Delaney. "The Sunday editions are only one day later than they were in Mobridge."

"He doesn't read the Wallace paper...not sophisticated enough," said Blalock.

"Is that true?" said Harry Archer.

"No, I'm only kidding," said Blalock. "He reads everything...even those ridiculous advertisements for cure-all tonics."

"People swear by California fig syrup," said Jimmy Delaney.

"California fig syrup?" said Harry Archer. "What is that?"

"Just what it sounds like," said Blalock. "It's also possible that whatever is in the bottle has never seen a fig."

"God knows what it has seen," said Harry Archer. "You actually look at all those advertisements?"

Jimmy Delaney shrugged. "I look at everything in the paper," he said.

"So, back to your schooling," said Harry Archer. "You're interested in college, are you?"

"Aye," said Jimmy Delaney.

"Engineering, the law..."

"A broad knowledge of everything," said Jimmy Delaney.

"Everything?" said Harry Archer. "You don't ask much."

"Others have done," said Jimmy Delaney.

"Men of leisure, wealth...men not required to earn their way," said Harry Archer.

"It is different from finding work, if I understand you," said Jimmy Delaney. "I can always find work for pay. It is a necessity, but it has no other value."

"And the value of knowing everything?" said Harry Archer.

"It is an unattainable goal," said Jimmy Delaney. "It need not have value beyond satisfaction of the attempt."

"Now you sound like my other brother...my younger brother," said Harry Archer. "You're nothing like him, but you sound like him."

"I did not know that you have brothers," said Jimmy Delaney.

"Oh yes...two," said Harry Archer. "My younger brother...accounting is a drudge and engineering is an applied substitute for real mathematics...went to a liberal arts college back in New York. He teaches classics at a boarding school. His name is Sherman, although he bears no resemblance to the army general for whom he is named. While we are on the subject of generals, I am named after Light Horse Harry Lee and my older brother after George Armstrong Custer. So, you see, we are two generals and I believe a colonel...or maybe he made general. So much for being named for generals...I avoid the military when possible, one of my brothers is afraid of his shadow and the other has no idea how the world works and no desire to know."

"You might be surprised," said Jimmy Delaney.

"I doubt it," said Harry Archer.

"Some do not choose to interact with the world," said Jimmy Delaney.

"You have to know something to choose," said Harry Archer. "Be that as it may, though, college opens doors. I can help you get into a good one in New York, if that's what you want. I started there before transferring to the Rensselaer."

"They will listen to you?" said Jimmy Delaney.

Harry Archer laughed. "They will listen to my father's endowment," he said.

"You have never mentioned your family before," said Jimmy Delaney.

"It never came up," said Harry Archer. "My father and his partner made a fortune in railroad stock. He retired when his partner died and lives with my mother in Albany. He threatens periodically to start another brokerage firm but never will. His partner was the brains and my father the mechanic. He was a good mechanic but still a mechanic. He does not admit that, of course, but he knows it, which is why he won't start another firm. Did you graduate from a high school?"

"I finished the public schooling in Ireland," said Jimmy Delaney.

"That's equivalent to what?" said Harry Archer.

Jimmy Delaney shrugged, shook his head.

"Well, it probably won't do," said Harry Archer. "I expect you'll have to sit an entrance examination. That requires a tutor...and tutors work for a fee...and the college will require a fee for the examination and there is no refund if you fail."

"I won't fail," said Jimmy Delaney.

"You're sure," said Harry Archer.

"Aye, I'm sure," said Jimmy Delaney.

"Are you really that tough?" said Harry Archer.

"He's Irish," said Blalock. "Pigsty Irish, I believe, was the last thing I heard. And with that, we should go to the fight."

"That's right, we'll miss the fight," said Harry Archer. "You shouldn't pay any attention to me, Jimmy...I always make things sound worse than they are. We'll come back here after the fight for a beer. How's that sound?"

"Good to me," said Blalock.

"Listen, Jimmy, I'm going back to Minneapolis for a

meeting to finish the trestles," said Harry Archer. "After the meeting I may possibly expect that girders and trusses will be shipped to Idaho instead of Iowa....God knows that would be a welcome change. Can you wrap things up in Wallace and meet me in Missoula in about two weeks?"

"Aye, it's just packing the trunks," said Jimmy Delaney.

"All right, I'll reserve a compartment on the Limited and send a wire with the date...should be no more than two weeks," said Harry Archer. "I just had an idea...my younger brother is the best tutor you can get."

"He will do this?" said Jimmy Delaney.

"Of course...he lives for this sort of thing," said Harry Archer. "In three weeks time, you'll be in Massachusetts preparing for college."

Twenty-Seven

"I thought you always knew."

"I'm going to the room and get my coat," said Jimmy Delaney. "I'll catch up."

Blalock waved and ran after Harry Archer. They hurried through a light rain and vaulted onto the elevated sidewalk in front of the El Rey Hotel and Saloon. Even without the barber shop, post office and hospital, the El Rey was larger than the Old Crow Saloon by half again. A sign by the door reminded passersby that the El Rey was the largest hotel in Grand Forks and had the only elevated sidewalk as well as imported whiskey, honest faro tables and agreeable barmaids.

Harry Archer laughed and rapped his knuckles on the railing.

"What?" said Blalock.

"The sign," said Harry Archer. "Accentuate the positive."

"If there is one," said Blalock. "Wait, the stew was pretty good...I'll give you that. This kid, Paddy O'Brien... he's as good as you say?"

"He is," said Harry Archer. "He's a big kid...two-fifteen or so...always moving forward in a tight crouch. In Taft he fought a guy who outweighed him forty pounds. He worked his way inside and knocked the guy silly with a straight right that didn't travel more than six or eight inches."

"Seen that before," said Blalock. "A guy like that put an end to my fight career...mercifully, I might add."

"You were a prize fighter?" said Harry Archer.

"Years ago," said Blalock. "Not very good...flailing away like an idiot. I finally got in the ring with a real fighter. He put an end to that nonsense...knocked me into next week."

"How well do you know Jimmy?" said Harry Archer.

"I've known him about two years...ever since he came to Wallace," said Blalock. "He's a smart kid and careful... and determination comes early and stays late."

"I can see how you are friends," said Harry Archer.

"Of course," said Blalock.

"I should think you would want him in the union," said Harry Archer.

"I do...it's not his line of work."

"I take it this has not been a source of friction."

"Why should it be?" said Blalock. "I don't expect everyone to be a union organizer and I don't make enemies without good reason."

"Touché," said Harry Archer.

"You have not tried to make him into an engineer?" said Blalock.

"As you say, it's not his line of work," said Harry Archer.

"I like Jimmy," said Blalock. "I liked him the moment I met him...gave him my sternest treatment and it didn't faze him."

"It wouldn't," said Harry Archer.

"I cannot imagine not having him as a friend," said Blalock. "But it's the strangest thing...I don't know what he cares about. I'm sure it's more than he talks about."

"I expect so," said Harry Archer.

"He thinks I care more about horses than people," said Blalock.

Harry Archer laughed. "Do you?" he said.

"Mostly," said Blalock.

"And yet you work for the union," said Harry Archer.

"Jimmy said the same thing," said Blalock.

"It seems incongruous," said Harry Archer.

"Isn't everything?" said Blalock.

"Raining," said Jimmy Delaney, jumping from the mud onto the sidewalk.

"Speak of the devil," said Harry Archer. "We've been talking about you."

"Nothing good, I hope," said Jimmy Delaney.

Of course not," said Blalock. "Let's go in and get the lay of the land."

The bartender met them at the door. He looked them over and made his decision.

"If you gents are here for libation, just step over to the bar or take a table," he said. "If you want a room, we're all full up. If you're here for the fight, admission is two bucks each...coin, notes or silver certificates, no difference to me."

"That's a little steep," said Blalock.

"It's a free country...I don't see no ball and chain on your leg," said the bartender.

Blalock smiled without showing his teeth and handed the bartender a gold half eagle and a one-dollar note.

"Right through the curtain," said the bartender. "You got about ten minutes...all bets handled in the back."

"Let me," said Harry Archer.

"You got dinner...I'll get this," said Blalock.

"It's a lot of money for a fight," said Harry Archer.

"Here," said Jimmy Delaney, offering two one-dollar notes.

"You can get the beer after the fight," said Blalock. "Let's go."

The back room of the El Rey was dim and noisy. The smell was a blend of cigar smoke and sweat. The ropes forming the boxing ring were held in a square by iron posts bolted to the floor. Men pressed against the ring, shouting and waving money over the top rope.

"Still offering three to one," said a man inside the ring. "It's still three to one. You like your man? Triple your money."

"Twenty dollars at four to one," said a man in the crowd.

"You're killing me, but I'll take it," said the man in the ring, accepting a wad of paper money. He counted the money, stuffed it into a leather satchel, wrote the amount on a slip of paper and handed the marker to the gambler. He moved quickly and expertly. "Two more minutes," he said. "It's four to one now...lay down ten, make forty...twenty-five, make a hundred."

"I've seen that fellow before...same checked suit and derby hat," said Harry Archer. "In Taft he was offering the same odds on the local guy...no bets on O'Brien."

"He's into these guys for hundreds of dollars," said Blalock. "Did you see that gallows out back? He must be pretty sure of himself."

"Gallows?" said Harry Archer.

"Right out back on the creek bank," said Blalock. "You didn't see it through the alley on the way down here?"

"I was running to get out of the rain," said Harry Archer.

"Well, this dandy's going to be running if his man doesn't win this fight...maybe even if he does," said Blalock. "If I was managing O'Brien, I'd tell him to stretch it out. There's a lot of money on the line...this could end up in a riot or worse. What happened up in Taft?"

"I told you," said Harry Archer. "O'Brien knocked the local guy into next week, as you say, but now that you mention it, the fight lasted maybe three or four rounds."

"You see?" said Blalock. "Spar a while, maybe take a few shots, then get inside and boom...lights out...take the money and run."

"These men do not have to bet," said Jimmy Delaney.

"No, I guess not," said Blalock. "What's your point?"

"The man in the ring cannot force anyone to bet," said Jimmy Delaney. "If these men lose, they have no cause for complaint."

"My God, Jimmy, he's enticing them with odds they can't pass up," said Blalock.

"If that is true, why don't you place a bet?" said Jimmy Delaney.

"Because I know who's going to win," said Blalock.

"Are you sure?" said Jimmy Delaney.

"Of course, I'm sure," said Blalock. "Harry has seen O'Brien fight."

"But you know nothing of the lumberjack," said Jimmy Delaney. "It is no more logical than these other men. Either way, no one has cause for complaint."

"This dandy in the suit doesn't know anything about the lumberjack either," said Blalock. "He doesn't need to."

"They are being foolish and if their man is knocked out, they will blame the man in the ring rather than admit that they are foolish," said Jimmy Delaney. "It is the way of things."

"Sometimes you drive my crazy, Jimmy," said Blalock. "This guy is taking advantage of men with whiskey in their guts, money in their hands and nothing in their heads."

"It is the way of things," said Jimmy Delaney.

"What do you think, Harry?" said Blalock.

"I'm not putting any money on the lumberjack," said Harry Archer.

"Jesus, now it's both of you," said Blalock.

"The lumberjack doesn't have a prayer," said Harry Archer.

"You know, Jimmy, I've often wondered what you care about," said Blalock. "Now I know."

"I thought you always knew," said Jimmy Delaney.

Twenty-Eight

Incident at the El Rey

"Time's up," said the man in the ring. "Where's the management of this establishment?"

"Right here," said the bartender, standing by the curtain.

"Bring in your boy," said the man in the ring.

The bartender parted the curtain. "Right here," he said.

The lumberjack came through the curtain. He was about twenty-five years old, shirtless, barrel-chested and taller than six feet. His head and square jaw were shaved. He smiled, revealing strong teeth. His gloved hands punched the air. He walked toward the ring and men stepped aside and slapped him on the back.

"Jesus, he must weigh two-fifty," said Blalock. "He doesn't look like a pushover."

"He doesn't have a prayer," said Harry Archer. "When he wakes up, he'll wonder if he walked in front of a train."

The man in the ring tipped his derby hat. "You're a hell of a specimen, son...a worthy opponent from the look of you," he said.

The lumberjack scowled and continued to punch the air.

Paddy O'Brien had come through a door from the bar in the corner of the room. He stood motionless in the shadows of the corner, watching the lumberjack. He was of medium height and carried his two hundred pounds without effort. His chest expanded perceptibly over a flat, hard stomach and his thick red hair was slicked back over his head. He wore a gray leotard tied with a narrow green sash and black high-top boots of soft leather which followed the contour of his calves. He made his way to the ring. He did not acknowledge the crowd.

Jimmy Delaney stiffened. "Could it be?" he said.

"What?" said Blalock.

"Nothing...he seems to make his presence felt," said Jimmy Delaney.

"I told you," said Harry Archer. "That boy is going to be the heavyweight champion of the world."

"The contest will be conducted under Queensberry rules," shouted the man in the ring. The referee is Mister Sawyer, chosen by our host, the manager of this establishment. I am assured that Mister Sawyer is impartial, knows the rules and has not laid a bet on either contestant."

"On either contestant?" said Blalock. "There aren't any bets on O'Brien."

"A matter of clarity," said Harry Archer.

"Hunh," said Blalock.

"Mister Sawyer, the ring is yours," said the man in the checked suit.

Sawyer motioned both fighters to the center of the ring. He shook hands with Paddy O'Brien and then the lumberjack.

"Three minute rounds, one minute between rounds," said Sawyer. "No butting, biting, low blows or anything else I don't like. The fight is over when a man is down for the count of ten or retires voluntarily. My pocket watch is the official time piece. At the end of three minutes of boxing, I will call time and each man will retire to his corner for one minute of rest. Back to your corners now and come out boxing at my signal."

The first four rounds were familiar to Harry Archer. Paddy O'Brien attacked with sharp left jabs from a stooped crouch, looking for an opening to move inside. The lumberjack threw heavy blows, which Paddy O'Brien deflected with his gloves. By the middle of the fifth round the lumberjack was tiring, his face had noticeably reddened and blood trickled from his nose. Stalking his opponent from the crouch, Paddy O'Brien's left jab struck from a shorter range, snapping the lumberjack's head back.

"It won't be long now," said Harry Archer.

"This is a slaughter," said Blalock. "Look at the way he moves...and that jab would crack a brick wall. He's been throwing a few rights...powder puff. He's holding back, stringing this guy along. When does he throw the big one?"

"Don't worry," said Harry Archer.

In the sixth round a wild punch to the side of Paddy O'Brien's head sent him careening into the ropes. Cheers erupted from the crowd. Paddy O'Brien anchored himself with his powerful legs. The lumberjack lunged forward and Paddy O'Brien's right fist crashed into his jaw. The crowd gasped as the lumberjack staggered briefly and fell to the floor.

"Oh, Christ," said Blalock.

"Well, that's that," said Harry Archer.

Paddy O'Brien walked to a corner of the ring and waited. Sawyer did not start the count; he waved his hand, indicating that the fight was over. Three men who worked for the bartender revived the lumberjack with a rag soaked in spirits of ammonia and helped him to his feet. The man in the checked suit and the bartender, armed with a shotgun, came into the ring.

"We'll have no trouble," said the bartender. "The first man in the ring gets a face full of buckshot."

"So, the bartender is in on it," said Blalock. "Did this happen in Taft?"

"No," said Harry Archer. "The fight was outdoors and the crowd more dispersed."

The bartender, the man in the checked suit and Paddy O'Brien left the ring. They were joined by three more men with shotguns and moved in the direction of the door to the bar. The bartender and his three men walked backward, aiming the shotguns toward the crowd. They disappeared through the door.

"This is a fix," someone yelled.

"Get the lumberjack...what's his name? He threw the fight."

"Out of here...now," said Blalock.

He pushed Harry Archer and Jimmy Delaney through the curtain. The man in the checked suit and Paddy O'Brien were on the stairs to the upper floor. The bartender and his men stood at the bottom of the staircase.

"Go on...out of here...back to the hotel," said Blalock.

"Wait," said Jimmy Delaney.

"Wait, my ass," said Blalock. "No waiting...these fools could do anything."

"I'll catch up," said Jimmy Delaney.

"You'll catch up?" said Blalock. "What are you talking about, Jimmy...you can't stay here. That mob..."

"Move on," called the bartender.

Jimmy Delaney pulled his arm from Blalock's grip. He walked toward the bartender.

"Jimmy," said Blalock.

The bartender leveled the shotgun. "No closer," he said.

"I would like to see Mister O'Brien," said Jimmy Delaney.

The bartender laughed. "You must be nuts," he said. "Get the hell out of here while you still can."

"Christ, Jimmy, what are you doing?" said Blalock.

"This is not a good idea, Jimmy," said Harry Archer.

"Send one of these fellows up to Mister O'Brien's room," said Jimmy Delaney. "Tell him Jimmy is here."

"Boss, it's awful quiet back there," said one of the men. "You think they all went out the back?"

"One thing at a time," said the bartender. He regarded Jimmy Delaney. "You just stay where you are," he said.

"Should I go up, boss?" said the man.

"No, look out back," said the bartender.

The man walked across the room. He pulled back the curtain with the barrel of the shotgun.

"Nobody," he said. "They all went out the back. You don't think they strung up that lumberjack fellow, do you?"

"I don't care what they do, long as they don't do it in here," said the bartender. He had not taken his eyes off Jimmy Delaney. "What's O'Brien to you?" he said.

Jimmy Delaney hesitated. "I must be mistaken," he said. "We will go now."

"Yeah, you do that," said the bartender.

Twenty-Nine

Paddy O'Brien

The rain had stopped, leaving silhouettes of lingering clouds against a full moon. Shouting and laughter and the tinny sound of an upright piano filled the street from the Old Crow Saloon. Blalock paused at the head of the narrow alley next to the El Rey barber shop. He peered into the darkness toward the gallows deep in the alley on the bank of Cliff Creek.

"Well, it looks like they didn't hang the lumberjack," he said.

"Here's what I think happened," said Harry Archer. "That bartender, who's a lot more than a bartender, gave the lumberjack or the referee a certain sum of money to spread around when the trouble started. If we go across the street and look in on the party, we'll see one or both of them buying rounds for the house."

"You don't say," said Blalock.

"I do say," said Harry Archer.

They looked over the swinging doors of the Old Crow Saloon. The piano player had stopped and the railroad men had gathered around the lumberjack for his next account of the fight. Barmaids moved among the men, filling their beer mugs.

"I'd like to have that bartender in the union," said Blalock.

The Bon Ton was empty. Blalock, Harry Archer and Jimmy Delaney took a table in the back near the doorway to the kitchen. Harry Archer called the waiter and asked for three mugs of Anheuser beer. Jimmy Delaney laid money on the table. Harry Archer clipped the end of a cigar.

"So, what the hell was that back at the El Rey, Jimmy?"

said Blalock. "You walked up to four men with shotguns asking to see Paddy O'Brien."

Harry Archer struck a match and touched the end of the cigar. He shook out the match, dropped it to the floor and stepped on it.

"You haven't noticed the resemblance?" he said.

Blalock's eyes widened. "No, you're not serious," he said.

"How long since you've seen your brother, Jimmy?" said Harry Archer.

"It's seven years...before I came across," said Jimmy Delaney. "He was only twelve...almost thirteen."

"O'Brien...half brother?" said Harry Archer.

"His name is Michael," said Jimmy Delaney. "O'Brien is our mother's maiden name."

"I see," said Harry Archer. "You don't know why he's using that name and that's why you cut it off with the bartender."

"Aye," said Jimmy Delaney.

One of the bartender's men came in the front door. He scanned the room and approached the table.

"Paddy wants to see you," said the man.

"He cannot speak for himself?" said Jimmy Delaney.

"He has to be careful," said the man.

"As we all do," said Jimmy Delaney.

"Look, it's no skin off me," said the man. "He wants to see you...yes or no?"

"I'll be here for a while and then at the Anheuser Hotel across the street," said Jimmy Delaney.

The man nodded and left. Paddy O'Brien came in a few minutes later. The man in the checked suit and derby hat and another man dressed in a black three-piece suit were with him. Paddy O'Brien wore heavy worsted pants, a wool sweater and a wool cap. His eyes swept the room. He motioned for the other men to leave.

"Do you mind?" said Jimmy Delaney.

"We'll be at the hotel," said Blalock.

Paddy O'Brien approached the table, nodding toward

Blalock and Harry Archer. He sat in Blalock's chair, took off the cap and laid it on the table.

"It's a long time," said Jimmy Delaney."

"Aye, Jimmy, a long time," said Paddy O'Brien. "You'll be wondering about the name. Who would pay to see Michael Delaney in a boxing match?"

"You're very good," said Jimmy Delaney.

"I'm not running from the coppers or anyone else," said Michael Delaney. "It's like a stage name."

"A beer?" said Jimmy Delaney.

"I swore off it," said Michael Delaney, waving toward the waiter.

"Paddy O'Brien in the Bon Ton," said the waiter. "I saw the Morton fight in Spokane...you took him apart, I'll say. Are you going up against Johnson? It ain't right, him being the champ, and you're the one to take him."

"Could you bring me some coffee," said Michael Delaney. "No beer...in training, you know."

"Right away, Mister O'Brien, right away," said the waiter.

The waiter hurried away. He disappeared through the kitchen door and returned with a mug of coffee. Michael Delaney pointed to the coins on the table.

"A little something for you, as well," he said.

"Oh, no...Paddy O'Brien don't pay in my place," said the waiter. He looked toward Jimmy Delaney. "And his friends don't pay either," he said. "Can I get you another beer?"

"I'll just finish this one," said Jimmy Delaney.

"Well, I'll leave you to your privacy," said the waiter. "I'll see nobody bothers you. Just call if you need anything else." He backed away.

"Is it always like this?" said Jimmy Delaney.

"He's harmless...just a fellow who likes boxing," said Michael Delaney. He took a sip of coffee. "Ah, good... strong and hot," he said.

"Boxing...is it not dangerous?" said Jimmy Delaney.

"I'm fighting bums...big and slow and without skill," said Michael Delaney.

"It's the crowds," said Jimmy Delaney.

"You were there...you saw how it's done."

"Aye," said Jimmy Delaney. "It seems to me a close thing."

"Pa's dead, Jimmy...pickled liver," said Michael Delaney. "Johnny's in Castlerea still...he's to study for the priesthood."

"I hardly knew Johnny," said Jimmy Delaney. "He was just nine when I came across."

"I hated you for a long time," said Michael Delaney. "I hated you for Ma's death...and then I found out Pa lied about everything. He went to his grave with a lie on his lips...he's burning in hell."

"Legends are a burden to their sons," said Jimmy Delaney. "What do you know of your grandfather?"

"Big Tommy?" said Michael Delaney. "Pa did not speak of him. The old ones say he was a force of nature."

"And the one son left could not embrace it," said Jimmy Delaney.

"I came across two years now...just after Pa died," said Michael Delaney. "I went looking for you. The address in New York was in Pa's papers. I learned of his lies from Bill Bannister."

"Bill helped us through a hard time," said Jimmy Delaney. "Sure he told you about Tim being killed. We were in a foreign world with nothing to grasp. Pa went to pieces. Bill Bannister gave me the breathing room we needed. They don't come much better."

"At first I didn't believe him," said Michael Delaney. "And then I knew it was true."

"All of that is over now," said Jimmy Delaney.

"Sometimes I see Pa's face in the men I fight," said Michael Delaney.

"Let go of it," said Jimmy Delaney. "It is a poison that eats away your life from inside out."

"You don't know the things he said...I have written Johnny with the truth, but he will not hear it."

"He never will," said Jimmy Delaney.

"What do you mean?"

"You have to let go of it," said Jimmy Delaney.

"Don't you care that he killed Ma and blamed it on you?" said Michael Delaney.

"He was weak," said Jimmy Delaney.

"He was warned," said Michael Delaney.

"There is nothing to be done," said Jimmy Delaney. "Ma left the glen but not the foul ritual that does not allow escape from destruction."

"Doomed?" said Michael Delaney. "Is it doomed you're saying?"

"Pa had the right of a husband," said Jimmy Delaney. "Even Bill took this right as just...it is engrained."

"Right, you say," said Michael Delaney. "He was warned. What of Ma's right?"

"That is the foulness of it," said Jimmy Delaney. "Ma could not refuse him or leave him. In her world, it was the way of things."

"What world?" said Michael Delaney. Pa had a choice and he was not man enough to make the right choice."

"Hating him will not change that," said Jimmy Delaney. "You can only harm yourself."

"Why didn't you do something? You were there."

"I was too young and too late."

"Not too young to kill him."

"You can say that now," said Jimmy Delaney. "Could you have said it then? And can you say there was not burden enough to go around?"

Michael Delaney's brow furrowed. "You blame yourself?" he said.

"Even if not, can you say it would not have killed Ma in another way?"

"Aye, you're right...I know you're right," said Michael Delaney. "You always had the logic."

"I suppose," said Jimmy Delaney.

"Bill Bannister said that you attacked a priest," said Michael Delaney.

"I have not attacked anyone since then," said Jimmy Delaney.

"Do you hate the church?"

"I don't think about the church," said Jimmy Delaney. "In Ireland, I would hate it."

"I don't understand."

"I knew a man from Derry," said Jimmy Delaney. "He was sure the lads would rise up against the British. That day may come and yet it will not free them from the church. With no way to see from a closed room, the Irish are tormented by sin, waiting for death. Ma could not escape destruction by the church. If I offend, I'm sorry."

"It's nothing to offend...I don't practice it," said Michael Delaney. "You don't put any blame on Pa, do you?"

"You say he died with a lie on his lips," said Jimmy Delaney. "Did he refuse the rites?"

"Aye, he did," said Michael Delaney. "How did you know?"

"Payment...his only way to forgiveness for the unforgivable," said Jimmy Delaney. "When did Johnny decide on the priesthood?"

"Just after Pa died," said Michael Delaney. "Now I can see it."

"Payment...the sins of the father...always payment," said Jimmy Delaney.

"Enough of that, he's dead," said Michael Delaney. "Tell me about yourself. What have you been doing? I guess you can see what I'm doing."

"It's not much to tell," said Jimmy Delaney. "I've been two years working as a telegrapher for the railroad. I have a stake now...for college. My friend, Archer, an engineer for the railroad, has a brother...a teacher in Massachusetts. He will be my tutor for the entrance examination."

"I can't remember when you weren't studious," said Michael Delaney.

231

"Were you able to finish your schooling at the orphanage?"

"Aye, I received my certificate," said Michael Delaney. "When Pa returned, I was working in a brewery in Castlerea and learning to box. Pa went back to the village...digging the peat. After he died, I went to Galway, earned passage by boxing and came across."

"My friend, Archer has heard that you will challenge for the championship," said Jimmy Delaney. "Is it true?"

"I've not had experience enough with professionals," said Michael Delaney. "These tour matches with lumberjacks and construction workers will not get me to the title. Johnson is fast and smart...he wears everyone down. I have the stamina and power to knock him out... it's the skill I need to get inside his defenses. He's to fight Jeffries later this year or next. I will be there."

"The fellows who were here when you came in," said Jimmy Delaney. "Blalock thinks Jeffries will win and Archer says not."

"Jeffries is the great white hope...hoping against hope," said Michael Delaney. "Johnson may fall and break his leg getting into the ring."

"You sound like Archer," said Jimmy Delaney.

"It's just a payday for everyone," said Michael Delaney.

"How can you arrange matches with professional boxers?" said Jimmy Delaney.

"Another manager," said Michael Delaney. "Andre, Andre LaPlante...not his real name, of course...we have made money, but he cares only about money, not the championship."

"Who was the other man?" said Jimmy Delaney.

"Bartok?" said Michael Delaney. "LaPlante has enemies."

"His enemies are not your enemies?"

"It's not to worry, Jimmy...I'm careful."

"He looks menacing."

"Bartok is a thug," said Michael Delaney. "He is paid from LaPlante's share. He stays away from me."

"May I say something?"

"Aye, of course."

"This LaPlante...he has no loyalty to you," said Jimmy Delaney.

Michael Delaney laughed. "I don't expect loyalty from LaPlante, Jimmy," he said. "After the tour, I will have a good stake. I will cut loose and go back to New York. First-class gyms have first-class trainers and good trainers know good managers."

"He will let you go without argument? Without you, what is he?"

"The tour ends in two months time," said Michael Delaney. "I will be in New York in the summer. How will I find you? Where will you be?"

"I will write to Bill," said Jimmy Delaney.

"Aye, a good idea," said Michael Delaney. "Your tour ends where?"

"Somewhere on the coast," said Michael Delaney. "It's a good stake I'll have...worth it, fighting all these bums. I'll treat myself to luxury accommodations and fine dining on the train." He took a sip of coffee and grimaced. "Um, cold," he said. "It's as well I shouldn't drink this...can't sleep."

"Where do you go next?" said Jimmy Delaney.

"A place called Tekoe," said Michael Delaney. "We need to get there early so LaPlante can get the lay of the land, find another bum and raise a crowd."

"You'll take care?" said Jimmy Delaney.

Michael Delaney picked up his cap, rose and held out his hand.

"I'll see you in New York in the summer," he said.

Jimmy Delaney rose and took his bother's hand. Michael Delaney's grip was firm.

Thirty

The Journal

The *North Coast Limited* stopped under the train shed at Minneapolis Union Depot with a slight lurch. Harry Archer had traded his khakis for a three-piece suit. He put the well-worn fedora on his head, slid his arms into an overcoat and lifted his valise.

"Well, here I am, ready to do battle for the trestles," said Harry Archer.

"Someday I would like to hear the story of your hat," said Jimmy Delaney.

"Do you think the hat has a story?" said Harry Archer.

"Aye, it does," said Jimmy Delaney.

"Let's say for now that this hat goes where I go," said Harry Archer. "You have your tickets to Amherst?"

"Aye, I'm thanking you for the accommodations," said Jimmy Delaney.

"Don't forget...you have the compartment all the way to Springfield," said Harry Archer.

"And they will move the car in Chicago from Union Station to LaSalle Street Station and attach it to the Boston train which will stop at Springfield the next morning," said Jimmy Delaney. "And I will take a connecting train from Springfield to Amherst and then a coach to the school."

"You wouldn't think I can walk out on a trestle two hundred feet above a gorge and check rivet joints," said Harry Archer. "But I do it all the time."

"You worry for others," said Jimmy Delaney. "It is not a bad thing."

"Did you check your trunks through to Amherst?"

"Aye, all the way through," said Jimmy Delaney.

"Well, I'm off," said Harry Archer. "Give my regards to

my idiotic sibling. He's expecting you. Oh, and remember me to your brother when you see him...hell of a fighter."

Jimmy Delaney took Harry Archer's extended hand. Harry Archer released his grip and went through the door into the aisle.

"I'll be stuck in Idaho until we finish the trestles," he said. "After that, I don't know...with the railroad finished, I'll probably be building bridges for all the new roads they're putting in these days. I'll let you know where I end up."

"You know where I'll be," said Jimmy Delaney.

Harry Archer rapped on the window of the compartment from the platform. Jimmy Delaney waved and watched until Harry Archer disappeared into the crowd.

The Mississippi River towns of Winona Junction, La Crosse, Prairie du Chien, East Dubuque and Savanna gave way to farms separated by patches of forest and then to row houses and factories in the western fringe of Chicago. The *North Coast Limited* entered the north concourse of Union Station just after noon. Jimmy Delaney's Pullman car was towed through a maze of switches, backed into the train shed of LaSalle Street Station and parked to await assembly of the *Twentieth Century Limited* for the overnight run to Albany, where the train would split into sections for morning arrivals in New York and Boston.

Jimmy Delaney answered the knock on the compartment door.

"Does you want to get out?" said the porter. "We don't leave 'til three forty-five."

"I have work," said Jimmy Delaney. "Does it disrupt your duties for me to stay here?"

"Oh, no, it don't bother me," said the porter. "Power generator plugged in...all your lights, heating, everything. The other fellow that got out at Minneapolis...does you want fresh linen on that bed for tonight? I can put fresh linen on that bed."

"Oh, no...I have the upper I used last night," said Jimmy Delaney.

"Well, some folks, they doesn't care for climbing the ladder and 'specially they doesn't like climbing down at night," said the porter. "Most folks prefers the lower."

"The upper is fine," said Jimmy Delaney.

"All right, then, there's fresh coffee at the end of the car," said the porter. "And just so you know, they's going to be some jostling around in a while when they start making up the Century."

"Aye," said Jimmy Delaney.

"Beg your pardon...is you from Ireland?" said the porter.

"Aye, seven years now," said Jimmy Delaney. "How about you...are you Irish?"

"You joshin' me?" said the porter.

"Aye, I am," said Jimmy Delaney.

"Is I from Ireland," said the porter. "Is they any black peoples in Ireland?"

"Just ruddy faces with red hair, like me," said Jimmy Delaney.

"My friend, Joe Murphy...he a dining car steward... he come over from Ireland. He say the Irish is held back. They white peoples but they still held back. How does you fair...being here, that is?"

"People have helped me...both Irish and not...but that's not always the way things are," said Jimmy Delaney.

"I has an easy feeling about you," said the porter. "You know any black peoples?"

"Aye, Willy Gantz...we rode the freights together," said Jimmy Delaney.

"You a bindle stiff?" said the porter. "You joshin' me... bindle stiffs don't ride in no compartment."

"Only for a time," said Jimmy Delaney.

"Now I has an uneasy feeling," said the porter. "Nothin' bad happen, did it?"

"Nothing bad happened," said Jimmy Delaney. "Willy Gantz went back home...he had been away a long time."

The porter nodded. "Sometime it seem like goin' back might be the best thing," he said. "Well, the Century sold out and we got some spillover. I best be cleaning these rooms."

"Come back if you get the chance...a late night coffee, if you like," said Jimmy Delaney.

"That mighty nice, but it against the rules," said the porter. "The conductor...if he come through...well..."

"I understand," said Jimmy Delaney.

The porter nodded and backed out of the compartment. The door closed with an audible click.

Jimmy Delaney took a loose-leaf notebook from the rucksack and laid it out flat on the compartment table. He had started the journal during the first winter in Wallace. The entries were generally chronological with narratives connecting the stories in time and substance. The sections were labeled Big Tommy, Big Jimmy, O'Donnell, A Coachman in Galway, Murphy, Roache, Bannister, Weiss, Monaghan, Gantz, Man in a Hobo Camp, Men in Trains, Hessler, Sluman, Blalock, Archer and Paddy O'Brien, the most recent entry.

Jimmy Delaney turned the pages, reading casually. He settled into the upholstered chair and took a pencil from the rucksack. He began to write:

May, 1909 - Wallace to Amherst
Note to Willy Gantz

Well, Willy, I am really riding the cushions now, thanks to Archer. This compartment has a couch which expands into a bed, an easy chair, another bed that comes out of the ceiling, a dining table and a toilet with a wash basin. Archer prefers a drawing room, enough space for four people, but he cannot overcome the guilt. To alleviate the guilt, which he claims to be a figment of my imagination, he settles for compartments.

He will not book anything smaller and thus does not travel in bedrooms, roomettes or berths and the prospect of riding in coach would be cause for panic. In South Dakota he once rode a flatcar from Mobridge to McLaughlin - 26 miles - and thereafter he decreed that all trains between these two points would carry a caboose with a chair - a chair with a cushion, not a straight-back chair with a flat wooden seat and certainly not a crate turned on end. So, in case you wonder why I am traveling in a moving hotel room, it is Archer. Actually, my distress is amusing, don't you think?

Since my last note, I have met my younger brother, Michael. It was a chance meeting, two years now since he came over from Ireland. Michael is a stout lad of nineteen who earns his living as a boxer. He has a yen to go far in boxing and he certainly is a good boxer. Still, I would sooner he took up coal mining or factory work - his associates are the kind of men one should keep at arm's length. I know, you needn't give me that look - I should have enough to do seeing to my own affairs.

Jimmy Delaney read what he had written and laid the pencil on the table. He went to the end of the Pullman car and ran hot coffee from the urn into a mug. The car lurched. He stood in the vestibule to watch the route over track and switches as his car was assembled into the *Twentieth Century Limited.*

The premier train of the New York Central Railroad – mail cars, sleeping cars, lounge cars and a diner – waited in the train shed of LaSalle Street Station behind a locomotive with six eighty-inch driving wheels and its tender loaded with thirty-six thousand pounds of coal and twelve thousand gallons of water. Another train, the *Pennsylvania Special*, flagship of the Pennsylvania Railroad, waited in the south concourse of Union Station some blocks away. The trains left minutes apart, counted down on the synchronized watches of conductors, engineers and dispatchers, passed beneath the overpass which carried Roosevelt Road and converged at Englewood Station in Chicago's South Side. There, sitting side by side, the trains waited for highballs to commence the daily race out of the city through the Indiana countryside. At the signal, the two contestants plunged into a corridor of parallel tracks cleared of all other traffic. When the tracks of the Pennsylvania Railroad diverged to the south, Jimmy Delaney waved to a man on the *Pennsylvania Special* and returned to the compartment.

Allegiance

There are certain men who give life to strength and weakness, kindness, revolution, fear and revenge and despair, confusion and resolve in the service of good and evil, if such things exist. Can my knowledge of men I admire ever be the equal of men I do not? Even if I cannot find respect for Big Jimmy, I can find sympathy for the son of Big Tommy and attribute this awakening to the hardness in the face of my brother. I can find sympathy for the man who kills the man who kills his father, even if that man is condemned to despair in payment for revenge. I can find the coachman from the underclass clinging to the false dignity of a uniform, the fear that causes an old man to jump from a train and the demands on a conductor who leaves his body by the track. I can find the vanity that causes one man to shun a stranger of lower station and the liberation of another to aid that same stranger and the motives that cause a man to murder

239

another man and join that man's comrades only to betray their trust. I can find both justice and retribution in the destruction of that man at the hand of those he betrays. I can find all of this, but how do I find O'Donnell, Murphy, Bannister, Weiss, Monaghan, Gantz, Blalock, Archer? There is no detachment in allegiance.

Note to Myself

Willy Gantz does not believe in a god and he does not believe in man. I can think of nothing to explain his interest in me unless he is partial to the Irish for a reason he did not mention. If you were to say, "Well, the white man can just walk away," Blalock would laugh in your face. Willy Gantz would say, "I sho hates to give up that garden patch."

"Yes, come in," said Jimmy Delaney in response to a light tap on the compartment door.

The porter opened the door enough to extend his head into the compartment.

"The diner is serving dinner now...three cars ahead... or they has waiters serving all the rooms," said the porter. "Does you care to eat here or go to the diner?"

"Here, if they don't mind," said Jimmy Delaney. "Something light...just soup and bread and coffee."

"They has a good potato soup with ham," said the porter.

"That sounds fine," said Jimmy Delaney. "I'm thanking you."

The door closed. A few minutes later a dining car steward brought a tray with a large bowl of thick potato soup with diced ham, bread, iced lettuce with cucumber and tomato and a pot of coffee.

Jimmy Delaney read through the journal, making

notes as he ate. He left the tray in the aisle outside the compartment and sat next to the window under the blue night light. He stared into the darkness. After two hours he returned to the journal:

A Scent of Destiny

Long ago, it seems now, O'Donnell said that destiny is something you say because chance does not bring comfort and ever the master of shaded meaning, he also said that destiny is what you make it. It has occurred to me that destiny may not be what you make it - if free will is not free, what follows is destiny. Bannister could not leave the city, Pa could not cope with Big Tommy, Ma could not save herself, Willy Gantz went home to recover his past. In all of this is the past. Is destiny the past lingering in memory?

A few minutes before two in the morning the *Twentieth Century Limited* passed slowly through a deserted train shed and came to stop in a service area. Jimmy Delaney made his way to the vestibule and opened the window. The night air was cold and damp. The locomotive vented steam as the night crew filled the tender with coal and water. The lights along the train shed were shrouded in early morning mist and the aura of tranquility seemed unmindful of men rushing to service the water and waste tanks of the sleeping cars. After ten minutes the train eased out of the yard into the night. Jimmy Delaney closed the window and returned to the compartment. His bed swayed with the steady rhythm of high speed and the music of rails beneath him hastened sleep.

241

Thirty-One

Citadel

The professor, holding a sheaf of papers, stood by the window gazing on an unbroken chain of fields and forests from the hilltop. He had never tired of autumn in the Mohawk Valley just before the first snow. He turned and held up the sheaf of papers.

"Mister Slater, what did you think of Mister Delaney's story?" he said.

"Rubbish," said Slater.

"Indeed," said the professor. "And on what do you base this judgment?"

"Sentimentality," said Slater. "The poor waif befriended by the sailor just before he dies...his last act a noble gesture. What rot."

"A last act of noble gesture," said the professor. "And how did you find this theme?"

"The sailor befriends the waif and then dies in a storm," said Slater.

"Mister Slater, you amaze me," said the professor. "The sailor had no foreknowledge of his death."

"Maybe he did," said Slater. "Maybe he goes around doing good deeds because he could die at any time and he wants to go to heaven. Maybe he dons clean underwear every morning for the same reason."

"I see," said the professor. "Read the relevant passages supporting these conclusions."

"It's just my opinion," said Slater.

"Unsubstantiated opinions are of no use to us, Mister Slater," said the professor. "Why don't you simply say that you don't like the story?"

"I don't like the story," said Slater.

"Why?" said the professor.

"Do I need a reason?" said Slater.

"Why are you attending college, Mr. Slater?" said the professor.

"I am expected to attend college before assuming control of my family's company," said Slater.

"I see...four years of seasoning up here on the hill," said the professor.

"Yes," said Slater.

"Someone else," said the professor. "Mister Edwards, what is the central theme of Mister Delaney's story?"

"Gratitude," said Edwards. "It is a simple tale of a good deed remembered. The remembrance is symbolized by the sailor's coat."

"A boy starved for kindness dwells on a single act of compassion," said the professor. "Isn't all this rather sentimental?"

"Yes, but it is not necessarily a flaw," said Edwards. "The example is Dickens...that Oliver Twist receives his reward for purity of heart does not detract from the social conditions the author is attempting to expose."

"So, Mister Edwards, you do not subscribe to the notion that Dickens is writing to the sensibilities of his audience."

"In what way?" said Edwards.

"Hope, Mister Edwards, hope...that most necessary of sensibilities," said the professor. "In the midst of depravity there is hope...the villains and scoundrels receive their just punishment and Master Twist is returned to his rightful place. Do you see another theme in Mister Delaney's story?"

"I don't think so, no," said Edwards.

"Oh, come now, Mister Edwards," said the professor. "Why did the sailor take the boy to the engine room?"

"Frankly, I thought of those scenes as padding," said Edwards.

"I'll put it another way," said the professor. "The sailor and the boy are both Irish."

"Just to irritate the Scotsman in the engine room?" said Edwards.

"And to indoctrinate the boy with a subversive view of the British," said the professor. "The sailor is recruiting. Now, what is the boy's motive?"

"Curiosity?" said Edwards.

"And that his Irish descent is coincidental," said the professor.

"Are you saying that the main theme is not compassion?" said Edwards.

"Yes, of course, kindness and appreciation of kindness are themes," said the professor. "However, as I see it, the main theme is the interplay of motive."

"How do you mean?" said Edwards.

"Human behavior is not simple, Mister Edwards," said the professor. "The sailor cares for the boy and at the same time solicits the boy for the revolution. The boy, who cares nothing for the revolution, uses the sailor to satisfy his curiosity and at the same time remains grateful for the sailor's kindness and the gift of the coat. It does not have to be one thing or another."

"I disagree," said another student. "The main theme is guilt."

"Explain, Mister Markham," said the professor.

"There is a subconscious clash of wills won by the boy at the expense of the sailor and the price of winning is guilt," said Markham.

"How so?" said the professor.

"The sailor, attempting to solicit the boy, is unaware that he himself is solicited for curiosity. The boy, whose goal is the engine room, never reveals his disdain for the revolution and thus wins the clash of wills. It is only after the death of the sailor that the coat gains significance. The boy's attachment to the coat symbolizes guilt, not gratitude."

"Interesting," said the professor.

"What do you say, Delaney?" said Edwards.

"It is not for me to say," said Jimmy Delaney. "You may take from it what you will."

"And with that, we shall adjourn," said the professor.

Jimmy Delaney packed his rucksack amid the rustle of papers, the sliding of chairs on the wooden floor and the din of talk. Averse to the involuntary flow of crowds, he was usually the last one to leave a room. When the room had almost cleared, he stood, straightened his tie and habitually pulled his waistcoat taut before sliding his arms into the sleeves of Murphy's coat. At the door he heard his name called and turned.

"Was it gratitude or guilt?" said the professor.

Jimmy Delaney smiled.

"Don't forget our appointment at three," said the professor.

Jimmy Delaney nodded and walked toward the stairs. Outside the building he drew a thin watch from his waistcoat pocket and rubbed his thumb along the gold fob, a gift from Sherman Archer. He put the watch away and started across the campus toward the common dining hall.

"Hello, Jimmy," said a voice from the portico of the chapel.

Jimmy Delaney turned and walked toward the voice.

"Blalock," he said. "Where have you been? It has been so long...I was afraid something had happened to you."

"I'm fine...just moving around a lot," said Blalock. "I was in the neighborhood...you have time?"

"Of course," said Jimmy Delaney. "You would ask me that?"

"Well, I'm out of my element here," said Blalock.

Jimmy Delaney took Blalock by the arm and led him to a concrete bench next to the sidewalk. They sat on the bench and Jimmy Delaney lowered the rucksack to the grass.

"Sometimes I think I am as well," he said.

"What...out of your element?" said Blalock. "You were born for it, Jimmy."

"I haven't heard anything," said Jimmy Delaney.

"I didn't know what to think...I was afraid the Pinkertons..."

"Oh please, Jimmy, a Pinkerton can't find his own ass," said Blalock. "You're looking good...suit and tie... and you still have the seaman's coat, I see."

"The dress is formal here, at least in class and dining hall," said Jimmy Delaney.

"How do like college?" said Blalock.

"I've just started my third year," said Jimmy Delaney. "I miss some things and there are too many laudy daws, but this is what I've always wanted."

"Laudy daws?" said Blalock.

"An old Irish expression...those from wealthy families and a high opinion of themselves," said Jimmy Delaney. "They don't bother me much any longer. How about you... are you still with the union?"

"You're the only college man I know, Jimmy, said Blalock.

"You know Archer," said Jimmy Delaney.

"Archer...how is he?" said Blalock.

"He's building mountain roads in Colorado," said Jimmy Delaney. "He's been through here several times. His parents live in Albany...they're getting on now."

"Archer is a top-notch man," said Blalock.

"I know," said Jimmy Delaney.

"I don't know if I should bring this up," said Blalock. "Old wounds and all...but I was sorry as hell to hear about Michael."

"He's working in a steel mill, but not being able to box makes him angry," said Jimmy Delaney. "He went to the gym for a time, but then gave it up. How did you know of his trouble?"

"I was in Pittsburgh when it happened," said Blalock. "There was a piece in the paper...they said his hands were smashed with a hammer."

"The bones in his hands were broken," said Jimmy Delaney. "He has good use of his hands for most things, but he can never box again. That is what they intended."

"Why did they do it?" said Blalock.

"It's a question like that...from you?"

"I guess not," said Blalock.

"Don't worry about Michael," said Jimmy Delaney. "He can't box but he can work himself into something else."

"It's just a damn shame, that's all," said Blalock.

"A lot of things are, Blalock," said Jimmy Delaney. "You know it more than most."

"Yeah...well..."

"Have you gotten back to Idaho?" said Jimmy Delaney. "I've almost forgotten what Wallace looks like."

"Once, a little over a year ago...before the fire," said Blalock. "I've heard the fire burned down the whole south hill...everything on Bank between First and Fourth and most of the east end as well...didn't get to downtown, though. Charlie is fine and Belle and the depot and union hall."

"Archer told me there was not much damage to the railroad," said Jimmy Delaney. "He got the steel trestles done just in time."

"He was there?"

"No, he had already gone. You remember Grand Forks."

"How could I forget?" said Blalock.

"Gone," said Jimmy Delaney. "And with the railroad completed, it won't come back. We were a part of history, Blalock."

"Some history," said Blalock.

"So, Charlie...you saw him," said Jimmy Delaney.

Oh, yes, Charlie is fine," said Blalock. "He gets plenty of oats and light loads...morning rounds with the ice wagon and back to the barn. Some things go like you hope. And Belle, she was still walking down the street like a lady...head up, looking straight ahead."

"I always wondered if Belle realized that the fences in

front of her house and the brothel gave her away," said Jimmy Delaney.

"Same fence...scraped and painted white at the same time every year," said Blalock. "Sure, she realized it... putting up those fences the way she did was the whole point...kiss my ass."

"Sounds like Belle," said Jimmy Delaney.

"So, Jimmy, what are you going to do after college?" said Blalock.

"I've been writing," said Jimmy Delaney. "Short stories and class assignments so far...but if I'm any good, I think I have something to say."

"Well, you've certainly read enough and seen enough," said Blalock.

"You're a long way from the coal mines, aren't you?" said Jimmy Delaney.

"I took a leave of absence," said Blalock. "I'm going up to Lawrence, Massachusetts. There's trouble brewing in the textile mills, Jimmy. The union up there wanted me to lend a hand."

"Do you think I've stopped reading the papers?" said Jimmy Delaney. "The Wobblies have been in Lawrence for some time now and there are probably more Pinkertons than Wobblies. Why did you leave Idaho? I must have forgotten."

"No, the skilled workers," said Blalock. "You know what I think of the Wobblies...pie-in-the-sky dreamers. Those idiots don't even believe in written contracts...they take the edge off the class struggle, don't you see. I'll tell you though, Jimmy, somebody is going to have to do something about the immigrants in the mills. They live like rats in a cage on bread, molasses and beans. Half of them are dead by the age of twenty-five and half of their children before the age of six. The mills just drag out the bodies and round up more on the Boston docks. That kind of thing...it's barbaric."

"You've always had a steady hand, Blalock," said Jimmy Delaney.

"The hell with that, Jimmy," said Blalock. "The more you try to be reasonable, the more they stomp on you. It's time they got stomped."

"They will bring in the army," said Jimmy Delaney. "What happened to your mother and brothers..."

"The public will be outraged," said Blalock.

"No, they won't," said Jimmy Delaney.

"Well, how do you stop it?" said Blalock.

"I don't know," said Jimmy Delaney.

Blalock took a deep breath and blew out the air slowly. He stood.

"Well, maybe we can get a decent contract for the skilled labor," he said.

Jimmy Delaney stood. "Do you have to go so soon?" he said. "Can you take time for lunch?"

"I'd better get back to the train station," said Blalock. "They're expecting me up there in Massachusetts tonight. Walk with me down to the road."

Jimmy Delaney and Blalock waited at the end of Campus Road for the carriage which connected the college to the village along College Hill Road. The carriage came into view at the crest of the hill. Blalock stepped into College Hill Road and held up his hand. The coachman pulled up and Blalock opened the carriage door and put his foot on the running board. After a firm and wordless handshake, Blalock settled into the seat. Jimmy Delaney closed the door and nodded to the coachman, who snapped his rein lightly. The carriage continued down the hill toward the village.

After a troubled lunch in the dining hall, Jimmy Delaney went to his residence hall and took out the journal.

October, 1911 - Blalock

Blalock stopped by today. I have not seen him since Grand Forks and our turn around Adair Loop for the railroad trestles. Blalock is thinner, gaunt almost, and nervous. He laughed a bit about Belle McNair's fences, but he is restless and troubled. I don't bring it up - he would deny it in any case. He travels to Lawrence, Massachusetts. He is consulting with the union representing skilled workers in the textile mills and yet he talks of the unskilled immigrants. He still denounces the Wobblies as inept, but the trade unions ignore the immigrants who have no skills, do not speak English and whose numbers grow steadily. Blalock is a man of steady temperament versed in the art of the possible, but he will never forget what happened to his family - he despises the system he is obliged to serve. The plight of the immigrants and the willful stupidity of the mill owners build in a man like Blalock and will test him as nothing else I can imagine. He enters the maelstrom and I fear for him.

At three in the afternoon Jimmy Delaney knocked on the door of the professor's office.

"Come," shouted the professor.

Jimmy Delaney opened the door and went in.

"Ah, Mister Delaney, have a seat," said the professor.

Jimmy Delaney sat in the straight-back chair in front of the professor's desk.

The professor opened a drawer and took out a sheaf of papers. He straightened the sheets and laid them on the desk.

"This is a type-written copy of your seaman's story," he said. "I would like to publish it in the college magazine. As you know, the magazine has wide circulation in the literary world."

"Thank you, I'm very grateful," said Jimmy Delaney.

"Your work has improved steadily since you were in my English composition class two years ago," said the professor. "Frankly, with your background, I didn't hold out much hope...a snobbery for which I admonish myself every time I do it. In any case, this story shows subtlety and maturity. You must work very hard."

Jimmy Delaney did not reply.

"Well then, that's all," said the professor. "I will send you a proof when the edited version is ready."

"Edited?" said Jimmy Delaney. "If I may ask, how will the story be edited?"

"In the usual way...grammatically and for clarity," said the professor.

"The seaman is Irish," said Jimmy Delaney. "His manner of speech..."

"I am aware of dialect, Mister Delaney," said the professor.

"I'm sorry, I did not mean..."

"It's all right," said the professor.

"If I may ask one more thing," said Jimmy Delaney. "How will the story be edited for clarity? How is it unclear?"

"It is difficult to discern your meaning, as was evident in class this morning," said the professor.

"That is how I intended it," said Jimmy Delaney.

"You do not wish to be understood?" said the professor.

"I have tried to allow for different points of view," said Jimmy Delaney. "You may take from it what you will."

The professor leaned back and swiveled his chair toward the window. He cleaned his glasses with a handkerchief from his coat pocket. After a few moments he turned his chair back toward Jimmy Delaney.

"How many drafts did you write?" he said.

"About twenty, I would say," said Jimmy Delaney.

"All right, Mister Delaney, I will have the story published as it is," said the professor. "You are aware, of course, that it will be reviewed. What will you do if the critics do not understand it?"

"I had not considered that," said Jimmy Delaney.

"Well, you may be compelled to consider it," said the professor. "Or you may not. We will publish the story and gauge the reaction."

"Thank you," said Jimmy Delaney. "I had hoped to have something in the magazine eventually."

"What are you working on now?" said the professor.

"Two men traveling on the rails encounter another man in a hobo camp," said Jimmy Delaney.

"Give me a summary," said the professor.

"I'd rather not at this time," said Jimmy Delaney.

"May I see the finished story?" said the professor.

"Of course, thank you," said Jimmy Delaney.

"Well, on your way, Mister Delaney," said the professor. "I will send you proofs in about one week."

Jimmy Delaney rose, pulled his waistcoat taut and buttoned Murphy's coat. He ran his hand along the sleeve, smoothing the nap of the wool.

"Thank you again," he said.

"Is that the coat?" said the professor.

"Yes, it is," said Jimmy Delaney.

"You pass your hand over the wool in a very deliberate way," said the professor. "I have seen you do it before."

"I wasn't aware of it," said Jimmy Delaney.

"The coat is never far away," said the professor.

"No," said Jimmy Delaney.

"Good day, Mister Delaney," said the professor.

Jimmy Delaney nodded and went through the door. He walked along the corridor toward the stairs, carrying himself more erect than usual.

Thirty-Two

Bread and Roses

A man wearing overalls and a heavy coat traveled from Lawrence by train in a snow storm. The man knew Jimmy Delaney's residence hall and room number. He climbed the stairs to the third floor and knocked on the door. Twenty minutes later the man trudged through blowing snow to the intersection of Campus Road and College Hill Road, took the carriage to the village and the trolley to the train station. There he waited for the next eastbound train to Albany and then Boston and then Lawrence. He did not long tarry on the way, thinking himself needed in the strike of bread and roses.

March, 1912

Dear Harry,

I feel so low and angry. Blalock is dead. If you have kept up with the Lawrence textile strike, you know that the Wobblies have been moving the children of striking mill workers out of town. You will also know that the militia and police converged on the train station with clubs and started beating the women and children and dragging them away. A friend of Blalock's came all the way here in the snow to tell me that Blalock was one of men trying to stop it. He was clubbed and then shot by the police. I'm just angry at everything right now, Harry - the Wobblies, whose only goal is revolution and if they were to gain power, could not govern an outhouse - the trade unions, playing into their hands - the shortsightedness of the mill owners, the brutality of the police. I even find myself angry with Blalock, who knew that all authority is self-serving. He always hoped that these atrocities would outrage the public. Shakespeare would say that public outrage is full of sound and fury, signifying nothing. And therein is the fallacy of hope - the death of our friend is meaningless, Harry. I cannot stop thinking of our time in Grand Forks. It was a moment so brief and it will never come again . Goddamn it, Harry, Goddamn it.

Thirty-Three

The Drawing Room

May, 1916

Dear Harry,

Your letter arrived today. I have not kept up with events in Ireland and all I know of the Easter Rising comes from the newspaper. However, one thing is certain - the stupidity of the British in executing the leaders will ensure their sainthood and embolden the Sinn Féin.

You remember when I told you that Michael left Pittsburgh for New York. Bill Bannister tells me he became involved with the Irish Republicans and just last week went back to Ireland. He could never find a place for himself outside of boxing. I'm afraid he will be drafted into the British army and die on some French battlefield or join the Sinn Féin and die in a civil war. Why do men search so diligently for a way to die? Well, Michael is 26 years old and I cannot live his life.

Like you, I have discovered that I cannot just build roads and bridges forever. My time in college was everything I thought it would be and my extra three years here have been very productive for me. I have stories in good magazines and the Willy Gantz novel is well along, although I think the end will be a hard slog. So where is the rub? My life is too sedentary and I am not cut out to be a tutor or a teaching assistant. You were right, of course - Sherman is at home in the cloistered life, but for me it is tedious and routine. I suppose my place is among men who struggle rather than *those for whom success or failure has no lasting consequence. Old Teddy once said that only men in the arena can know triumph and if they fail, at least they are not timid souls who know neither victory nor defeat - fearless words, even if somewhat hollow from a man born to money.*

My trunks are already gone - posting this letter will be the last thing I do before boarding the train for California. I have a compartment, of course, not wishing to inherit from you a case of drawing room guilt - oh, I forgot, that is a figment of my imagination. I will settle in Sacramento for the time being and work as a free-lance reporter and finish the book. Let me know your plans - General Delivery in Sacramento for now. I will send an address when I have one.

As always, Jimmy

Halos encasing the lights highlighted the humid air in the train shed. The rucksack from County Roscommon and a small suitcase lay on the brick platform at Jimmy Delaney's feet. Murphy's coat and a wool cap from Donegal dulled the chill of early evening.

The locomotive began as a silent bright light in the distance and entering the station vied for the ear against the iron wheels of luggage wagons and the names of cities echoing through the train shed from public address speakers. Jimmy Delaney hung the rucksack over his shoulder and picked up the suitcase as the locomotive passed him. Venting steam spilled across the platform, driving the curious from the track. Jimmy Delaney waved to the engineer and walked along the platform. His home for the next three nights was the fourth car behind the tender. A porter wearing an overcoat stood on the platform beside the stair well. He had just finished cleaning the handrails with a cloth. Jimmy Delaney presented his ticket.

"Compartment A for Sacramento," said the porter. "Well sir, you will be pleased to hear that somebody messed up...compartment A was sold again to a Denver passenger getting on in Rochester. You has been assigned to our drawing room...no extra charge."

Jimmy Delaney laughed.

"It's a fine room, sir," said the porter.

"Oh, I'm sure it is," said Jimmy Delaney. "I was thinking of a friend of mine who would like to travel in drawing rooms but doesn't."

"Well, this here our finest room...spoil you for sure," said the porter. "And you has it all the way to Sacramento."

"That's fine, thank you," said Jimmy Delaney.

"Take a right, straight on down the aisle past the berths," said the porter. "The drawing room is at the end of the aisle. Be facing you...DR right on the door."

"Thank you," said Jimmy Delaney.

"The dining car is serving...two cars back," said the porter. "You can put away your things and go right on back. Just swing around into the aisle past the two compartments and the men's lavatory and keep going through the next sleeper. After you has had your dinner, I'll be around to get you set up for the night."

Jimmy Delaney opened the drawing room door. To his left was a door to the closet and toilet facilities. To his right was a couch backed by a wall against the aisle with recessed lighting. In front of him was a table with two easy chairs. A pewter vase with a red rosebud and a water pitcher with four stemmed glasses had been placed on a linen cloth in the center of the table. A double bed, turned down, occupied the outside wall beneath two windows with the shades drawn. The pillow lay under a reading light mounted in the forward wall. The room was comfortably warm.

Jimmy Delaney tossed his hat, the rucksack and

suitcase on the couch and hung Murphy's coat in the closet. He sat in one of the easy chairs.

"Well, Willy, this looks like the top of the mountain," he said. "If I let slip and Harry Archer finds out, I'll never live it down. On the other hand..."

Steadying himself against the motion of the train, Jimmy Delaney pulled his waistcoat taut and opened the door into the dining car. A steward carrying a menu approached. His hair was trimmed to a moderate length and parted in the middle. He wore a white shirt with a high stiff collar and black bow tie, a dark blue vest and black trousers. Behind him were rows of tables for four on one side of the car and tables for two on the other. Pewter vases with red rosebuds sat on the tables next to the windows. The car was paneled in red mahogany and the dining chairs were upholstered in maroon velvet. Each table was lighted by a chandelier suspended from the ceiling. The aroma of roast beef and a low din of conversation permeated the warm humid air.

"Welcome to the Commodore," said the steward. "Are you dining alone?"

"Yes, I'm alone," said Jimmy Delaney.

"We have a table with another gentleman," said the steward. "Will that be satisfactory?"

"Fine," said Jimmy Delaney.

Jimmy Delaney followed the steward to a table for two. The table cloth was white linen, the dinnerware was bone china and the silverware was heavy and polished. The man sitting at the table was clean-shaven with a middle-aged face and wayward streaks of gray in his hair. He wore an expensive three-piece suit. He extended his hand.

"My name's Carlyle," he said.

Jimmy Delaney accepted the handshake, sat down and took the menu from the steward.

"Delaney," he said. "What's good?"

"I had the roast beef three days ago on the eastbound," said Carlyle. "It was excellent...I'm having it again."

"All right, sounds good," said Jimmy Delaney.

A waiter took their orders for two roast beef dinners and bottle of red wine.

"So, what is your occupation, Mister Delaney?" said Carlyle.

"I'm a writer," said Jimmy Delaney.

"Oh, what kind of writing do you do?"

"Newspapers," said Jimmy Delaney.

"A reporter," said Carlyle.

"More of a feature writer," said Jimmy Delaney.

"How does one get started in that?"

"There are a number of ways," said Jimmy Delaney. "As for me, I had a professor in college with connections in the publishing industry."

"That seems to be the case, whatever you do, doesn't it?" said Carlyle.

"I guess it's the way people are," said Jimmy Delaney.

The waiter brought a tray and laid out the roast beef dinners and poured the wine. The liquid swayed rhythmically in the glasses. Jimmy Delaney looked out the window into the darkness; the Mohawk River shimmered in the moonlight.

"What would you say is our speed?" he said.

"About seventy or seventy-five," said Carlyle. "Even in winter, the train makes good time. We're usually into Chicago by seven in the morning...about fifteen minutes early. This is really good roast beef."

"It is," said Jimmy Delaney. "I've been eating cafeteria food. It certainly isn't the same."

"There's nothing like good food prepared well," said Carlyle. "What paper do you work for?"

"I will be writing for papers in California," said Jimmy Delaney.

The train slowed and stopped under a train shed. Jimmy Delaney leaned toward the window.

"Rome," said Carlyle. He drew a gold watch from his

waistcoat pocket. "Eight o'clock...right on time," he said. "What train do you catch for the west?"

"I have a Pullman car going all the way through," said Jimmy Delaney. "Three different railroads operate the car after Chicago...the Burlington to Denver, the Rio Grande to Salt Lake City and the Western Pacific to California. I'll be on the train for some time."

"They just attach your car to another train?" said Carlyle.

"Yes, they tow the car over to Union Station for the Burlington train," said Jimmy Delaney.

"California...I've never been there," said Carlyle. "I've heard that it is quite different from other places."

The train moved with a slight lurch. Jimmy Delaney watched the station disappear and drew back from the window.

"I haven't been there before either," he said.

"Just moving around, I suppose," said Carlyle. "It is good that young men do that...the settling down with responsibilities will come soon enough. Not that I regret anything, mind you."

"What is your occupation?" said Jimmy Delaney.

"Architect, from Chicago," said Carlyle. "We also have an office in New York...it seems I spend half my time on the train."

"One of my best friends is an engineer," said Jimmy Delaney. "He has told me a few things about bridge design."

"Architecture is a curse sometimes," said Carlyle. "Instead of just enjoying your surroundings, you're always looking around at things...trying to determine how to improve them."

"A few years ago I came east from Montana on a train with a much plainer dining car...newer and plainer," said Jimmy Delaney. "What do you think of the architecture of this car?"

"Victorian excess," said Carlyle.

Jimmy Delaney laughed. "I have heard that description before...the New York post office," he said.

"My God, Mullet's monstrosity...more like Gothic excess," said Carlyle. "Our New York offices are in the Park Row Building...I can't look out the window without seeing that eyesore. Clean lines and simplicity are the coming trends."

"A welcome change?" said Jimmy Delaney.

"In some ways," said Carlyle. "However, it is easier to forget attention to detail if there isn't any. Do you strive for detail in your writing?"

"Yes, the facts are necessary, but so is balance," said Jimmy Delaney. "Most readers are more interested in themes than details."

"I suppose architecture is too technical," said Carlyle. "For us, any piece of writing without the detail is useless."

"Well, I wouldn't think it is meant to be entertaining," said Jimmy Delaney.

"I don't see why you can't have both," said Carlyle. "You're not old enough to remember when Pulitzer and Hearst started the Spanish-American War with their so-called newspapers. No offense, but feeding entertainment to a gullible public is dangerous."

"No offense taken, Mister Carlyle," said Jimmy Delaney. "There is a place for entertainment and a place for objectivity."

"So there is, so there is," said Carlyle. "Sometimes I get carried away."

"Not necessarily," said Jimmy Delaney. "Sensationalism sells advertising."

Carlyle leaned back in his chair. He seemed to be considering his words.

"How about some coffee?" he said.

"All right," said Jimmy Delaney.

"Dessert?" said Carlyle.

"No, not for me," said Jimmy Delaney.

Carlyle called the waiter and ordered coffee. The

waiter cleared the table and brought a silver pitcher with hot coffee and two cups and saucers.

"You surprise me, Mister Delaney," said Carlyle.

"Do I?" said Jimmy Delaney.

"Such a young man," said Carlyle. "How old are you? Do you mind my asking?

"I'm twenty-eight," said Jimmy Delaney.

"How long have you been out of college?"

"Three years."

"Um, what did you do before college?" said Carlyle.

"I came across from Ireland when I was fourteen. I have worked in a grocery store and a stove factory, I was an able seaman's mate on a river steamer, I worked in the ice fields on the Hudson River for one season and I was a telegrapher for the railroad out west."

"Do you mind me asking these questions?" said Carlyle. "I mean no harm...just curious."

"No, not at all," said Jimmy Delaney.

"How did you find time for school?" said Carlyle.

"I finished public school in Ireland," said Jimmy Delaney. "At that time it was roughly the equivalent of eighth grade...about the same as here for most people."

"How did you get into college?" said Carlyle.

"My friend, the engineer, arranged a tutor for me and then an entrance examination," said Jimmy Delaney.

"Fascinating," said Carlyle. "I did nothing before college...perhaps I should have. My father was an architect with the same firm as myself. Do you think we're going to get into the European war?"

"The European war...I suppose I would not have been surprised last year when the Lusitania was sunk," said Jimmy Delaney. "Now it seems less likely."

"I think you're mistaken," said Carlyle. "Have you kept abreast of events in Mexico?"

"Somewhat...not very much," said Jimmy Delaney.

"Do you know of the raid in New Mexico two months ago?" said Carlyle.

"Pancho Villa?" said Jimmy Delaney. "I read about it."

"Sensationalist nonsense, no doubt," said Carlyle.

"The stories did not favor Villa, if that's what you mean," said Jimmy Delaney.

"Well, this Villa, a two-bit revolutionary, raided a town in New Mexico...Columbus, a small village near the border...for reasons we will probably never know," said Carlyle. "We know what Wilson did, however...he used it as an excuse to invade Mexico. We will end up fighting both the revolutionaries and the Mexican army, as Wilson well knows. He's seasoning the army for intervention in the European war...and in case you doubt that, he also invaded the Dominican Republic not two weeks ago."

"I don't pay much attention to politics," said Jimmy Delaney.

"Well, you should," said Carlyle. "You're a young man and Wilson is in the same gaggle of criminals with the Kaiser and that warmonger Roosevelt...and if he thinks my two sons are going to be drafted and die for nothing, he's mistaken."

"I don't have sons, Mister Carlyle, but this country hasn't had military conscription since the Civil War," said Jimmy Delaney.

"Well, if I were you, I'd go back to Ireland if Wilson is elected again in November," said Carlyle.

"Maybe I'll just hide out in the hills," said Jimmy Delaney.

"You can laugh now, but you won't be when they pass a draft and come after you," said Carlyle.

Jimmy Delaney drank the last of the coffee in his cup. He pushed back the chair and extended his hand.

"I don't mean to belittle your position, Mister Carlyle," he said. "I hope you're wrong."

Carlyle rose and took Jimmy Delaney's hand. His handshake was firm, as before.

"I get carried away," he said. "This war, my sons...I can't sleep nights."

"I hope you're wrong," said Jimmy Delaney. "History is against a draft."

"Good night, Mister Delaney," said Carlyle, releasing Jimmy Delaney's hand. "The dinner is on me...your money's no good here."

"Mister Carlyle..."

"I insist," said Carlyle. "Good luck to you in California."

"Thank you," said Jimmy Delaney.

The sleeping car porter was in the vestibule of the dining car. He was leaning against the wall looking out the window and smoking a pipe.

"Be in Syracuse in a few minutes," said the porter. "A short stop and then I'll be along to get you set up for the night."

"I'm fine," said Jimmy Delaney. "The bed is turned down and it's the best room I've ever had."

"I keep coffee in the vestibule," said the porter.

"I know, thank you...maybe I'll take a chance and have one last cup."

"The diner is open five-thirty to six-thirty for breakfast, but they ain't no need to wake up 'less you want to," said the porter. "I go off in Chicago but this car here gets towed over to Union Station for the train to California. You has about six hours in Chicago, plenty of time to have your breakfast in the station and walk around if you're a mind."

"Thank you, I'll do that," said Jimmy Delaney.

"You been to Chicago before?" said the porter.

"Oh, yes...a while back," said Jimmy Delaney.

"Well, good night to you," said the porter. "Sleep well."

May, 1916 - The Train to California

It is past midnight and the train is quiet and has the feel of speed. Because a telegraph wire was not sent or not logged, I am traveling to

California in a Pullman drawing room. I am wallowing in opulence that Willy Gantz and I would not have dreamed possible. Even Harry Archer, who thrives on opulence as a respite from work, would be embarrassed. I suppose I should just enjoy it, as it is unlikely I will pass this way again.

I told Harry that Michael has gone back to Ireland. He will take it hard that Paddy O'Brien has to exist as Michael Delaney. Archer always takes it hard when a man is pushed - his instinctive dislike of Hessler back in Mobridge is a testament to his manner when a man is being pushed. He will probably think Michael is better off in Ireland. I have said what I know and guess and worry about and have nothing to add.

I doubt that Harry will be surprised by the move to California. It is curious that he has known all along that I would tire of the inactive life. I hope to hear from him soon - he seems weary of going from job to job, but does not say what he will do instead.

Before sleep, there is a final entry that leaves me ill at ease. I had dinner with a man in the diner tonight - Mr. Carlyle, an architect from Chicago. He is well informed, obviously prosperous and fears that his sons will be conscripted for the European war. I suggested that history does not favor a draft - he would have none of it and advised that I should leave the country if Wilson remains in office. Although Mr. Carlyle seemed somewhat conspiratorial, he did not seem delusional. I had not considered a draft. I have a vague sense of dread.

The train was not moving. Jimmy Delaney opened the window shade and saw a concrete platform and passenger cars on the adjacent track. The time was nine in the morning. He washed and dressed in denim work clothes, having put away his suit the night before. He encountered the porter on the platform.

"We're in Union Station, I would guess," he said.

"We sure is," said the porter.

"I'm in the drawing room," said Jimmy Delaney. "I must have died last night."

"Yes sir, they towed you over here from La Salle Street and when I come on at seven-thirty, you hasn't moved. They's a good restaurant in the station if you want some breakfast and I'll make up your bed while you're gone."

"I think I will and then I'll walk around," said Jimmy Delaney. "We have until one-thirty?"

"Yes sir, they'll be making up the Denver train about noon and we pull out at one-thirty."

Jimmy Delaney had ham and eggs and black coffee and left the station into Canal Street. Crossing the bridge at the end of the south concourse, he walked along Adams and turned right into Dearborn. The clock tower of Dearborn Station half a mile to the south dominated the skyline, as it had seven years before. Jimmy Delaney walked along Dearborn, crossed Van Buren under the El and turned right into Harrison Street. Two blocks beyond the south end of La Salle Street Station, he crossed the river, walked two more blocks, turned right into Canal and returned to Union Station. The clanging bells of the streetcars, once the dominant sound, were absorbed in the clamor of cars and trucks and gasoline had conquered the smell of horses.

Jimmy Delaney awoke suddenly. Sensing smooth straight rails and high speed, he pulled back the shade; the flat farmland of Nebraska rushed by in the pre-dawn twilight. He dressed and walked along the aisle between the drawn curtains of the berths to the vestibule and poured hot coffee into a mug. He returned to the drawing room, took a manuscript from the suitcase and laid it on the table. He settled in the chair, read the last page and wrote on a blank sheet of paper:

When the boy awoke in the boxcar, Willy Gantz was gone. He had left the fruit jar half full of water by the door. The boy pulled the door open and felt a brief wave of nausea against the humid air heavy with the odor of stockyards. The boxcar was two feet from a high fence made of heavy wire twisted into squares. The fence separated the track from an open field of waist-high weeds which almost concealed scattered piles of discarded machinery. The boy sat in the open doorway and drank water from the fruit jar. His mind's eye could not follow Willy Gantz on the southbound freight before dawn.

Thirty-Four

The Rainbow's Edge

May, 1916 - Approaching Sacramento

The Rocky Mountains between Denver and Salt Lake City are spectacular. I had forgotten how much the mountains lift your spirit. After Salt Lake City the land is bleak: briny flats, dry lake beds, monotonous plain. The reward is the Sierra Nevada.

The train has stopped in the Oroville station, one and a half hours from Sacramento. Since leaving the snow this morning in the mountains, the weather has become clear and mild. The Oroville station is a long narrow building with arches supporting the roof over the platform. Like many other structures here, it is built with a light brown clay-like substance and has a red tile roof. I think we will follow the Feather River through a valley now. I think I will like it here.

The train crossed the bridge over the American River into Sacramento. Jimmy Delaney, dressed in the denim work clothes and his Donegal cap, looked around the drawing room and went to the vestibule. The nose of the locomotive eased up against the L Street crossing; the train lay across K Street, J Street and half of I Street. Jimmy Delaney's Pullman car rested directly in front of the Mission Revival depot and freight house occupying a city block bounded by J Street, K Street, Nineteenth Street and the Western Pacific track.

Jimmy Delaney shook hands with the porter, leaving a half-dollar in his palm, and walked into the depot under the grand arches over the brick platform. He crossed the tile floor to the adjoining freight house and learned that his trunks would arrive in three days. He copied the addresses of several boarding houses from the notices on the bulletin board and left the depot into J Street. On the third stop, he found a front room on the second floor of a Victorian house dating from the Gold Rush. The room was large and airy with two windows facing N Street near the Capitol. He paid one month's rent. After a welcome bath, he walked into a brick building in J Street between Second Street and Firehouse Alley in the waterfront district, the oldest part of town on the Sacramento River.

The newspaper editor took the folder and laid it out on his desk. He read the summary sheet of Jimmy Delaney's work history and education and looked at the list of stories published in literary magazines.

"Your credentials as a writer are excellent, but you don't have any newspaper experience," said the editor.

"I will submit articles on a trial basis," said Jimmy Delaney. "If you publish them and they are well-received, we can talk again."

"Fair enough," said the editor. "Did you know that we once sent Mark Twain to Hawaii to do travelogue pieces?"

"Yes, I've read them," said Jimmy Delaney.

"Well, I will bet that you didn't know that most people thought he wrote those articles right here in Sacramento," said the editor. "The paper has made money from time to time selling the desk where Mark Twain sat."

Jimmy Delaney laughed. "No, I did not know that," he said.

"Well, I have a paper to run, said the editor, extending his hand. "By the way, my name is Weaver."

Jimmy Delaney accepted the hand shake, gathered his papers and stowed them in the rucksack. He nodded and backed away from the desk.

"That rucksack looks like it's seen a better day," said Weaver.

"Yes, I've had it a long time," said Jimmy Delaney.

"I'll be looking forward to seeing something," said Weaver.

"I'll have something soon," said Jimmy Delaney. "I'll leave it with your secretary."

Jimmy Delaney walked around the city and rode the interurban streetcars to explore the towns through the valley and foothills of the Sierra Nevada. The newspaper published his brief biography of Louis Brandeis, the new justice of the Supreme Court, and another article on the design of the stone wall and guard tower of Folsom Prison. He read about a man named Ishi who had recently died in San Francisco. The man was the last member of the Yahi tribe of Yana Indians and thought to be the last aboriginal American Indian. He had walked out of the mountains five years before and surrendered himself to slaughterhouse workers near Oroville. The man was rescued by professors at the university in San Francisco, where he lived out his life as a janitor in the anthropological museum. Jimmy Delaney could not discover anything new after two weeks of research. He began to consider stories relating to the Gold Rush and the transcontinental railway.

"Come in," he said in response to a knock on the door.

The landlady opened the door and said, "It's the telephone for you."

Jimmy Delaney accompanied the landlady to the main hallway on the first floor. The telephone was mounted on the wall. He put the receiver to his ear and answered.

"Can you go to San Francisco for the Preparedness Day Parade next Saturday?" said Weaver.

"A straight reporting job?" said Jimmy Delaney.

"No, I want the essence of the thing," said Weaver. "The Wobblies and every other radical in California are out in force and the Chamber of Commerce has organized what they call a law and order committee. You get the picture."

"The Wobblies again," said Jimmy Delaney.

"You've dealt with them before?" said Weaver.

"Not directly, no," said Jimmy Delaney. "I'll come down to the paper and we'll talk about it."

"Come ahead," said Weaver.

Jimmy Delaney spoke to the secretary and went through an open door into the editor's office. He settled into a chair in front of Weaver's desk.

"So, can you go down to San Francisco?" said Weaver. "The parade is Saturday. I'll pay you fifty dollars for a four-column story, plus expenses."

"That's a generous offer," said Jimmy Delaney. "What is your interest in this parade?"

"What do you mean?"

"There are two ways to think of it," said Jimmy Delaney. "It is a focal point for isolationists and everyone else opposed to the war and on the other hand, it drums up support for intervention. So, what is your interest?"

"What angle would you take?" said Weaver.

"War is good for business," said Jimmy Delaney. "Otherwise there would be no parade."

"Our subscribers think the Germans must be stopped," said Weaver.

"Then the story is not for me," said Jimmy Delaney.

"I didn't say we had to go along with that...not necessarily," said Weaver.

"I can do a balanced piece, but it has to include the reasons for interventionist sentiment," said Jimmy Delaney.

"What reasons?" said Weaver.

"Investments...sales, loans and credits for armaments and supplies...I don't have to tell you that," said Jimmy Delaney. "If Germany wins, all of that is lost. Russia is going to collapse and the Germans will transfer everything to the western front. Who's going to stop them?"

"How do you know Russia is going to collapse?" said Weaver.

"The Tsar is a fool...Lenin isn't," said Jimmy Delaney.

"Listen, Mister Weaver, the radicals are not all anarchists and lunatics...some of them are well-educated and they are over there and writing about what they see."

"Why do you believe what they write?"

Jimmy Delaney laughed. "Because it is exactly what you would expect," he said.

"I should have known from your Brandeis piece," said Weaver. "I didn't know you were so interested in politics."

"I'm not interested in politics," said Jimmy Delaney.

"You could have fooled me."

"So, what would like me to do?" said Jimmy Delaney.

The newspaper editor shrugged. "Go to San Francisco," he said. "Write a four-column story and earn fifty dollars."

Jimmy Delaney prepared to leave for San Francisco three days before the parade, time enough to read background material and walk the proposed route at least twice. He packed a change of clothes in the rucksack, spoke to the landlady and left the boarding house wearing his Donegal cap and Murphy's coat against the wind off the bay. He walked to the interurban station on the waterfront and bought a ticket to San Francisco on the Sacramento Northern Electric Railway. At the Long Wharf at the foot of Seventh Street in Oakland he took a Southern Pacific ferry across the bay and checked into a hotel for three nights near the Ferry Building in San Francisco.

Jimmy Delaney was standing on the north side of Market Street across from the new Southern Pacific Building when the first of more than fifty thousand marchers turned into Market from Steuart Street. About two dozen men carrying a large American flag that spanned Market Street had just passed when a piece of metal from an explosion across the street shattered the plate glass window behind Jimmy Delaney's head.

The smoke and acrid smell of dynamite dissipated

in the light breeze within minutes, leaving the corner of Market and Steuart littered with glass and bits of metal and bodies. Jimmy Delaney and other onlookers who had scattered into the parade route ran back into the melee and the day manager of the Alameda Cafe in Steuart Street brought waiters and customers with pitchers of water and table cloths and aprons for bandages.

After the ambulances had gone, Jimmy Delaney went into the Southern Pacific Building and sent a wire to Weaver summarizing what he knew: a bomb had exploded on the corner of Market and Steuart near the Ferry Building, killing ten people and wounding forty. He bought a new change of clothing and extended his stay in the hotel. Six days later he returned to Sacramento and handed Weaver a four-column story on the bombing and the aftermath.

"A time bomb in a suitcase, huh," said Weaver.

"Packed with sash weights," said Jimmy Delaney.

"Christ," said Weaver.

"Read on," said Jimmy Delaney.

Weaver looked up. "They've offered seventeen thousand dollars to anyone claiming to have seen someone leave the suitcase?" he said.

"They're buying testimony," said Jimmy Delaney. "Charles Fickert, the District Attorney, has arrested three men and a woman...all militant radicals."

"The witnesses are lying?" said Weaver.

"Yes," said Jimmy Delaney.

"How do you know?" said Weaver.

"They could not identify anyone in police lineups," said Jimmy Delaney.

"Do you know that for a fact?"

"Yes."

"How?" said Weaver.

"As you know, I was once a telegrapher," said Jimmy Delaney.

"You've seen the wires?" said Weaver.

"I am sure the story is true," said Jimmy Delaney.

"Christ, they're going to trial with that?" said Weaver.

"That is my understanding," said Jimmy Delaney.

"Can you go back down there and cover the trial?" said Weaver.

"I'm sliding into something I don't care to do," said Jimmy Delaney. "I'm not interested in politics, I'm interested in literature. I'm not a reporter."

"The hell you're not," said Weaver.

"No, I would like to continue our arrangement before I became involved with this," said Jimmy Delaney.

"This is a big story, Delaney," said Weaver. "Of course, they'll never hang the woman, but if I understand you, they're going to railroad these labor guys to the gallows."

"They will do that whether I go back to San Francisco or not," said Jimmy Delaney.

"All right, listen," said Weaver. "Cover this one story and we'll go back to the human interest stuff. You can't pass this up...I'll pay you one hundred dollars plus expenses to cover the trial."

"That is a lot of money," said Jimmy Delaney. "Why me...you have reporters who have been with this paper for years."

"You saw the wires on the lineups," said Weaver. "You have a source who gives you the inside stuff."

"Let's understand each other," said Jimmy Delaney. "Anything..."

"Of course," said Weaver.

"I'm serious."

"I know you are," said Weaver.

February, 1917 - The Mooney Trial

The trials of Thomas Mooney, his wife, Rena, and his associate, Warren Billings, as well as Israel Weinberg, a jitney bus driver, are over. Mooney and Billings were sentenced to death by hanging; Rena Mooney and Weinberg were acquitted. I have just wired Weaver the fourth and last dispatch regarding these trials along with a firm statement that I will not do this kind of work again. I record it here as a reminder.

Charles Fickert is an ambitious criminal who panders to war fever while posing as a district attorney. The two witnesses who claimed to have seen Billings plant the bomb and then meet Mooney and his wife a few minutes later are perjurers. I have learned that Fickert chose these two men from dozens attracted by the reward. One initially said that two men whom he could not identify had left the suitcase on the sidewalk and the other was not in San Francisco at the time of the bombing. Both were bribed with reward money to implicate Mooney and Billings, the main targets. Countering this testimony, to no avail, the defense presented a photograph showing Mooney and Rena watching the parade eight minutes before the explosion, as recorded by a clock tower in the photograph. They were more than a mile from the corner of Market and Steuart and thus could not have been seen there by Fickert's witness. I have also learned that Fickert's master is Martin Swanson, a former Pinkerton. Swanson has tried twice before to frame Thomas Mooney - Billings and Weinberg were tried because they refused to implicate Mooney in a previous bombing.

I do not expect Weaver to publish my last dispatch. The truth of these trials will not be known for years, if ever. I've not the temperament for this kind of work.

275

May, 1917 - Dies Irae

It is mandated that men between 21 and 30 will register for military service. Conscription will begin in three weeks time. During the past three months I have given Weaver four stories. The last one related the illusions of a bank teller from Illinois during the Gold Rush. I called it "Pipe Dreams."

Thirty-Five

Balance Due

The trunk on the porch held journals and the culled remnant of a book collection which began with a leather-bound copy of *Walden and Other Writings* from a shop in Hester Street. The other trunk with discarded books and a suitcase packed with two three-piece suits, dress shirts, ties and shoes lay against the wall on the receiving dock of the shelter near the Capitol.

Jimmy Delaney stood on the porch beside the trunk. He wore Murphy's coat over denim work clothes, heavy brogan boots and the well-worn Donegal wool cap pulled down to the top of his eyebrows. His red beard had grown into a dense fullness. His pocket watch and gold fob from Sherman Archer and a manila envelope containing cash from his bank account were out of sight in the inside pocket of Murphy's coat. The rucksack with toiletries and two changes of clothing hung on his shoulder.

A truck resembling an ice wagon stopped in front of the boarding house. The driver slid across the seat and peered through the open window.

"You hire a delivery to the dock?" he called.

"Aye, the trunk and myself to the ferry dock at the foot of L Street," said Jimmy Delaney.

Jimmy Delaney and the driver lifted the trunk into the back of the truck. The driver guided the truck through the early morning traffic and parked in the loading area in front of the ferry dock on Front Street. Jimmy Delaney paid the driver and hired two boys on the dock to carry the trunk to the baggage room in the terminal. He bought a one-way ticket to San Francisco on the stern-wheeler *Pride of the River*, leaving within the hour.

Most of diners in the boat's cafeteria were older, well-dressed businessmen who would not give up the stern-wheeler for the interurban railway. Jimmy Delaney had breakfast alone at one of many empty tables and then climbed the wide stairway to the promenade deck and stood on the starboard side of the bow by the rail. From there he could hear the familiar commands of the first mate through a megaphone and feel the pulsing of the steam engine through the deck planks as the boat turned in the river to face the south.

Men working the soil waved to the steamboat, trailing black smoke and towering over the fields, and then the farms gave way to the Montezuma Hills which faded into marshes forming the top side of Suisun Bay. The boat docked at Vallejo in the Carquinez Strait and with new passengers steamed into the wide expanse of San Pablo Bay. After Pinole Point the boat turned hard aport in the narrows at San Rafael and entered San Francisco Bay. The city lay on the bow.

The captain, once a man of the sea in sailing ships, guided *Pride of the River* through the crowded channel. By the feel of the boat abeam of the Ferry Building, he called for reverse and then neutral wheel abeam of the last ferry slip and then hard astarboard into the dock against Pier 14. The boat secured, the captain sat on a high stool in the pilot house and resumed reading a book he had started the previous day. The voyage back to Sacramento would begin as soon as the passengers were aboard and require an extra hour against the current.

Jimmy Delaney watched the docking maneuvers beneath the clock tower of the Ferry Building and descended the stairway to the main deck. He nodded to the first mate at the gangway and checked the trunk at the baggage station in the Ferry Building. He crossed the pedestrian bridge over the streetcar turnaround on the Embarcadero, descended into Market Street and walked to a familiar hotel near the corner of Market and Spear.

"Welcome, Mister Delaney...a new assignment?" said the desk clerk.

"Just the one night for the time being," said Jimmy Delaney.

"Well, we're finally in the war and about time too," said the desk clerk. "The Huns will really squirm when our doughboys get over there...especially with Black Jack Pershing showing them the way."

"Yes, I'm sure he can do the job," said Jimmy Delaney.

"Four-fourteen in the front?" said the desk clerk.

"That's fine," said Jimmy Delaney. "I'm not sure if I will be in the city tonight. If I don't return by six o'clock, you can go ahead and rent the room to someone else. Do you require a deposit?"

"Oh, no," said the desk clerk. "We shall be happy to hold your room until six."

"Thank you, I appreciate it," said Jimmy Delaney.

The waterfront was crowded with closely spaced structures built on landfill and rubble pushed into the bay after the great earthquake. Jimmy Delaney made his way through wagons, trucks, rail cars and longshoremen, passing between warehouses, cheap hotels, boarding houses, cafes and bars on the inland side of the Embarcadero and piers identified by bulkhead buildings of stone and brick along the bay. He read the flyers on the notice board inside the bulkhead building at the head of each pier. He walked along the side of the railroad track serving the south dock of Pier 17 and approached the gangway of a ship.

"First mate handy?" he said to a man on the gangway.

"Looking for a berth?" said the man.

"Aye...from the notice," said Jimmy Delaney.

"That notice is old," said the man. "They were filling out the crew on *Santa Cecelia* this morning...Pier 19."

Jimmy Delaney nodded. "Aye, I'll look into it," he said.

The *Santa Cecelia*, tied up on the north side of Pier 19, occupied just more than half of the 800-foot dock.

The ship had a single stack amidships and carried five masts and a 100-ton boom. The deck was loaded with a steam locomotive and tender and stacks of finished lumber. Jimmy Delaney walked around longshoremen stacking lumber from rail cars on the boom platform. He approached the ship.

"Looking for a berth?" said a man on the gangway.

"Aye, able seaman's mate," said Jimmy Delaney.

"We had two crewmen got killed last night, but they got replacements this morning," said the man. "Something might come up though. We're stuck here 'til we find a Marconi operator and some of the boys might ship out on another berth."

"I can handle Marconi," said Jimmy Delaney.

"Well, looks like we'll be out of here by morning," said the man. He scanned the ship. "Up there on the bridge deck," he said. "First mate is the guy with the wool cap."

Jimmy Delaney adjusted the rucksack on his shoulder and crossed the gangway. He climbed the stairway to the bridge deck and approached the first mate.

"I understand you need a Marconi operator," he said.

"Aye...would that be yourself?" said the first mate.

"Railroad telegrapher," said Jimmy Delaney. "I'm rusty, but I'll recover my fist quickly."

"What are you called?" said the first mate.

"Delaney...Jimmy Delaney."

"Your accent's almost gone," said the first mate. "Been here a long time?"

"Aye, a long time," said Jimmy Delaney.

"Flynn's my name," said the first mate. "A long time as well. Still have a sister lives in Cork though...see her from time to time even. You got any people?"

"Passed away," said Jimmy Delaney.

"Well, we're carrying a locomotive to Mexico and finished lumber to Cuba through the canal," said Flynn. "We also have thirty passengers, mostly for Balboa. The

Marconi shack is behind the bridge...your cabin is off the shack. You can handle cables for the passengers, but the official cables come first...ironclad rule since the Titanic disaster. After Cuba, we'll be working the Caribbean and Brazilian coast. Does that fit in with your plans?"

"No plans," said Jimmy Delaney. "I have a trunk at the ferry terminal. Can you spare a couple of men?"

Flynn took a pad from his pocket, wrote on a sheet and tore it off.

"No need," he said. "Go down to the terminal and give this to one of the agents...they'll send the trunk up here on the belt railway. I'll have some crewmen take it to your cabin."

"I'm thanking you," said Jimmy Delaney, nodding.

"You have a pile of cables in the shack that'll take you half the night to sort out," said the Flynn.

"Who took the cables?" said Jimmy Delaney.

"The Marconi operator...before the damn fool got killed in a bar fight last night," said Flynn.

"I'll see to the trunk and get the cables organized," said Jimmy Delaney.

"Before you go, send a wire to the company...Grace Line...the book is in the shack," said Flynn. "Tell them we have a Marconi man and they needn't send one. Oh, and send a wire to the harbor master as well...they think we're still sitting here waiting."

"Aye," said Jimmy Delaney.

"I'll fill you in on the mess schedule for ship's officers and other things later," said Flynn. "The passengers board tomorrow morning at seven and we're underway as soon as you get a clearance from the harbor master."

"Aye, I'll have the shack organized by then," said Jimmy Delaney, backing away.

"Welcome aboard," said Flynn.

Jimmy Delaney nodded and descended the stairs to the main deck.

The fog had begun to break into pieces of sunlight when Jimmy Delaney copied the message from the harbor master. He took the message to Flynn, who gave the order to cast off the lines. The *Santa Cecelia* backed out of the dock into the bay, took a northerly heading and turned hard aport at Treasure Island. Jimmy Delaney stood on the bridge deck against the railing. He opened the collar of Murphy's coat to the wind and allowed his hair to fly in disarray. On the bow lay the Golden Gate and the open sea.

LaVergne, TN USA
28 July 2010
191294LV00001B/45/P